Bones

by Larry Allen Lindsey

© Copyright 2023 Larry Allen Lindsey

ISBN 979-8-88824-150-9

Published by

◤ köehlerbooks™

3705 Shore Drive
Virginia Beach, VA 23455
800-435-4811
www.koehlerbooks.com

BONES

A SISTER'S REVENGE

BONES

A SISTER'S REVENGE

Inspired by a True Story

LARRY ALLEN LINDSEY

VIRGINIA BEACH
CAPE CHARLES

"Good friend, for Jesus sake forbear
To dig the dust enclosed here.
Blest be the man who spares these stones,
And cursed be he that moves my bones."

Shakespeare's Epitaph

This book is dedicated to Sue Esper, who was always able to motivate this grateful author with a single, signature word: "So?"

And to the memory of our beloved corgi, Geoff,
who was the best dog in the whole wide world.

PREFACE

The true story that suggested this novel

Born in Olster, Ireland, in 1761 and raised in remote County Londenberry—not far from the shores of Lough Neach—Charles Byrne, dubbed the "Irish Giant" later in life, had grown to his full height of seven feet seven inches by his seventeenth birthday. Legend has it he was conceived atop a ten-foot haystack, a fact that many locals at the time believed contributed to his extreme height. His parents were not that tall, but his mother was considered to be a "stout woman" by neighbors. One of eight children, Charles was afflicted with gigantism, an abnormal growth of the pituitary gland that damages the skeletal system and leads to high blood pressure.

Troubled with consistent and intense growing pains from birth, his frequent driveling resulted in him being ostracized by other children. Although sickly, Charles later supplemented his family's meager income by lending his awesome stature to several theatrical ventures. He was a gentle giant with a thunderous voice, large, square jaw, and wide forehead, and by twenty had become a popular figure in English freak shows.

John Hunter, London's preeminent surgeon and anatomist (later known as the father of modern surgery), attended several of Charles's performances and became obsessed with him, wanting to include his bones in his macabre cabinet of curiosities. Knowing that individuals suffering from gigantism never lived long, he offered the Byrne family a substantial sum for Charles's body when he died.

Charles spent the rest of his short life trying to avoid Dr. Hunter and his many agents. Hounded unmercifully, he suffered a nervous breakdown in 1783, and by his twenty-second year, his popularity had faded, nudging him toward alcoholism. Eventually he contracted tuberculosis in May of that year. Fearing the end was near and that Hunter and his minions would desecrate his body, he arranged for three local fishermen to transport his coffin to the middle of the Irish Channel, where, loaded down with rocks, it would be dropped into the sea off Margate.

Charles struggled onstage—gaunt and penniless from his illness—for his final show, only to see Dr. Hunter grinning from the back row. During his last days, family and friends gathered around the gentle giant's deathbed to swear that the doctor would never lay his hands on Charles's remains. Unbeknownst to them, however, Hunter had bribed the undertaker to switch coffins. When Charles's friends were drunk at his wake, Hunter's agents spirited the real coffin away.

Hunter, fearful of being discovered, chopped Charles's body up and boiled it in a copper tub until nothing but the bones remained. He then waited four years until the Irish Giant's notoriety faded before showcasing the reassembled skeleton in his museum of oddities. Today the bones of Charles Byrne are still on display at the Royal College of Surgeons in Dublin.

Rumor has it that late at night, when the room gets real quiet and there's no one else around, if you put your ear close to the glass enclosure and listen real hard, you can hear Charles whisper out a raspy request: "Please . . . let me go."

ONE

Somewhere in the hills of Eastern Tennessee

High atop a remote ridge in the Smoky Mountains stands a majestic, weather-beaten oak tree. Hidden from view, a huge human skeleton lies cradled in its upper branches, in life at least two heads taller than the average man. It was lifted from its shallow grave by the tree in a miraculous burst of growth over eighty years ago and now rests peacefully a hundred feet above the forest floor. Swaddled by a protective veil of verdant leaves, the position of the bones is reminiscent of Michelangelo's *Pieta*. From a distance it looks as if the regal oak is offering up a sacrifice to the heavens.

The skeleton's right hand clutches a flat river stone. On that stone is a simple inscription. A century's worth of wind and rain has blurred all but three letters: A, N, and G. Whatever the original passage meant is known only to God—and maybe the spirit of the man-child whose flesh had been supported by those same bones long ago. Perhaps also his revenge-seeking sister, who, at her advanced age, is not long for this world.

Hattie Sexton's place was the final tortuous stop on Vardy Miser's mail route. The twenty miles of winding dirt road up the steepest incline in the Clinch Mountains always pushed his fifteen-year-old four-wheel-drive Jeep to its limit. The real killer, however, was the cliff-hanging half-mile hike he had to make through the thickest forest in eastern Tennessee. Over a footpath only a mountain goat could stomach. A single misstep at Hangman's Gulch, and Vardy's body would be lost forever at the bottom of a 300-foot drop to the jagged rocks of the Clingman River below.

Despite the ordeal, Vardy looked forward to chatting with Miss Hattie. Granted, he usually did most of the talking. But after just ten minutes in her beatific presence, he always felt world's better about himself and life in general. Hattie had a way of cutting to the quick, getting to what was really important to Vardy, who was only a year away from putting in his retirement papers. Cheaper and more efficient than a citified shrink.

Today Vardy's arthritic left knee was acting up on him again, making this morning's pilgrimage more difficult than most.

Shifting his mail pouch to his left shoulder, he leaned against the nearest trunk to wipe his brow. With the surrounding vegetation choking off all hope of a cooling breeze, the mountain air had taken on a thick, green hue. The humidity on this hot summer day rivaled that of a steam bath, laboring his breathing even more. Thankfully, fifty yards ahead lay Hattie's moss-covered cabin, nestled in a copse of overhanging trees. Today especially, it was a welcome sight.

On the sagging porch stood Hattie herself, gnarled with age, a cane in her right hand. Although the postman's arrival times varied, Hattie always sensed when he was on his way. Not once in all these years had Vardy had to knock on her door. No surprise there; most mountain folks knew Hattie "was told things" by critters in the forest. Who or what was coming and going. What was going on around her. In this world and the next. Vardy was one of those folks.

"Be right there, Miss Hattie," he called out. "Just give me a second to catch my breath. These tired old legs of mine ain't what they used to be. It might be my imagination funnin' with me, but the trail to your place seems to get longer every month. Steeper, too."

"Take your time, Vardy," said Hattie. "I ain't going nowhere. You got my magazine?"

"Right here in my pouch. Got a letter for you, too."

Usually Hattie's deliveries consisted solely of her *TIME* magazine. Five years ago, Vardy had wised up and began to weed out all the

Visa applications and other junk mail. With Hattie's approval, of course. No sense in lugging extra weight up the mountain. As if Hattie Sexton would ever buy anything on credit.

"A letter, you say," said Hattie. "Who from?"

"It's from Burl Wiggs, your cousin down in Kyles Ford."

At the porch, Vardy handed the letter up to Hattie, then plopped himself down on the first step to prop his pouch against a railing. Hattie held the letter up to the sun for a second or two. Stuck it in a skirt pocket.

"I'll read this later," she said. "No doubt Burl's letting me know about his wife's passing. I'm glad she's finally at peace. Poor Prudy had a rough time of it this past month."

Hattie never left her property. Hadn't ventured more than two football fields from her cabin in ten years. And she didn't cotton to modern gadgets of any kind, including telephones. A cellphone? Not on your life! Her only outside touch with civilization were the tidbits her few neighbors occasionally brought her, and her magazine. Which she read religiously, and slowly, from cover to cover. "To keep myself abreast of what's going on in the rest of the world," she liked to say. For things closer to home, she relied on the good nature of her four-legged, and sometimes feathered, woodland friends to keep her up to speed.

TWO

"Sorry to hear about Missus Wiggs," said Vardy. "She sick for long?"

"A couple of months," said Hattie. "Bone cancer, the doctors said. Burl came to visit a few months back. Asked if I could work up a special something that would help her any." Hattie shook her head. Looked off to the north. "Not much I could do, though. I gave him some powder to ease her pain and said a prayer or two for Prudy. Powders must have helped her last this extra month. Not so sure about the prayers."

Vardy sucked air in through his teeth. "Cancer's a damn rotten way to go. Once it gets into your bones, that's all she wrote."

"Burl bawled like a baby when I told him I couldn't help her," added Hattie. "Gruff as a grizzly on the outside, but inside, he's all mush. Man's gonna miss his wifemate something fierce. Been married fifty-some years. It tore me up, not being able to save her. But some things are beyond me and my medicines."

"Some things maybe, Hattie. But not all that much. That salve you gave me two months ago stunk to high heaven, but it sure worked real good on my arthritis. Better than anything the doctors over in Sneedville prescribed."

"You need more?"

"Now that you mention it," said Vardy, "I am running a bit low." Bending over to rub his leg: "This left knee of mine has been acting up this past week. Getting older is a bitch, and that's a fact. I may not be worm bait just yet, but nowadays I have to think twice before starting in on a thick book."

"I hear you loud and clear," said Hattie, heading inside. From a shelf above the sink she pulled a small jar. Held it up to the light to make sure it was the right one. Then returned to hand it to Vardy. "That should hold your knee for a while."

She leaned her cane against the wall. Sat in the porch's only rocking chair. Creaked it back and forth twice. "Got time to chat for a spell?"

"For you I'll always make time, Hattie."

"What do you hear from your brother Coose? Last we talked, he was in trouble with the law."

"He still is," sighed Vardy. "Sometimes I think Coose ain't got brain one."

"What's he gone and done now?" asked Hattie.

"You know how he can't handle his liquor?" said Vardy. "Well, just last Saturday he got drunk as a skunk and tore up the Feed and Grain. Cost me a hundred bucks to bail him out of the Stuggersville jail. Another two hundred for damages. My brother is ornery enough when sober. Put a few beers in his belly, and he turns downright mean. And even more stupid. If that's possible."

"My dear poppa, may God rest his soul, was much the same way." Hattie nodded. "Never could handle his moonshine. But when Poppa had a few too many, he turned silly, not mean."

"Silly doesn't get you in as much trouble. I love Coose dearly, but there are times when I'd like to knock some sense into his sorry ass."

Hattie leaned forward to put a hand on his shoulder. "You're a good brother, Vardy. Nobody can deny that. How old is Coose, anyway?"

"Sixty-nine."

"You'd think he would've learned by now."

"Family curse, I guess," said Vardy. "Until I saw the light ten years ago, I wasn't much better. Booze has been the bane of we Misers as far back as I can remember. My grandpappy lathered himself up one night and got the notion he could fly. Jumped off Deadman's Drop to prove it. Laughing like a hyena, he flapped his arms like a bird all the way down. Lucky for him that pine tree broke his fall, or he would have broke his neck for sure."

Hattie tugged at an ear. "I remember that tomfoolery of his. Good thing the Lord looks out after drunks and fools."

"Ain't that the honest-to-God truth. And my grandpappy was a bit of both."

A snowy egret took flight from a tall oak tree across the way. Vardy watched it glide out of sight. After a comfortable minute of silence, he stretched out his back, sighed, then slapped both thighs.

"Well, I suppose I better be heading back. This mail pouch of mine ain't gonna deliver itself. Here's your *TIME* magazine, Hattie. You might want to check out the article on page forty-two. It's about how America's getting to be a nation of geezers."

Hattie grinned. Peaked an eyebrow. "Are you calling me old, Vardy Miser?"

"Wouldn't think of it," said the mailman. "You'll probably outlive us all."

"Already doing that." Hattie grinned.

Vardy let out a grunt as he hefted his bag to his shoulder.

"Need anything from town, Hattie?"

"Not that I can think of. But thanks for asking."

"Then I guess I'll see you next week. Don't take any wooden nickels."

"Or copper quarters," said Hattie.

For twenty years it had been their parting shot. Seemed to work as well as anything. At the edge of the forest, Vardy stopped to turn around.

"I'll want to hear what you think of that article, Hattie. That author's got a fine way with words."

A final wave, and he was gone.

Usually Hattie read her magazine from the beginning. That night, however, she skipped to page forty-two. Vardy Miser had been right. The article was both well written and insightful. And more importantly, respectful of the elderly. The author's name was John March.

"Well, Mr. John March," said Hattie, to no one but herself. "You do have a right nice way with words. I think it's you I'll be telling my story to."

Outside her cabin window, a full moon, ripe and punkin' round, was sneaking a peek over the treetops, like an alabaster eye keeping watch on its minions below. A time of peace in the mountain forest. In a few minutes Hattie would be fast asleep, content with the decision she'd just made.

Except for one last loose end, Hattie Sexton was ready to die. Had been for the last four decades. After she turned a hundred, life had become sort of, well, redundant. Been there, done that. These days she was looking forward to meeting her maker face-to-face, looking Him—or Her—in the eye, and asking, "What the hell was that all about?"

Suicide had never been an option for Hattie. After all, she was a God fearing woman. Always had been, always would be. The Lord would take her in His (Her) own sweet time.

And that was good enough for Hattie Sexton.

THREE

Boston, Massachusetts

When I boarded the Thursday-night red-eye back to Boston, I was at the end of my rope. A five-day fact-finding mission in the nation's capital will do that to you. Other than New Orleans on Ash Wednesday, or maybe Paris on a spring weekend, Washington can be the most exhausting city in the world. No surprise there: our government planned it that way.

My person of interest that trip had been a crackpot congressman. Under indictment for misuse of public funds, he had cracked unwise in what he thought was a private tweet, saying, "Everyone in Washington has his price, and mine is dirt cheap." Not the smartest thing a sitting public servant can put out on the airwaves.

Up until then, his diehard constituency—mostly good ol' boys from the Deep South—had been willing to forgive his many shortcomings. They even overlooked the sneaked snapshot of him staggering out of a local watering hole, three sheets to the wind with his road-kill toupee hanging from one ear. In one misstep too far, however, he had been caught on tape telling a friend, "If I ever get caught, I'd run on the crooked and crazy platform from prison." At least he was honest about his dishonesty.

I've never been comfortable with flying. Being cooped up with a hundred or so other nervous human beings in an aluminum cylinder doesn't sit well with my constitution. Doomed by *TIME*'s Spartan expense accounts to fly cattle class, I always book midnight flights. The plane is never full, so I can spread out. Being on the other side of six feet, it's a big plus for my knees. One of which I recently wrenched during a vigorous game of racquetball.

Arriving bleary eyed at Logan International at two in the

morning is nothing new to me, but I still hate the early hour. So does my accommodating wife, Abby, who, after the first few times picking me up at zero dark thirty, decided it would be better for our marriage (to which I agreed) if I sought alternative means of transportation on these nocturnal excursions.

I also hate long cab rides. If Boston cabbies aren't bitching about a late fade of the Red Sox, they're bending your ear on how far the once mighty Celtics have fallen. Both topics too painful for a diehard sports fan like me. Married to me for twelve years now, Abby—bless her forgiving heart—has learned to live with my getting home well after midnight and falling asleep sprawled across the couch with my clothes on. Which was what I did last night. Rule #1 in the *Husband's Book of Survival*: "Never, ever wake up a sleeping wife. Unless it's a matter of life or death."

I probably shouldn't have gone to work the next morning. I looked like shit and felt worse. In the back of my mind, however, I knew if I stayed in bed, my boss would be on the horn bright and early, asking me about my trip to DC. So, before I could take a sip from my first cup of coffee, I found myself standing in front of Helen Collette's half-open door. I couldn't blame her for the early summons. As managing editor of *TIME*'s Boston office, Helen was only doing her job. She has to be on top of things. And one of those things includes grilling her favorite, if overworked, investigative reporter.

I knocked on her door twice, then pushed my way in, dodging past the four hanging ferns and a whiteboard easel. I came to stand hat in hand between a well-worn leather couch and overstuffed easy chair—squarely in front of her aircraft-carrier-sized, highly polished mahogany desk. Stifling a yawn, I chanced a glance through her corner window at the Boston skyline. A view that always impressed me and sometimes calmed me down.

"You wanted to see me, Helen?" I asked.

"Welcome back, John," she said, a half grin on her face as she came out from behind USS *Birdfarm*. "Another late night, I see."

Leaning on a desk corner, she bent down to pick up her Persian cat, Oko. Constant companion and predatory scourge of the office. "Did you corral what you needed in Washington?"

"Enough to nail Congressman Schillings to the wall. I'll bang out a first draft over the weekend. More importantly, I ran across a titillating tidbit that could lead to a blockbuster scoop. A verifiable source says a certain investigative committee is about to lower the boom on the president's scumbag son-in-law. Something about shady dealings surrounding the delayed oil-drilling rights in the Gulf of Mexico. My guy says sonny's hands are beyond dirty and that there's no way he can escape prosecution this time. He even dropped a thinly veiled hint that there may be connections to the 'head honcho.' Says he gleaned those very words from an email."

"I can't wait to read your draft," said Helen. "And I agree with you that someday the president will finally get what's coming to him."

After two strokes, she set the cat aside. Oko gave me a haughty look, then bounded away. Helen looked out the window. Rubbed her eyes.

"But for now," she continued, "I'm putting your piece on hold. And as for the son-in-law thing, we both know he's a loser, a total waste of sperm. However, given the current political climate that's clogging all our arteries, I can't risk going after him at this point. Upper-management priorities"—she threw up finger quotes—"if you know what I mean."

I pursed my lips. Nodded an eye roll. "Sadly, I do."

Helen crossed her arms. Began to pace as she gathered her thoughts. Half an inch short of six feet tall in flats, immaculately groomed, tucked and lifted in all the right places, Ms. Helen Wentworth Collette was an impressive physical specimen. Although in her late sixties, her pale-blue eyes and knockout legs still turned every male head in the room. And quite a few of the women's. She was a driven businesswoman who'd exhausted three husbands—and swore there wouldn't be a fourth—and was accustomed to getting her way.

"Have a seat, John," she said, motioning to the chair. "Something came up while you were gone."

I didn't like the sound of that. After inhaling slowly, I smiled and sat down. Helen and I have always been on good terms. Sometimes even friendly terms. But usually when the boss says, "Have a seat," it means a ream job is on the way. Grinning on the outside, inside I was sweating bullets.

"Should I bend over and assume the position?" I asked.

One of the nicer things about Helen is her genuine laugh. Void of pretense, it comes from the belly. Puts you at ease, even if you're expecting the worst.

"Am I that predictable?" she said, elevating a slow-motion eyebrow. "No ream job is headed your way. Just a minor adjustment of priorities. Something has come across my desk that's right up your alley."

I crossed my legs. A subconscious move to protect my genitals.

"'Right up your alley'? Seems to me you've used that cliché on me more than once before," I said. "But go ahead. Lay the bad news on me."

"While you were in Washington, I received a hot tip from our Memphis branch."

I was not a big fan of coonskin caps or country music. A question inched onto my face. Punctuated by a grimace. "I didn't know we even had a branch in Memphis."

"Contrary to what James Dickey might say, they actually read and write in Tennessee. And those that do often buy magazines. Including the latest edition of *TIME*."

Crossing her own legs to advantage, Helen looked to the window again. It was turning out to be a beautiful day. Despite the bomb she was about to drop on me.

"According to the branch manager," she continued, "there's a recluse woman down there who claims to be a hundred and forty-three years old."

FOUR

Sometimes my hearing isn't the greatest. I'd been a second-string swimmer in college. Water in the ear, that sort of thing.

"Come again?" I said.

Helen smiled that feline grin of hers. When Oko jumped in her lap, she stroked her several times behind the ears. A vague vision of Blofeld, the old James Bond villain, swam through my head.

"You heard correctly, John. I know it sounds implausible, and perhaps a long stride beyond the willing suspension of disbelief, but I have it on good authority the woman's been alive for almost a century and a half."

"But that would make her—"

"The oldest human being on the planet."

"By over thirty years at least," I added.

Having researched the subject for my last story, I was well aware of the facts. The record for longevity currently belonged to a Japanese lady living in Tokyo. At the ripe old age of 114, she was a whippersnapper compared to this woman in Tennessee.

"Can this lady verify her age?" I asked.

"Supposedly she can. And she wants to talk to one of our reporters as soon as possible. And not just any reporter. She asked for you by name."

"Why me?" I asked. More dumbfounded than flattered.

"Apparently she read your article last month on aging in America and was impressed with your style. Said, and I quote, 'He's got a bodacious way with words.' Whatever that means. Bottom line, she's got a story to tell and wants to tell it to *TIME*'s star reporter."

"Just what I don't need," I said. "Another blue-haired fan."

"It would be a great follow-up to your article, John. Might even win an award. If it has legs."

Resolved to my fate, and now more than a little bit intrigued, I uncrossed my legs.

"Suppose she is as old as she says. That means she was born . . ."

"When maybe Ulysses S. Grant was president," filled in Helen. "Think of the tales she could tell, her perspective on history. On life in general. I smell a Pulitzer, John."

Damn it, I can too. I hate it when the boss is always right.

I shrugged. "When do I leave?"

"I've already had my secretary book you on the next flight to Knoxville. It leaves a few hours before sunrise tomorrow morning."

"Tomorrow? But I just got back from Washington late last night. Haven't even opened my suitcase. Barely had time to kiss the wife hello."

"Then you're all set to go. You won't have to repack."

"You realize you'll be named in the divorce proceedings."

"Won't be the first time."

"But why Knoxville?" I asked. "I thought you said Memphis."

"This woman lives in the eastern part of the state. High up in the hills somewhere. Never comes down off her mountain."

"I'll have to track her down? Climb a friggin' mountain? You know I'm afraid of heights. What's worse, I have a lousy sense of direction. I can get lost in a closet."

"Not to worry. You'll have a guide."

"What about background? I need to do some research. Scope this woman out. Find out more about—"

"Already taken care of." Taking my arm in hers, Helen escorted me around the ferns. Sidestepped the easel. "Your intern has all the info you'll need. I took the liberty of putting her on it yesterday."

At the door, she shook my hand. Leaned over to kiss me on the cheek.

"I'm sure you'll do a bang-up job on this, John. You always do."

"You can butter me up all you want, but my kids are going to kill me," I groaned. "I promised them I'd take them to the zoo this weekend. Crossed my heart and hoped to die. This won't sit well with them. I've begged off twice now. The last time was just before this junket to Washington you sent me on. You should have seen their puppy-dog expressions."

"Sorry, but this will have to make three." At least Helen's eyes were sympathetic. "As I've said many times, time waits for no man. Especially at this aptly named publication."

I stuck a finger down my throat. Faked a gag. "God, I hate that line. You really should come up with something new when holding my feet to the fire."

"I may overuse it a tad," said Helen, "but it's still tried and true. And you have to admit, it works."

With that, Helen nudged me further out the door.

"The zoo will be here next weekend," she added. "A hundred-and-forty-three-year-old woman might not. In this business, you have to strike while the iron is hot."

"Is there no end to your platitudes?" I half laughed. "Have you no shame?"

Before she closed the door on me, she blessed me with a wink. "Have a good flight, John. Make sure you keep your powder dry in Tennessee. And don't do anything I wouldn't do."

Thanks a pantload, I thought.

FIVE

Reeling from Helen's fast shuffle, for several seconds I just stood there, staring at her closed door. Way too late, I finally came up with a witty comeback. But even if I'd thought of it in time, it wouldn't have been enough to save me. I took a deep breath. Made an abrupt about-face and headed for my office. Another day, another dollar.

"One of these days, John," I mumbled, "you've got to stand up to that woman."

When frustrated, I often talk to myself. Sometimes it helps. Today it didn't.

"Yeah right, numbnuts," I added, "and someday pigs will fly."

"I see by the lipstick smudge on your cheek things went well in there," said William, not Will or Bill, Helen's well-meaning secretary. He handed me a steaming cup of coffee. Black, with one teaspoon of sugar, just the way I like it.

Like his boss, William Jonathon Cornwall was also in his sixties. Also tall, handsome, and well groomed, he was the Marlboro man in a three-piece suit, a former all-Ivy middle linebacker from Cornell, and tastefully gay. He spoke Spanish, French, and German fluently. And had a working knowledge of Russian. Overqualified for just about any job in the civilized world, he was the perfect buffer to the sometimes abrupt Ms. Collette. To top it off, he made the best cup of coffee in all of Boston. His salary was rumored to be at least twice mine, and he was worth every penny.

"Bless you," said I, cradling the warm cup in both hands. I savored the bitter fluid as it slid down my throat and let out a grateful sigh. "I needed that."

William laid a sympathetic hand on my shoulder.

"I thought you might. Tough break on the quick turnaround, John."

Helen never did anything without first consulting William, so I wasn't surprised he knew the specifics of her latest blindside.

"Nothing she hasn't done before," I said.

"At least she handed you a plum of a story."

"More like a prune."

Like his boss's, William's laugh was also genuine.

"Considering your subject's age, you have a point," he said. "On the plus side, how often does one get the chance to interview a one-hundred-forty-three-year-old hermit?"

"That may be, but I have to trudge through the back hills of Tennessee, to a place nobody's ever heard of."

"I'm sure you'll enjoy the trip. I hear the Smokies are beautiful this time of year."

One of William's many fine qualities is his positive attitude. Unlike grumpy old me, a half-empty kind of guy, his glass is always at least half-full. I took a final sip of my coffee, set the cup down.

"Thanks for the coffee. Better than anything Starbucks could concoct, as usual."

"Glad I could be of service. Have a safe journey, my friend."

Heading for the men's room, I wondered why anyone as sharp as William would settle for a secretary's job. *Different strokes, I guess.* Then again, other than Helen, I couldn't think of anyone in the office who has more influence on our magazine than William.

Standing in front of the washroom mirror, I gave my image a critical eye. I tend to avoid mirrors. Given my late hours, I'm never pleased with what's staring back at me,

Well, John, I thought, *maybe you only speak one language moderately well, but you've done pretty well for yourself. Bottom line, you're a semi-successful writer. At least in some circles. You've got a sexy wife, two beautiful kids, and a fairly new car that's almost paid for. So what if it's a Honda Accord? All things considered, life is good.*

Turning to profile, I glanced down at my beltline. A frown inched onto my face. I sucked in my gut.

"Okay, okay," I said, apologizing to the guy in the mirror. "Maybe I'm closer to forty than thirty. So what? Everyone my age puts on a few pounds."

I leaned forward to check out this month's crop of gray hairs. Pulled at the bags under my eyes. Getting home at four in the morning does that to you. But I still had a full head of dirty-blond hair. Maybe I couldn't run the hundred-yard dash in ten seconds flat anymore, but I didn't smoke, do drugs, or cheat on my wife. Thanks to the competitive swimming I'd done at BU, I was still in halfway decent shape. Better than most of my former classmates, anyway. I recycled religiously, counted my calories, watched my cholesterol intake, gave to the poor, and braked for furry animals of all kinds. Even humans. These days, that had to count for something.

Connie Blanchard, my hardworking intern, was waiting for me in my office. Interns are what upper management gives you after ten years of faithful and impeccable service—in lieu of a raise.

"Welcome back, boss," she said, way too much cheer in her pale-blue eyes.

I tossed my tweed jacket, complete with elbow patches, toward the coat rack in the corner. Missed as usual. My non-ergonomic chair let out a painful squeak when I plopped into it. Leaning forward on my dinghy-sized desk, I aimed a grumble Connie's way.

"Don't welcome back me, you Jezebel." Faking a frown.

"I take it you've heard about your new assignment," she chuckled. The third genuine laugh of the day, and the morning was still young.

"From the horse's mouth," I said. "The least you could have done was give me a heads-up. Interns are supposed to look after those who sign their report cards."

Mildly attractive in her oversized Harry Potter glasses, ponytail, and minimal makeup, Connie set a thin folder on the paper chase that was coagulating on my desk. She is a graduate of the Columbia School of Journalism and has been my right-hand person for over a year. I don't know what I'd do without her. Her coffee doesn't compare to William's, but that's okay since I've never asked her for a cup. Add politically correct to my résumé of glowing attributes.

"Not my fault," she said, still grinning. "I called you twice, but someone I know never bothers to answer his messages. Or even check his phone. Besides, Ms. Collette gave me strict marching orders." She tapped the folder twice with her index finger. "I had to have this ready by the time you returned. 'Or else.' Her exact words."

"Helen can definitely turn a phrase," I said. "Alright, what have you got for me?"

Connie adjusted her glasses to reading position and pulled out the top sheet from the folder. "Lots of good stuff. First of all, do you happen to know what a Melungeon is?"

"A tropical fruit? An Italian sports car?"

"Good guesses both, but no cigar. Melungeons are a backwoods people indigenous to the eastern mountains of Tennessee."

"You mean hillbillies?"

"More than just hillbillies."

SIX

Connie scanned the sheet, gathered her thoughts, then looked up at me. "The hot skinny is all here. Two separate theories, more like legends, have been passed down over the years. Melungeons are alleged to be either descendants of a band of deserters from DeSoto's expeditionary force in the mid-sixteenth century, or they're the last remnants of the Lost Colony of Roanoke."

Connie returned the sheet to the folder. Grinned.

"Me? I prefer the Roanoke angle. Makes for a better storyline. Either way, over the next two centuries the Melungeons migrated west to the hills of Tennessee, where they crossbred with slaves, maybe outsiders from a local Indian tribe, to form their own culture. In time their descendants became known for their dark skin, light hair, and pale-green or blue eyes."

Connie closed the folder. Handed it to me. Raised an eyebrow.

"Very interesting," I said. "But how's all that tie in with the woman I'm supposed to interview?"

"She's probably the last pure Melungeon alive."

"Pure? I thought you said their culture was based on crossbreeding."

"Pure by flatlander standards," said Connie.

"Flatlander? Now, that's a word I haven't heard in ages. Not in Boston, at least."

"Better get used to it. Because you definitely are one. And not to rain on your parade, but there's a fifty-fifty chance you'll get called worse when you get there. A lot worse."

"Sticks and stones."

I retrieved the sheet she'd read. Scanned the first paragraph. Stopped abruptly at the woman's name.

"Hattie . . . Sexton?" I asked.

"Sexton is a common Melungeon name," said Connie. "Much like Miller and Zook are common names in the Amish culture. If it's politically correct to call them a 'culture' these days. Of course, given how separatist they are, I doubt they'd give a damn what anyone calls them."

I continued my scan. When I got to Hattie's age, I paused again. There it was in black and white. Seeing it written down made it seem even more outlandish.

"One hundred and forty-three years old?!" I marveled. "How could any human being live that long? For that matter, why would anyone want to?"

Connie gave a slow nod.

"Amazing, isn't it? As far as I can tell, though, she's the real deal. According to the county clerk I talked to in the town nearest to where she lives, they have her birth record on file. When I mentioned her name, he perked up. His voice raised a full octave. As if she was a full-blown celebrity."

"At least in the backward hills of eastern Tennessee," I said. Something else caught my attention. "What's this? She's a witch doctor?"

"More like a shaman," said Connie. "Or rather, a sha-woman. The clerk said Hattie is known for her homegrown medicines. Also incantations, potions, spells, and the like."

"Spells and incantations? Sounds like voodoo to me. And voodoo's not exactly my cup of tea. You know I don't like spiders and snakes. And things that go bump in the night. Maybe Helen should have outsourced this assignment to Ann Rice. Too bad she's dead."

"It's too late to back out now," said Connie. "Besides, Rice was only interested in vampires. She never did voodoo. And remember, Hattie Sexton was specific. Mentioned you by name. She wants you, and nobody else."

Connie settled into the other ratty chair in my office. Hooked a long leg over a mended arm.

"One more thing: I canvassed a few of the old-timers in the office, and it seems back in the early seventies, we sent someone to Appalachia to do a human-interest piece on Melungeons. An eccentric hard-charger by the name of Bill Turner."

"Bulldog Turner?" I asked.

"The one and only. You know him?

"Mostly *of* him," I said. "He was way before my time. Ten years ago, I met him in a bar after he retired. Interesting guy, but a bit of a blowhard. Then again, after four or five beers, aren't we all? He told me he got shot covering the Tet offensive in Vietnam. In the ass, of all places. Even dropped his drawers to show me the scar. It made a lasting impression on our waitress."

"I hate to cast aspersions on anyone's tall tales," said Connie, "but according to our archives, Turner never went on a military assignment. Not once in all the years he worked here. I went through his history thoroughly. If he went to 'Nam, it was on his own. And considering all the travel restrictions at the time, not to mention how much it would have cost him, that's highly unlikely."

"But what about his butt scar?" I asked. "I saw it with my own two eyes. Pretty hard faking something as gruesome as that. I didn't take the time to count, but it had to be at least twenty stitches' worth."

"The company's insurance records indicate he got that down in Tennessee. A Melungeon supposedly shot him. Filled said butt full of buckshot. Which is why I brought him up."

Connie pulled out her notebook. Flipped a few pages.

"To make sure, I called one of his coworkers. According to him, the day Turner left for the Smokies, he had a full head of jet-black hair. When he came back, it had turned alabaster white. Right down to his eyebrows and chin whiskers. After getting his butt patched up, he refused to write the story. Never spoke of his trip again. To the day he retired, the word 'Melungeon' never passed his lips."

I ran a nervous hand through my own locks. Took a second to

digest this latest tidbit.

"I suppose there's no record of who he interviewed. Or tried to interview."

"Nope," said Connie. "Not a word. If he came back with any notes at all, they were lost or destroyed long ago. Or he conveniently shit-canned them himself."

"Can't really blame him. It's what I would have done were I in his shoes. Maybe I should ask him myself what happened down there, concerned journalist to retired gentleman of the press. I'd hate to get blindsided in Tennessee. White hair is not a good look for me."

"Won't do you any good," said Connie. "He'll just clam up and look away. Maybe throw his drink in your face. A year after he got back, he punched out a persistent editor who pressed him on the matter."

"So, Helen expects me to drop everything, hightail it down to who-knows-where, and listen to a ridiculously old woman ramble on about who-knows-what?"

"Yep," said Connie. "That about covers it."

SEVEN

Hands behind my head, I leaned back to stare at the ceiling. Said hello to the brown stain on a corner tile for the umpteenth time, the one maintenance had promised to remove two months ago. In the dim light, it looked like a profile of Joe Biden eating an ice cream cone. Contemplating my fragile future, I inhaled deeply through my nose. Let it out around a groan.

"Why me?" I asked. "What did I do to deserve this assignment?"

"You should be honored," said Connie. "You'll be the first reporter to ever interview Hattie."

"But how lucid could she be?"

"The town clerk says she's sharp as a razor. And from the tone of his voice, twice as dangerous."

"Dangerous?" I snorted. "At her age, what's she going to do? Hit me with a bag of wrinkles?" However, resolved to my fate, I asked, "When do I leave?"

"You depart Logan tonight. Or rather, early tomorrow morning. Four in the morning, to be exact."

"Another kick to the plums! Who in his right mind gets up that early?"

"Apparently you're about to. You'll arrive in Knoxville at five. I've reserved a rental car at the airport. I've also canceled your racquetball game. You won't have enough time."

"Good thinking. I forgot all about it. You'll make somebody a wonderful wife, Connie."

"I'm not counting on it."

Connie put both feet back on the floor and leaned forward.

"I almost forgot. Hattie Sexton will be asking you for two small favors."

An electric shudder shot up my spine. *Beware the man bearing gifts. And run like hell from any woman asking for small favors.* Especially a woman well over a hundred years old.

"I don't like the sound of that. What kind of favors?"

"She didn't say," said Connie.

"This is getting better by the minute." I tilted my chair back to study the ceiling again. No answers there. Joe hadn't moved an inch. "The things I do for this magazine."

Connie smiled at me. Normally her smile lights up a room. But not this time.

"To minimize the impending blood loss when you tell your wife," said Connie, "I've taken the liberty of ordering flowers for Abby. Two dozen red roses should cover all the bases. They're being delivered as we speak."

"Bless you, my child. You're a lifesaver. My kids, however, aren't going to be bought off so easily. They were looking forward to the zoo this weekend."

"Maybe you could stop at a toy store on your way home."

"Oh, my aching wallet!"

"Isn't that what padded expense accounts are for? Sure wish I had one."

"Good looking, efficient, and appropriately devious. You'll go far in this business, Miss Blanchard. If I wasn't in a serious relationship, I'd marry you myself."

"Already spoken for, kind sir."

"I didn't know you had a steady beau," I said.

"Neither does he. When the time comes, however, I'll fill him in on where he stands."

"And they say it's a man's world." I leaned forward on my elbows. "I just had a brilliant thought. Why don't you go in my place? You're a big fan of all things eccentric. And I hear the Blue Ridge is beautiful this time of year."

"Sorry, no can do, boss. I've got two hungry cats to take care of. I suggest you leave work before Helen dumps something else on you."

After a quick skirt adjustment, Connie headed for the door.

"Coward!" said I to her vapor trail.

"Have a memorable trip!" She waved from the corridor. "One more bit of advice. Don't drink anything that comes in a Mason jar while you're on Hattie's mountain. I hear Tennessee joy juice can put more on your chest than hair."

I watched her walk down the hall. All the way until she turned left at the water cooler. Quite a package, Connie Blanchard.

I swiveled around to stare out the window at the wall across the courtyard. Focusing on my favorite brick, my thoughts turned to Tennessee. In rapid succession, three colleagues had wished me a good, safe, and memorable trip. With best wishes like that, I had nothing to worry about.

As it turned out, un-truer words were never spoken.

EIGHT

L oose ends can strangle any reporter, even the better ones. And I had more than my fair share of loose ends hanging over my head after the Washington turkey shoot. I ended up wasting most of that afternoon mired in paperwork. By the time I'd deciphered the last of my scribbles from DC, I was a scant ten minutes ahead of the rush-hour commute, a precarious pole position if one wanted to make it home in time for dinner.

In hurry-scurry mode, I dashed down the three flights of stairs two steps at a time (faster than waiting for the ever-so-slow elevator, and also a better form of exercise), then hot-footed it to my Honda Accord. Thank goodness upper management had had the good sense to grant me reserved parking two spaces from the exit. Out of the garage in second gear, I zoomed past the new Garden/FleetCenter at well above the speed limit.

I still can't believe they tore the old Boston Garden down. It was hotter than hell up in the cheap seats, but I'd grown up sweating blood for the Celtics. I remember my last Celtics game there like it was yesterday. The 1980 championship finals against the hated Lakers. Me and my dad getting our hearts torn out by Magic Johnson's damn baby hook shot. Ten seconds left, and the son of a bitch sticks a dagger deep into the city's collective heart, smiling as usual. Great player, but how we Bostonians hated that guy! I was so pissed off I punched a hole in my bedroom wall when we got home. So did my dad in his.

What's next to go? Fenway's fabled Green Monster, old stomping ground of my all-time favorite ballplayer and the game's greatest pure hitter, Ted the "Splendid Splinter" Williams? Not in my lifetime, I hope.

Blinkers on, I angled to the right onto a traffic circle, then shot off at the first exit onto the Longfellow Bridge. Halfway across, I noticed a cabin cruiser beneath me making its way up the Charles River. Probably headed for an evening of sport-fishing out on the bay. I put the window down to savor the hint of saltwater in the air, take in the view. One of these days, if I ever get that promotion Helen's been promising me, maybe I'll buy a boat. Nothing fancy, just big enough to take the family fishing. Maybe water-ski the kids.

Free of the bridge, I hung a left on Memorial Drive. A slow curve to the right, and I was home. I pulled up the abbreviated driveway to my two-story brownstone and parked next to my sorry excuse for a lawn. My attention was drawn to the middle of the river. Out on a practice run, the Harvard heavyweight crew was picking up its pace.

I watched their progress for a minute or so after getting out of the car, appreciating the coordination required to propel a skittish craft like a scull in a straight line. In my college days, I'd thought about going out for the team, but the muscles required for rowing differ from swimming. Besides, two sports would have been a drain on my study time. And I am far from what you might call brainy. I had to work my tail off just to graduate.

When the scull disappeared beneath the bridge, my mind returned to the daunting task at hand. Telling the family I would have to bail on them this weekend wouldn't be easy. Working up my courage, I gave my sanctum sanctorum a critical eye.

In the grass to my right lay my son's ball glove, the one signed by Big Papi. Alongside was Davey's faded ball cap. I picked both up. An avid Red Sox fan, the one goal so far in Davey's ten-year-old life was to pitch a no-hitter against the hated Yankees. Like father, like son; at that same age, my goal had been to knock a walk-off homer over the Green Monster in the top of the ninth to beat the bullies in pinstripes.

The grass out front was getting high, and the porch banister tilted a bit to port. The shutters could stand a coat of paint, and the roof needed fixing. But in two more years, my humble home would all be mine. Or rather, our humble home.

My wife, a successful lawyer (I think I'll keep her), is actually the bigger breadwinner in the family. Some men can't handle their better halves earning a larger paycheck, but I'm definitely not one of them. Abby's friends call me an enlightened man. A proponent of gathering rosebuds both when and where you may, I prefer the term "pragmatic realist." Bacon's bacon, no matter who brings it home. Other than our mortgage and Abby's college loan, which we'll also pay off soon, we're debt-free. So the future looks bright. Life is good. Despite my impending trip to Tennessee.

Comforted by the radiance of economic solvency, it took me all of three seconds to return to reality. I looked down to contemplate the shine on my shoes. Adjusted my tie. Glanced over at the river again.

Procrastination is not one of my better qualities.

NINE

I reached the porch steps mumbling a favorite mantra of mine: "Into the valley of death, cannons to the left, cannons to the right . . ."

A quick twist, a manly push, and in I went. On the hall table to my right stood a crystal vase, Abby's favorite, filled with roses. A good sign. I breathed a sigh of relief. Thank goodness the flowers had been delivered

"Bless you, Connie Blanchard," I muttered to the ceiling.

I peeked up our wooden staircase. Then down the hall. Nothing stirred. I heard the refrigerator door open. The clink of glasses. Abby was in the kitchen.

"Hi, honey. I'm HOO-oome!" My best Ricky Ricardo imitation. Probably the only one I'm good at.

From the kitchen: "Hey, John. How about a cold one?"

I set the glove and ball cap beside the vase. Headed into the living room.

"Sounds great."

Wearing white shorts and a tank top, Abby padded in barefoot. She had a killer set of legs. Long, flaming-red hair, porcelain-smooth skin, and Irish-green eyes—no matter what she wore, or where she was, she always took my breath away. Why she settled for a slob like me is still a mystery. She handed me a long-necked Budweiser dripping with condensation. Nodded at the vase.

"Two dozen red roses? Connie has good taste. But she must think you stepped in something big-time."

Rotating the cold bottle across my forehead did wonders for my headache.

"With both feet," I said. "And up to my ankles. As soon as I got off the elevator at work."

"Let me guess. Helen called you into her office."

"You got it." I took a swig of beer. Swished it around in my mouth before swallowing. "Didn't even have my first sip of coffee. And you know what a grinch I am without coffee."

"You got that right. No doubt she laid a hot new assignment on you. Something that can't wait."

"Right again."

"And you have to leave tonight? Even though you just got back."

I tipped the Bud in her direction. "The lady is on a roll."

"One of these days, I'll have to have a serious sit-down with that woman," said Abby. "Helen's great, and I like her a lot, but sometimes she can be a bit . . . pushy. Maybe just this side of overly aggressive, as you men like to say."

"I think bitchy is the word you're looking for."

"I don't like what she's doing to you, John. To us, for that matter. All these last-minute ambushes cut into our quality time. You're on the road twice as much as anyone in your office."

"I guess I should be flattered she has so much confidence in me."

"*TIME* does have other reporters, you know," said Abby. She shook her head. Tried to hide a grin. We'd had this conversation before. I took another swig of beer and, tucking her arm in mine, steered her toward the couch.

"This time I was asked for by name," I said. "By a one-hundred-forty-three-year-old Melungeon hillbilly woman."

TEN

In five minutes, I had laid out the entire scenario for her, cutting a few corners here and there. I left out the bit about spells and incantations. And, of course, the Bulldog Turner incident. No sense in alarming my wife.

Although Abby passed the bar on her first try, she's not above having a few quirks, maybe even a superstition or two. She won't admit it, not to me and especially not to her colleagues, but she reserves a special set of lucky underwear for important court dates. Along with a lucky pen, purse, and umbrella. They must work, because she's a crackerjack lawyer. I can't remember the last time she lost a case.

When I mentioned moonshining, her only comment was a brief "No shit!" Finishing my story and my beer at the same time, I settled back to stifle a burp.

"How's that for an incredible tale of woe?" I asked her.

Abby let out a low whistle, then puffed out her cheeks like a chipmunk hoarding nuts.

"It's like something out of a Stephen King novel."

"Same thing crossed my mind," said I.

For a few seconds, we contemplated our living room's crown molding, one of the reasons we fell in love with the place. Finally, Abby gathered our dead soldiers and headed for the kitchen.

"Care for another?" she asked.

"Please."

"So, when do you leave?" she called from the kitchen.

"William booked me on a flight early tomorrow morning. A couple of hours before sunup. Talk about adding insult to injury."

She returned with two more beers.

"It figures," she said. "Helen must really think this woman's worth it."

This time Abs sat in the easy chair. Probably to look me in the eye.

"And what garden spot are you headed for this time?" she asked.

"Knoxville. As in Tennessee. From there I'll be driven up into the mountains."

"The Smoky Mountains?"

"Give the woman a cigar."

Abby's expression turned serious. And a bit worried. "Now I'll really have to kick Helen's ass."

Taking her hands in mine, I kissed her fingertips. "Hey! I'll only be gone for a day. Two at the most. What could go wrong in such a short period of time?"

"Promise me, no canoe trips while you're there."

"*Deliverance* was filmed in Georgia, not Tennessee." I raised three fingers. "But Scout's honor, I promise I won't come anywhere near a river."

I finally noticed we were alone.

"Where are the kids?"

"Davey's next door, playing video games with Billy. Tracy's at cheerleading practice."

"Do they know about me having to bail on them this weekend?"

"When the roses arrived, I had a hunch something was up, so I told them not to count on the zoo tomorrow. I hinted that Daddy might have to beg off. Again."

"How did they take it?" I asked.

"Tracy shrugged it off, said it was no big deal, that something always comes up. But she was clearly disappointed."

"And Davey?"

"He didn't say much. Nodded something about it being okay, then ran out the door to play with his buddy. But I could see the hurt in his eyes. He was really looking forward to seeing the zoo's new baby gorilla."

I felt like a first-class heel. To make matters worse, I'd forgotten to stop at the toy store.

"I'm lower than snail slime," I said. "I'm pond scum."

"You'll get no argument from me on that score," said Abby.

"How about I make it up to you by taking you out to a fancy dinner tonight? Name the place; sky's the limit. I'll even spring for Nine Knox. I know how much you love their rumaki."

A serious peacekeeping offer. It was the best I could think of on short notice. The cheapest thing on Nine Knox's menu cost twenty-five bucks. And that was a garden salad on the side.

Abby raised her own slow eyebrow.

"The Knox? You must be feeling big-time guilty."

"Intensive Care Unit guilty."

"Your offer is tempting," she said.

I waited for the "but."

"But don't you think you should spend what little time you have left with the kids? I'm a grown-up. I've learned to cope with life's little disappointments. I'll suck my thumb for a few minutes, whimper a bit, maybe break a glass or two, then I'll be fine. Trace and Davey aren't quite that mature yet."

First the boss, then my intern, and now my wife. I hate it when all the women in my life are dead-on right.

"I wasn't thinking," I said. "What can I do to make it up to them?" A light bulb went off. "I've got it! The Yankees are in town next week. Box seats should make Davey forget about the zoo."

"What about Tracy? You know she hates baseball."

"How about I buy her the new Taylor Swift album?"

"Not in the same league as box seats," said Abby.

"Okay, what if I throw in an MP3 player?"

"I think she'd prefer a smartphone."

I let out a groan. Then grinned. "What is this? One of your legal arbitrations? You know how I feel about teenagers and cell phones. Those infernal contraptions are the bane of my existence. You mark my word, they'll bring on the end of civilization as we know it."

"Don't blame me," said Abby. "I'm only the messenger. As your wife and chosen barrister, it's my duty to lay it on the line. And remember, in the court of disappointed children, there is no appeal."

And just like that, I'd lost my case. As the saying goes, anyone who represents himself in court has an idiot for a lawyer.

"Guilty as charged," I said. "Maybe we should all go to the movies before I leave. I hear the *Avatar* sequel is playing over at the Cinema Nine complex. That should appeal to both of them."

Abby kissed me on the forehead. Got up from her chair.

"A much better choice than any restaurant. Now, if you'll excuse me, I've got to finish making dinner. The roast should be about done. Any preference for dessert?"

"How about a large slice of humble pie?"

"Coming right up," said Abby.

ELEVEN

After staggering up to United's ticket counter two hours before the sun was even contemplating yawning its first hello to the world, I was told by an equally groggy counter guy that Helen had my ticket upgraded to first class. A pleasant surprise. Apparently she felt guilty about springing this last-minute trip on me. The prospect of having extra legroom on the flight did wonders for my mood. Almost made up for having to get up so early. But not quite.

Call me a cockcrow sourpuss, but I'm basically incoherent before 8 AM. And don't like to associate with anyone who thinks that's a respectable hour. People who rise and shine before the sun clears the horizon should be lined up and shot. Or at least sterilized so they can't foist their progeny on the sleepy masses.

A minute after takeoff, the plane banked steeply to the right. Through my window I glimpsed Point Shirley sliding under the wing. When Marine Park came into view, I loosened my grip on the armrest, and circulation returned to my knuckles. First class or not, I hate to fly.

When the "You may now resume breathing" sign came on, I tugged my recent purchases from my briefcase. A roll of Necco wafers and James Patterson's latest effort. He seems to put out at least one a month these days. I'd have preferred a Dean Koontz novel, but I'd read all three of the books on display in the gift shop. Like most frequent travelers, I can't go anywhere without something to read and an unhealthy supply of candy. Preferably something to suck on.

I was halfway through Patterson's tenth chapter—no great feat since his chapters are getting shorter and shorter—when my thoughts turned to Hattie Sexton and what awaited me in Tennessee. I glanced out the window and was shocked to see nothing but rolling green mountains beneath a still drowsy sun. A paltry twenty pages, and we'd left all traces of civilization in our contrails.

As the flight attendant handed me what the airlines optimistically call breakfast, this time a one-egg, light-on-the-cheddar omelet, she noticed my puzzled expression.

"There sure is a lot of green down there," she offered.

"As far as the eye can see," I said. "This omelet smells great," I added generously. It really didn't, but being a negative Nelly is the best way to shut down conversations. I like to talk when airborne to keep my mind off my nerves.

She nodded at the window. "Some people call that God's country."

"Very impressive," I agreed. "I've never seen so many trees in one place."

She set a juice container on my tray. Poured me a cup of coffee. Smiled.

"Sounds like something a New Yorker might say."

"Actually, I'm from Boston."

"Ah, yes. I should have recognized the accent." She poured the juice into a glass. "We're coming over the Blue Ridge now. It's beautiful this time of year."

"Speaking of accents, I detect a slight twang. You wouldn't happen to be from Tennessee, would you?"

"Born and raised a hundred miles east of Knoxville," she said. "In a small town called Jefferson City."

"What a coincidence. I'm headed in the same direction. To someplace called Sneedville. In Hancock County, I think."

She pointed to her name tag.

"Name's Bobbie. It's short for Bobbie Jean. Whenever we Southerners leave for the big city, we tend to drop a name or two."

The wink and heavier twang said we were on our way to becoming friends.

She added: "I've been through Sneedville a couple of times. It's a hog's holler across Cherokee Lake, up near Newman's Ridge. About thirty miles into the Clinch Mountains."

I assumed she meant nearby.

"What's Sneedville like?" I asked.

"Other than the county courthouse, there's not much there anymore. Most businesses closed down several years back when the coal mines petered out. A gas station, a Piggly Wiggly, and a Dairy Queen are all that's left. Maybe a hardware slash feed-and-grain outlet. The folks are neighborly, and the weather's nice enough, but I can think of better places to vacation."

"I wish I were on a vacation," I said. "This is just another business trip for me. Believe it or not, I'm supposed to interview a woman who might be the oldest person alive. Probably the oldest in history. With the exception of Methuselah."

"Hattie Sexton? You're going to talk to Hattie Sexton!"

TWELVE

My day had just begun, and already I was ankle deep into my second coincidence.

"You know the woman?" I asked.

"I know of her," said Bobbie. "Hell, everyone in Tennessee has heard about Hattie Sexton. She's flat-out famous. A woman for the ages. A bigger-than-life, living legend. In this part of the country, she's right up there with Davey Crockett and Patsy Kline." Bobbie's smile bordered on awestruck. "You're serious? Hattie's actually agreed to talk to you?"

"To me and my trusty recorder."

Bobbie shook her head. Clicked her tongue.

"If that don't beat all. I can't believe it."

"Cross my heart and hope to die," I said, making the motion. "She sent for me. Says she's got a story she wants to tell."

"Just one? She's probably got a million of them." Another headshake. This time slower. "She has to be well over a hundred and twenty years old. If you can believe the rumors."

"A hundred and forty-three, they tell me."

"Amazing."

"I understand she's something of a recluse," I added.

Bobbie laughed. Switched feet, scratched her head. "Recluse? Calling Hattie Sexton a recluse is like calling the Grand Canyon a big hole in the ground. She and her whole tribe are standoffish. Don't cotton to strangers. Go out of their way to discourage"—finger quoting—"visitors. If you know what I mean. They even got their own way of talking. Their own way of looking at things. They live high up in the mountains, in the thickest wilderness you can imagine. Some even say they're ghosts. You never see them, but you know they're there."

"Tribe?" I said. Connie must have missed something in her research.

"Tribe, clan, kinfolk," said Bobbie. "They call themselves Ramps. Educated flatlanders call them Melungeons. They're fiercely territorial and seldom come down from their mountaintops. And they never, ever invite anyone up. Outsiders are as welcome as ticks on a hound. They value their privacy and go to extreme measures to protect it."

I looked out the window again. The mountains below me suddenly took on a darker hue. I swallowed hard before asking the obvious. "Do you think I might be in any danger?"

Bobbie took a few seconds. Gave a little shrug. Not exactly reassuring.

"That's hard to say. Ramps are a strange people. At times they can be downright squirrely. And they're all crack shots. I sure as hell wouldn't mess with them. Plus, it's said their women have special powers."

"Powers? What kind of powers?"

"I know it sounds silly, but magical powers," she said. "Black-pot-potions, eye-of-newt, witchy kind of powers. They've been known to conjure up spells that sicken the living and raise the dead." Bobbie crossed herself. "Lord knows I'm not the superstitious type, but things go on up in those mountains of theirs that churchgoing folks can't explain. Most don't even try. If they know what's good for them."

"Are you talking voodoo?" I asked.

"Call it what you will," said Bobbie. "My grandmother, may she rest in peace, was descended from the Louisiana Redbones, an off-the-grid kind of people themselves. And she claimed the Ramps were as dangerous as anything that ever slithered out of the swamp. Every year, two or three tourists get lost north of Sneedville, and they're never heard from again. Gone without a trace."

Noticing the worried look on my face, Bobbie forced a smile back to her lips.

"But I don't think you have anything to worry about. If you received a personal invite from Hattie, you shouldn't be in any danger. Above Newman's Ridge, her word is law. She won't let anything bad happen to you. Nobody will mess with a friend of Hattie Sexton. Even if you're a city dude."

My mouth now dry, I swallowed again. "That's comforting to know. Your words would make interesting reading on my tombstone. 'Now he really has nothing to worry about.'"

Another shrug from Bobbie. "At least you're in for an interesting meeting."

"Yeah," I said, my smile on the feeble side. "Like Custer had an interesting meeting at Little Big Horn. But thanks for the heads-up. I'll make sure I keep my eyes open and my powder dry."

Bobbie adjusted her skirt and returned to her cart.

"Well, I'd better get back to work. Good luck on your trip, Mr. March."

I raised my juice glass in a toast. "Thanks. Here's hoping I won't need any."

Watching Bobbie head down the aisle, I thought back to yesterday's meeting with my boss. *You should have stood up to Helen, John. It wasn't fair, sending you out on such short notice. And it's damn inconsiderate of her, putting you in harm's way like this. I wish, just once, you'd have the balls to tell her what she could do with her precious assignments.*

I turned to the window. Let out a sigh.

"Yeah right, John. Wish in one hand, and shit in the other. See which one fills up first."

The gnawing sensation in my gut continued to fester, but there was no turning back now. Especially at thirty thousand feet. As Bobbie had so eloquently pointed out, I might have an interesting day ahead of me. Besides, what could Hattie Sexton do to me? Hell, she was almost a century and a half's worth of old.

Bobbie Jean's voice came over the intercom.

"We are now on our final approach into Knoxville Airport. Please secure your tray tables in the upright position and fasten your seatbelts. We will be pulling up to the terminal shortly.

"Final" and "terminal": two words that should never be uttered anywhere near an airplane. "Approach" is sufficient all by its lonesome. Attaching "final" to it conjures up images of last rights. Same thing for "terminal." Why can't they just call it a depot? Like the bus people do.

White-knuckle time again, I put Hattie and her clan of voodoo ghosts on hold and closed my eyes. On my long list of fears, landings rank right up there with takeoffs.

THIRTEEN

Following the advice of the helpful lady at the Avis rental counter, I bypassed the local interstate and took Highway 33 north out of Knoxville. She said I would avoid the morning freeway tangle while treating myself to some "bodacious" scenery. Must be a common word in these parts.

After shooting first through Maynardville, then its identical twin brother, Tazwell, I crossed Norris Lake Bridge and started to climb in earnest. In a few miles, when my Ford Explorer automatically downshifted a gear or two, I knew I was entering some serious hill country. I turned on the radio, and up came a Garth Brooks song. I pushed a button, and it was Tammy Wynette's turn to warble. A second push resulted in three little girls singing something I assumed was bluegrass. My third try treated me to the unmistakable strains of "Dueling Banjos," *Deliverance*'s unofficial theme song. Just what I didn't need to hear. Thinking back to Abby's warning, I hoped it wasn't an omen.

That's just great, John, I thought. *Look out, Ned Beatty, here I come. I hope squealing like a pig isn't in my immediate future.*

Finally, I settled on a local weatherman. But without relief.

"And it looks like we're in for another hot one today, folks. Temperatures in the city will reach over a hundred again. Slightly cooler in the higher elevations. It's going to be a perfect day to hit the beach. Yuk, yuk, that is, if we had a beach!"

"I guess that's what passes for humor in rural Tennessee," I said.

I turned off the radio. Glanced down at my watch. At least I was making good time.

Out the window I noticed a distinct lack of structures on either side of the road. So much for the suburbs. There was no longer a house in sight. Not even a fence. Nothing but trees, hills, and more hills from here to the horizon.

When I turned left on Route 31 ten miles later, the going got even steeper. My ears began to pop past the second mile marker. A battered sign half hidden by vegetation caught my eye, and I pulled over for a closer look: SNEEDVILLE 2 MILES, POPULATION 610.

Only 610? Kinda small for a county seat, I thought.

I pulled out my map to double-check. Perhaps I'd gotten myself hopelessly lost. Having no sense of direction whatsoever, it was a distinct possibility.

Route 33 across the lake, twenty miles left on Route 32 to Route 31 . . . Yep, I'm still on track.

"I guess this must be the place," I told the map.

Checking unnecessarily for traffic, I pulled back onto the road. After twenty minutes, three sharp, climbing bends, and another thousand-foot jab to my internal altimeter, I pulled into Sneedville's only lodging facility, a weatherworn 1950s-style motor court. When I'd called ahead for reservations—as if any were needed—I told the eager clerk I'd be checking out the same day, that I only needed the room for couple of hours. "To freshen up and get the kinks out," as my wife likes to say. Given my Italian background, my five o'clock shadow usually materializes around noon.

When I opened the car door, a wave of humidity heat hit me flush in the face. By the time I reached the front office step, I'd worked up armpit stains. *Five seconds out of air-conditioning and you're sweating like a stuck pig? Not a good sign, John.*

To the right of the office were five bungalows arrayed in a line like baby chicks following a mother hen. Not exactly five-star material. Thank goodness I wasn't staying the night. All I needed was running water, preferably hot, to shave and wash my face—and to put on an extra layer of deodorant. Maybe make myself more presentable for my meeting with Hattie Sexton.

Picturing a hayseed clerk with green teeth and the IQ of a

rutabaga, I opened the office door and walked in.

The hayseed clerk turned out to be a striking young woman with immaculate dental work and wearing a colorful gingham dress. After checking me in, she graciously directed me to bungalow #1. All the while using complete sentences, unlike any kind of vegetable.

Expecting a closet-sized room with purple walls decked out in velvet Elvis artwork, I opened the door to a shock. My second slice of humble pie in less than a day. The room was luxurious. A huge stone fireplace spanned the far wall, a fifteen-foot picture window the other. A tasteful Mondrian print hung over the bed, a Wyeth lithograph over the modern writing desk in the corner. And the room was even clean.

Never judge a book by its cover, John, I thought by way of apology.

The view from the window took my breath away. Fifty feet in front of me, a mountain stream cascaded off a towering cliff into an azure pool. *Better Homes and Gardens* couldn't have come up with anything better.

"Abby would have loved this place," I said to the drapes.

A bit discombobulated, I pulled out my notebook and plopped onto the king-sized bed. A first-rate mattress, not a lump anywhere. Too bad I didn't have time for a nap. First things first: I needed to check in with my contact, that local county clerk.

He answered after the first ring.

"Mr. Herkemer Bollinger?" I said. "This is John March, from *TIME* magazine. Connie Blanchard arranged our meeting."

"Ah, Mr. March," he said. "Welcome to Sneedville."

Bollinger's high-pitched voice caught me off guard. I'd been expecting a "good ol' boy," baritone Southern twang.

"Call me Herkie," he said. "Are your accommodations satisfactory?"

"Very much so. The view is surprising, to say the least."

"I thought you'd like it. I know you're on a tight schedule, so I'm available to meet with you anytime. At your convenience, of course."

"Give me a minute to freshen up, and I'll be right down."

"Excellent," said Bollinger. "I appreciate a man who gets down to business. I'll be waiting for you at the courthouse. You can't miss it. It's the only three-story building in town. My office is in the basement. Looking forward to meeting you in person, Mr. March."

"Please, call me John. See you in a few minutes, Herkie."

After hanging up, I headed for the bathroom.

Basement? And Herkie? I thought. *What kind of name is that for a grown man?*

I saw the overhead rain shower fixture and decided to indulge myself. When meeting the oldest person on the planet, one should be as clean as possible. And definitely not stink. It's only good manners.

FOURTEEN

Herkie Bollinger's description was dead-on. There was no way to miss the county courthouse. Sitting atop a sweeping mound in the center of Sneedville's town square, the white-columned, antebellum building dominated its surroundings. After I climbed the twenty-three front steps—I subconsciously count such things—I turned to look down at Sneedville's sleepy main street.

Like a snapshot out of history, the town probably hadn't changed much in seventy years. Except for the five late-model cars parked in front of the courthouse, it could have passed for a '40s diorama. And take away the cars, the telephone poles, add a smattering of horse-drawn buggies, and I could have been back in the Gay '90s. The tingling sensation of being engulfed in a time warp somehow comforted me. If out-of-the-way settlements like Sneedville could endure for centuries, maybe there was hope for the rest of us.

In front of the courthouse's two ponderous wooden doors stood a ten-foot-tall statue of General Thomas "Stonewall" Jackson, Confederate hero of Fredericksburg. Jaw firmly set, he sat astride a fiery-eyed steed pawing the air, an indication that the general had eventually succumbed to his battle wound. An avid Civil War buff, I knew that if Jackson had died of natural causes, his horse would likely have been shown positioned with all four feet on the ground. In Stonewall's right hand was the archetypal raised sword. His left sleeve was pinned at the shoulder, the only depiction I'd ever seen of him after he'd lost the arm.

I bent down to read the inscription: LET US CROSS THE RIVER, AND REST UNDER THE SHADE OF THE TREES, it said.

Jackson's last words brought a lump to my throat. They don't make heroes like that anymore.

Realizing I had my own river to cross, I pushed through the doors. The courthouse was even more impressive on the inside. A marble foyer led straight to a wide, polished, wooden staircase. To the right, a more mundane stone stairway led to the basement. An arrowed sign there pointed the way to the archives, where I was supposed to meet Herkemer Bollinger. Two centuries of pounding feet had taken their toll on the steps, rounding them down until they almost touched. They reminded me of some of the older buildings at Harvard.

At the bottom of the steps, another sign directed me to a room at the end of a long hall. Inhaling the musty order of shelf-tired books, I listened to the echo of my loafers clip-clopping on the tile while my imagination conjured up an image of someone who would call himself "Herkie." My thought process ended up somewhere between Gomer Pyle and the Phantom of the Opera.

The door to the archives had been left ajar. Peering in, I saw row upon row of box-laden shelves, all stretching to the ceiling. On the far wall was a battered rolltop desk illuminated by a solitary library lamp. Half expecting the ghost of Boris Karloff to suddenly appear, I knocked on the door.

FIFTEEN

"**H**ello? Anybody here?"

A head appeared from behind the shelves. Then an entire body.

"Mr. March, I presume," said the head. Two heartbeats later, its body came forward to extend a hand. "Welcome, welcome! I'm Herkie Bollinger. I can't tell you what an honor it is to meet you, sir. I loved your piece on aging last month. Great bit of writing. Factual and well thought out. Not at all what I've come to expect from the media these days."

Trim and maybe an inch or two over five feet tall, Bollinger boasted a head of flaming-red hair that added a dash of much-needed color to the room. As did the transparent green visor he was wearing. His close-set but not beady eyes, thin lips, and button nose reminded me of the baby ferret I'd seen the week before at our local pet shop. Looking like he'd stepped out of the Roaring Twenties, Bollinger was dressed in a white shirt with elastic arm bands, suspenders, a pinstripe vest, and a navy-blue bow tie. The canvas spats, round, wire-rimmed glasses, and Rudy Vallee haircut completed the "look." All that was missing from the crooner's ensemble was a megaphone. Knowing that Halloween was still two months away, I decided not to mention his attire and shook his hand.

"You flatter me," I said. "I can't take all the credit for the article, however. Most of the research was done by my talented assistant."

An ear-to-ear smile blossomed across Bollinger's face. He hooked his arm in mine to lead me around the corner. "According to Michner, you can only go as far as good research takes you. But I guess that's why you're here, Mr. March." Motioning to his desk: "And in that vein, I've found something you might find interesting.

A headline-scoop diamond in the rough, as you pundits might say."

On the wall above his desk hung three autographed black-and-white photos. Jean Harlow, Greta Garbo, and Will Rogers. Harlow's was signed, WITH ALL MY LOVE. Next to her was a framed cross-stitch that read, THE TWENTIES FOREVER!

I nodded at the montage. "I take it you're a fan of that period."

Bollinger ran a loving finger across the embroidery.

"To me the twenties were the golden age of America. A time that maybe we all should try to recreate. The country had style and class back then. A certain panache, if you will. The movie stars were bigger than life. Charlie Chaplin, Mary Pickford, Clara Bow, better known as 'the *It* Girl.' Real heroes dominated the silver screen. Swashbuckling types like Douglas Fairbanks and Buster Crabbe, the Olympic swimmer.

"People knew how to dress, how to entertain, how to live. Not like today where everything's Day Glo Nikes and designer jeans. Where you wear pajamas to Walmart, letting your butt crack hang out while you shop. Today it's all doom and gloom. Where everyone deserves a trophy for being mediocre."

I took a closer look at the Rogers photo. Will was standing in front of a sleek-looking airplane, shaking hands with a short, squat man wearing an eye patch.

"Rogers was a favorite humorist of mine," I said.

Bollinger pointed at the photo, then sighed as he crossed himself. "Will died in the same plane. Terrible loss, that. Lord knows we need more men like him today."

"So, that must be Wiley Post standing next to him."

"You know your history well, Mr. March."

"Please, call me John. I understand they ran into bad weather and crashed into a mountain. Somewhere in Alaska, if I'm not mistaken."

"Now I'm really impressed."

"Both died way too young," I said. "Rogers was a great humanitarian. Never met a man he didn't like."

Bollinger let out a soft chuckle.

"He wouldn't say that if he were alive today. Too much 'me too' going on. Too many power grabs in Washington. And don't get me started on what's happening out there in California. Talk about a bunch of whackos! That's why I prefer the flapper age. Things were much simpler back then."

"Simple, but sometimes costly," I said. "Don't most historians say the excesses of the twenties led to the bread lines, Hoovervilles, and dust bowls of the thirties?"

Bollinger raised an eyebrow. Cocked his head to the right.

"At least they didn't have rap music, opioid addictions, global warming, and cell phones. Not to mention eight percent inflation and the threat of nuclear war."

SIXTEEN

"**P**oint well taken," I said. "I also worry that my generation has gone overboard in their love of electronics. Last time I was in a restaurant, I saw a family of four sitting at a table across from each other, waiting for their food to arrive. All four had their noses buried in their iPhones, their thumbs going a mile a minute. For all I know, they could have been texting each other. Whatever happened to face-to-face communication? Talking things out man-to-man? Or man-to-woman? I may be a hopeless anachronism, but as for Twitter, I refuse to use a service that begins with the word 'twit.'"

"I hear and applaud you," laughed Bollinger. He pointed to an aged photograph in the center of his desk. Yellow and cracked along its edges, it had to be well over a hundred years old. "This is what I wanted to show you. It's the only known picture of Hattie Sexton. If the date on the back is correct, it was taken on her twenty-first birthday."

I bent down for a closer look. Fearful of damaging the brittle antique, I didn't even breathe on it. "It looks like a tintype of some sort."

"The Kodak Brownie was still a twinkle in George Eastman's eye back then," said Bollinger. "This photo is faded and out of focus, but you can still tell that Hattie was far from a raving beauty."

I noticed the sagging growths on Hattie's face, along with her alarmingly crooked posture. "That's so sad," I said. "What was wrong with her?"

"She was born with a tuberculin infection that damaged her backbone. Turned it into a lopsided *S*. Poor woman has had to rely on a cane since she was three."

"That had to be rough on a child," I said. "What about the deformities on her face?"

"As if the tuberculosis wasn't bad enough, she also had elephantiasis. As you can see, the tumors were confined to the left side of her face. She can't see well out of that eye. Mostly just blurs of light."

I couldn't take my eyes off the young woman in the photo. Despite the grotesque features, something about her good eye grabbed me. Even from a faded tintype, it seemed to bore into me, daring me to look away.

"With those afflictions, all the hardships she had to endure, it's amazing she's lived so long," I said.

"Especially considering her mother died at an early age. Mullie Moon Sexton was a legend in her own right. She weighed over eight hundred pounds when she passed away. Queen of the moonshiners they called her."

My imagination in high gear, I envisioned expanding the upcoming interview into a book. Maybe with a movie to follow. Hollywood was always on the lookout for oddball scripts. And this Hattie Sexton thing had all the earmarks of a gold mine. An eight-hundred-pound mother and her 143-year-old deformed daughter? Moonshine and voodoo? Sounded like an Oscar winner to me.

"Do you think Hattie wants to talk about her mother?" I asked.

"She didn't say so in her message," said Herkie. "But that could very well be. Then again, given the life she's led and the things she's seen, it could be about a hundred things."

"'Message'? So, you didn't actually see her? Talk to her in person?"

"Nope. Nobody here in Sneedville has seen Hattie face-to-face since before I was born. Some in town say she's covered with hair now. Turned herself into a bearlike creature with fangs. Others say she's sprouted wings and hunts the forest at night like a vampire."

A slow grin came to Herkie's face. Followed by a full-fledged laugh.

"A few swear she's grown another head and two more arms," he continued. "We hill people have a penchant for tall tales and nonsense. Supposedly a not-so-local postman is the only person from the valley who's seen her recently. And he's not talking."

"I guess that's the price one pays for being a hermit," I said. "Same thing happened to Howard Hughes. I just hope she isn't saving her pee in jars like he did. That could complicate the interview."

"Even though no one in town has seen Hattie in over fifty years, people take heed whenever she sends word down to us. No questions asked." Bollinger motioned to an empty chair. "Getting back to your original question, I'm sure she'll mention her mother eventually."

I took a seat.

"What else can you tell me about Hattie?" I asked.

"First of all, I'm flabbergasted she granted you a sit-down. Other than Vardy Miser, the postman I was talking about, she hasn't allowed anyone from the valley on her property in over a decade. You should be honored she sent for you."

"You're the second person to tell me that." I pulled out my pocket recorder. "Do you think she'd be offended if I used one of these to record our conversation?"

Bollinger took the recorder in his hand, turned it over. Thumbed a button or two, then handed it back to me.

"It's amazing how small they make these things these days," he said. "Foreign?"

I nodded. "It's a Sony."

"Smart people, the Japanese. How noisy is it?"

"You can hardly hear it."

"As long as it's quiet, I don't think it will bother Hattie. She's not much for loud." Bollinger touched a finger to his nose. "Of course, you never can tell what will set her off. Twenty years ago, she cast a spell on the mayor of Kyles Ford for ordering the demolition of an old bridge on her property. Hazard to public safety, he called it."

"A spell? Did anything happen to him?"

"Well, they never proved Hattie had a hand in it, but that very same year, poor Mayor Goiner's hair went totally white. Seven days later, it all fell out, and he was bald. One week he had a full head of hair, the next, slick as a cue ball. Hard to believe he was only thirty at the time. Wife left him three months later."

"And the bridge?"

"After what happened to the mayor, no work crews would go near it. It's still standing today."

I ran a nervous hand through my hair.

"In other words, you're telling me not to get on Hattie's bad side."

Bollinger reached over to pat me on the knee.

"You catch on fast for a city feller. But with your special invitation, I'm sure you have nothing to worry about, John. I'd still be on my best behavior, however. No sense in poking the bear. If you catch my drift."

He glanced up at the wall clock. Stood to extract a chained watch from his vest pocket and compared times.

"Well, we'd better get a move on," he said. "Hattie's punctual as the morning sun. If she sets an appointment, you'd best be on time."

"You're coming along?" I asked.

"I've got to. I could give you directions to her place, but considering you're a flatlander"—there it was again—"sure as shooting, you'd get yourself lost. No offense. I'll drive you as far as the turnoff to her property."

Herkie retrieved a button-down cap from the nearby hat rack. Donned it at a jaunty angle.

"From there, you'll be on your own."

SEVENTEEN

Outside in the parking lot, removed from the courthouse's color-sapping fluorescent lighting, I noticed Bollinger's Hollywood-caliber tan for the first time. In high school, way back, there had been three redheads in my senior class. One girl, two boys. And all three fried to a bright-red crisp after twenty minutes in the sun, their freckles peeling off the next day in flakes the size of candy wrappers. Looking at George Hamilton incarnate, curiosity got the better of me.

"Are you a sun worshipper, Herkie?" I asked.

"Sun worshipper?"

"Your Coppertone tan," I said. "It usually isn't associated with red hair."

"This isn't a tan," he laughed. "I was born this dark. I thought you knew. I'm one-sixteenth Melungeon." Something else Connie had failed to tell me. "From my great-grandmother on my father's side." He pointed to his crimson locks. "This head of hair I got from my mother's father, an Irish potato farmer fresh off the boat from Dublin. A strange gene pool for a backwoods hillbilly, don't you think?"

"I didn't mean to offend."

Herkie stopped a yard short of his car and smiled when he turned toward me.

"No offense taken. Here we are: my humble, if not so basic, form of transportation."

Sitting all by itself was a pale-blue 1952 Studebaker, the kind where you couldn't tell if it was coming or going. In immaculate condition, its chrome trim glistened in the sun. So did the four whitewall tires. Not easy to come by these days. Impressed, I let out a slow whistle.

"There aren't many of these old-timers on the road anymore," I said.

Bollinger pulled out a handkerchief to wipe a speck of dirt from a front fender.

"They didn't build that many," he said "And the lucky few that avoided the scrap pile are usually in museums. Ginger here, she's my baby. And yes, I named her after Ginger Rogers. I park her this far in the back to avoid dings. Matching the original paint can be a hassle."

"I've got a friend who does the same thing with his '55 T-bird," I said.

"Not a bad car in its own right," said Herkie. "But it's no 'Baker."

The car's interior was equally impressive. Bollinger had spent big bucks in maintaining the old girl. Another surprise, the engine started up with a throaty roar, then settled down to a well-tuned rumble.

"Ginger purrs like a kitten," I said. "And from the sound of her, she probably has all the moves of her namesake."

Bollinger patted the dashboard as he headed out of the lot. "It took me three years to restore her. Rebuilt the engine myself on weekends. It's amazing what a new crankshaft and a ring job will do for a seventy-year-old lady."

I ran an appreciative hand across Ginger's leather armrest.

"You did all this yourself? Again, no offense, but you don't strike me as . . ."

Bollinger arched one eyebrow. Chuckled again.

"The mechanical type?" he finished with a wink. "Just because I look like what some people call a dandy doesn't mean I don't like getting my hands dirty every so often."

"Dandy? Now, that's a term I haven't heard in years."

"I find it to be all-inclusive. And much more palatable than some of the things I've been called. Feel free to put it in your article."

Coming to an impossibly steep gravel road, Bollinger downshifted into second.

"Hold on to your hat," he said. "This stretch can get a little hairy."

Hairy didn't come close to what came next. The incline ahead looked challenging for a four-wheel drive with knobby tires, much less a vintage Studebaker on street slicks.

"You can't be serious," I half said, half groaned. "Is this the only way to Hattie's place?"

"There's one other way. But it involves hiking ten miles through thorny underbrush. Followed by a hip-deep wade into a snake-infested bog."

I glanced up at the hill we were heading for. It appeared to be getting steeper.

"We're going up that? I vote for the snakes and thorns."

"Sorry, John. No can do. It would take us at least an extra eight hours, and we can't spare the time. As I said, Hattie doesn't like to be kept waiting."

Bollinger spun the steering wheel hard to the right, then downshifted to pull us out of the hill's first turn. In two seconds, Ginger's hood ended up pointing at the sky, her engine straining under the load. When her tires began to spit gravel, we slipped a few feet to the left. For half a heartbeat, I thought we'd tumble over backward.

"Jesus H. Christ!" I all but bleated.

Unfazed by my outburst, Bollinger yanked the wheel back to the left and let off the gas. The back tires thankfully regained their grip, and the horizon reappeared. Airborne for two seconds, we returned to earth with a resounding thud. Herkie pulled to a stop and let Ginger idle for a few seconds, a big smile on his face.

"No problem. A little harsh, but nothing she couldn't handle."

My heart pounding out a double-time backbeat, I inhaled twice. Felt for a pulse. Checked my shorts. Thank goodness I didn't have high blood pressure.

"Little harsh? You've got to be kidding! I came this close to soiling myself."

Bollinger shot a thumb over his shoulder. "Rest assured that was the worst part. From here on, it's an easy climb to Mulberry Gap. Nice little town. You'll like it."

As we got moving again, I asked, "There's actually a town way up here? Somewhere at the end of this so-called road of yours? A road that isn't much wider than a goat path?"

"Can't argue with that."

Bollinger's hard left came just in time to avoid what looked to be a bottomless deep rut.

"Actually," he continued, "Mulberry is more of a cluster than a town. There's one business establishment, if you can call it that. And it's the only one for miles. But it's a great place to get you up to speed on Melungeon lore. It'll give you a taste of what's in store when you meet Hattie. The owner—or proprietor, as he likes to call himself—is a grizzled old cuss, name of Leaton Scump. I wouldn't stand downwind of him, but he knows everything that goes on in these hills."

I let the three mismatched syllables trickle over my tongue.

"Lea . . . ton . . . Scump? Odd name for a human being. Sounds more like a wood fungus," I said. Politely not mentioning Herkie's own name.

"It's no stranger than Elvis Presley, Whoopi Goldberg, or Englebert Humperdink," said Bollinger.

"Good point," I said. "I guess 'A rose is a rose is a rose is a rose.'"

"Gertrude Stein, right?"

"I see you know your American novelists, Herkie. Now I'm the one who's impressed."

EIGHTEEN

We'd gone less than a mile since our brush with death, but already I noticed something strange. The forest was changing right before my eyes. It seemed to be turning ominously darker, even more uninviting.

Long green vines now reached all the way from the ground to the treetops. At least three fingers thick, they were everywhere—on bushes, on the ground, covering rocks and boulders, wrapped around tree trunks. It looked as if a giant chlorophyllous spider had spewed miles and miles of thick green silk over the entire landscape. Up ahead, several of those angry-looking vines dangled across the road to form a webbed tunnel. As if they'd laid out a trap for us.

It felt like we were slowly being swallowed by an Appalachian version of the Twilight Zone. Filtered from above, the dimming sunlight was sleep inducing, almost narcotic, a verdant lullaby. Without realizing it, I had to stifle a yawn.

"What is all that green stuff?" I asked. "It looks like someone, or something, dropped a huge camouflage net over the land."

"That's kudzu," said Bollinger. "The fastest-growing weed in America. We call it the green menace." A downshift brought us to yet another steep bank. Reflexively, I held my breath. "It strangles everything in sight," he continued. "Even the tallest oak trees."

He slowed to point out a copse of emaciated trees to the right, their blackened branches gnarled and twisted like something out of a Tim Burton movie.

"See those maples over there? That's what happens after a few years. In time, the menace blots out the sky. Chokes the life out of everything in its path. Any plant beneath it can't get sunlight, so eventually it withers and dies. Kudzu is also a thirsty bastard. It sucks up all the moisture before other plants can get a drink. No sunlight, no water—so, in time, no more trees. Nothing's left but those damn vines."

"Can't anything be done to stop it?"

Bollinger shook his head. Scratched his chin.

"It's too expensive to spray. And it would take an army to chop the stuff down. Even then, it would grow back within a month. Burning is the only surefire way to control it, but that would be like throwing out the baby with the bath. Besides, at the first sight of a lit match, some say the kudzu would only pull up roots and run away. Over the years we've learned to live with the plague of the hills. Or rather, around it. It was here long before I was born. And unfortunately will probably be here long after I'm gone."

I stuck my head out the window to get a better view. High above me, a dense tangle of vines swayed gently in the breeze. It reminded me of a multitentacled predator trolling for its next meal. To the left stood another stand of dead trees, their broken branches extended toward the sky like a doomed congregation of lost souls praying for a sun that could never reach them.

"Despite all the damage kudzu is doing," I said, "in a scary sort of way, it's almost beautiful."

Bollinger raised an eyebrow. Shot me a quizzical look.

"In this case, beauty is definitely in the eye of the beholder. The green menace may be pretty to look at, though you're the first person to ever say that, but it's got no heart. Not much brains, either. Saddest thing of all, in a few years there will be nothing left to the forest but rotting skeletons. The kudzu itself will then die out, and the whole process starts anew." A wan smile crept onto his face. "I suppose it's another life-and-death cycle."

"Just nature's way, as the environmentalists like to say?"

Herkie nodded and looked away.

"I suppose," he said. "I guess there are days you just have to take a breath and count your blessings. Be thankful for what you've got. And not what's got you."

NINETEEN

W e rounded another bend, and a rusted-out road sign came into view. Dented by buckshot and drilled with a dozen or so bullet holes, it dangled from a single twisted bolt. It was so weathered I could barely make out its faded letters: MULBERRY GAP, POPULATION 27.

The "27" had been crossed out and a "26" scratched in. But before I could ask, Bollinger pulled into a small clearing to the left of the sign and turned off the engine.

"Well," he said, "here we are."

Resembling a faithful plow horse too long in the field, Ginger coughed twice, gave out a clipped wheeze, and died. Like me, the Studebaker's carburetor hadn't been calibrated for higher altitudes.

I looked around. Nothing but trees and more trees. And a lot more vines.

"'Here,' you say? There's nothing here but a clearing in the forest. And that Volkswagen-sized boulder over there."

Bollinger pointed to an indent in the far tree line.

"How about that business establishment over there? There stands the Mulberry Gap Mercantile and Feed. Best country store in five counties. That's where we'll find Leaton Scump. And if we're lucky, a few of his buddies."

I followed his finger to a building of sorts. And had to look twice to make sure I wasn't seeing things. Looking like it had sprouted out of the wilderness, the Mercantile's roof was covered with a thick layer of multicolored moss. Its ramshackle siding melded in perfectly with the trees. Two towering oaks seemed to hover over the store, as if protecting a younger sapling from the woodsman's ax. A warped front porch was missing several floorboards. Its steps were beyond repair. The entire structure hadn't tasted a drop of paint in decades, and I was one hundred percent sure a healthy sneeze would collapse the claptrap in a heartbeat.

"I wouldn't set foot in that hovel on a bet," I said. "No way, no how. Damn thing looks like it died a hundred years ago."

Bollinger smiled.

"Then I'd lay odds you wouldn't get your story. The Mercantile may not look like much on the outside, or smell much better on the inside, but don't let her appearance fool you. You can get just about anything you need in that so-called 'hovel.' Ask Leaton for a flumpus widget, and he'll ask if you want left or right handed. Besides, he and his cronies are fountains of local color. And isn't that what you're after? As the old saying goes, 'No guts, no glory.'"

"You make a good point, Herkie. No writer worth his salt writes articles without at least a smidgeon of local color."

I shook my head, thinking, *When in Rome*, then followed Bollinger toward the Mercantile. Cannons to the left of me, cannons to the right.

I stopped beside him at the first step. "You're the expert here, my friend. After you."

Bollinger navigated the four steps without mishap, so I followed in his exact footsteps. When he reached the front door, he turned to add a warning.

"One thing: if you want to stay on Leaton's good side, whatever you do, don't stare at his toupee. He sent away to Sears and Roebuck forty years ago for the thing. Although it's seen better days, he's still proud of it."

"Bad rug?" I asked.

"'Bad' doesn't do it justice. It's like he stapled a mangy dead cat to his head. That monstrosity of a wig, and anything to do with the Civil War, are two things you should avoid mentioning at all costs. And if he catches you staring at his Confederate flag on the wall, you're doomed. First he'll ask for your affiliation. And whatever your background, don't tell him you're from Yankee country. If you're lucky enough to get that far, he'll bore you to death with stories about his great-great-grandpappy. And how Gramps fought with Lee at Gettysburg."

"Is he one of those 'Stars and Bars' diehards waiting for the South to rise again?"

"Worse. He thinks Appomattox never happened."

I sucked in a grin.

"So, it might not be wise to whistle the 'Battle Hymn of the Republic' in his presence?"

Bollinger tugged at an ear. "Not unless your Blue Cross is all paid up. And you have a sympathetic doctor on speed dial."

With a nod, I opened the door for him. "'Dixie' it is."

Bollinger tapped a finger to his temple.

"Definitely a wiser choice of tunes. And don't forget about the toupee. Silence there is most assuredly golden."

TWENTY

A giant stride back in time, the Mercantile was more commodious than I'd expected. And a mind-boggling surprise. An aroma of strong coffee and hickory-cured ham undercut the sweet smell of pine. After my eyes adjusted to the dim light, I was bombarded with a kaleidoscope of sights from a century long past. Covered with a thin layer of sawdust, the store's pegged-oak floorboards had been worn smooth under the trod of probably a thousand hobnail boots. A variety of bridles, bits, stirrups, saddles, and other horse paraphernalia hung helter-skelter on the wall to my right. An assortment of what I assumed to be farm tools dangled from the left. I recognized a hand scythe and something that looked vaguely like an adze. I only knew about the adze because it was a favorite four-letter fill for crossword puzzles, another weakness of mine.

The far wall was covered by the biggest Confederate flag I'd ever seen. I remembered Bollinger's advice and tried not to stare. Faded, torn, and ragged around the edges, it looked old enough to have been owned by Jefferson Davis himself. The numerous bullet holes were an ominous sign.

Six rocking chairs ringed a dormant potbellied stove at the store's epicenter. To the stove's right stood a half-filled pickle barrel, its metal bands rusted to a rich reddish brown. A skinny, one-eyed black cat with a crooked tail leveled his wary eye at me from under the stove. Rumbled something from deep in his throat that could have been the start of a hiss. Three of the chairs were filled with Gabby Hayes impersonators whittling on sticks. Both years and miles out of place, suddenly I felt guilty for having all my teeth.

I breathed easier when I spied a new Black and Decker chain saw hanging in one corner. Even more reassuring were the brand names stacked on the store's shelves to my left: Cocoa Puffs, Skippy, Reynolds Wrap, Wonder Bread, and best of all, four bags of Cheetos. Crunchy style, my snack food of choice. Abby keeps telling me they're one of the most unhealthy things you can put in your mouth, so I have to sneak them at home.

I jumped when the cat arched his back and growled at me. I'd always thought only dogs could growl. Not that I was scared of the critter; it's just I'm more of a dog person.

Coming out from behind what looked like a meat counter, Leaton Scump spat tobacco juice at the cat. Hit the poor feline dead center between its eyes.

"Settle down, Archie," said Scump, wagging a finger in the cat's direction. "Is that any way to greet a guest?"

Obviously accustomed to such treatment, Archie merely curled up to wipe away the juice with a paw.

"That's much better," said Scump, readjusting his chaw to the other cheek. "Now go earn your keep. Catch a mouse or something."

As wide as he was tall, and probably in his mid to late seventies, when Scump smiled his nose almost touched his chin. He took off his soiled apron and settled into one of the vacant chairs. After getting comfortable, he waggled another finger at the cat.

"And from here on, mind your manners, Arch." Turning to Bollinger: "Long time no see, Herkie. Grab a seat and set for a spell. How's things in the big city?"

Big city? Sneedville?

Not having been introduced yet, I kept my thoughts to myself, trying not to stare at Scump's hairpiece. Or whatever it was he had glued to his head. It looked as if someone had run over a skunk, sprayed it with paint, and stapled the carcass to Scump's skull.

Herkie pulled up one of the chairs. After two rocks back and forth, he blended right in.

"Sneedville's pretty much the same," he said. "Bustling as usual."

Bustling? I thought, biting my tongue.

"I noticed the sign driving up," added Herkie. "The twenty-seven was crossed out. Somebody die recently?"

Scump launched another glob of tobacco juice. This one landed in a brass spittoon two yards to my left. The man was deadly accurate with his expectoration.

"Old Man Fritter bought the farm last week," he said. "Accidentally strangled himself fishing for bluegill up at Bottom Creek. Should have known better than to try his luck when the water was so high. But you know much Fritter loved his bluegill filets. Poor bastard stepped in a hole and got tangled in his own line. When they pulled his body out four miles downriver, he was wrapped up tighter than a Christmas present. Took 'em an hour to cut him free. For my money, they should have buried him as was."

Herkie nodded slowly, then shook his head.

"That's a terrible way to go."

"Better than some," said Scump. He shot a nod in my direction. "Who's the Florsheims, Herk?"

TWENTY-ONE

H erkie motioned me over. Pulled up the last chair for me.
        "He's a friend of mine from . . . er, out of town, Boys, meet
John March, a big-time reporter for *TIME* magazine. He's here to
interview Hattie."

Scump scratched his stubble. Gave me a quick once-over. Then
drilled another bull's-eye into the spittoon.

"So, you're the foolhardy feller. Funny, you don't look that stupid."

The three old geezers laughed so hard two of them farted. Out
of the corner of my eye, I saw Herkie stifle a snicker. To be honest,
I found myself grinning. Despite the brickbat he'd hurled at me, I
liked Leaton Scump immediately. Prickly as a barrel cactus—and just
about shaped like one—he reminded me of my grandfather. Gramps
never minced words either.

"I take it you're here to pick our brains, sonny," added Scump. A
quick wink at his cronies. "That is, what's left of them." He touched
a pudgy finger to his forehead. "The altitude in these hills tends to
affect the ol' gray matter. 'Specially when you get to be our age."

"I'm here to listen to whatever you've got to say, Mr. Scump."

"Ain't no misters here. Rules of the road. I'm Leats, you're John.
Fair enough?"

"Sounds good to me."

Scump nodded at the open chair.

"Then you'd better park it. We don't want to keep Hattie waiting.
She has a thing about being 'punk-chew-all.'" Another bull's-eye into
the spittoon. "I looked that up last night. It's my word for the day."

After testing the chair, I sat down. It was sturdier than it looked.
Even comfortable.

"You mentioned the altitude. Um, has it had any effect on Hattie?"

"Not by a long shot," said Scump. "She's sharper than the rest of us put together. When it comes to smarts, she runs rings around my friends and me. Probably give you a push or two."

"She still has all her faculties?"

"Faculties? Isn't that what they got at all them highfalutin universities?"

"I mean, is she still lucid?"

Scump looked at the ceiling, then pulled at his right ear. The one that looked like a half cauliflower.

"If you mean does she still have all her wits about her, my answer is yes. And then some! She may not have no fancy-schmancy degree, but there's more to being wise than book smarts. Hattie's sharper than any tack in the box. She knows what's important and what's not. And that's a hell of a lot more than most of your hoity-toity college graduates can lay claim to."

Scump obviously thought highly of the woman. Beneath the awe, however, I detected a tinge of fear.

"How old is she, anyway?" I asked.

"Never was much good at math," said Scump. "Don't rightly know Hattie's exact age, but rough calculatin' has her near a hundred and forty. All I know for sure is that she's been around since long before I was born. Hell, long before my pappy was born, even."

A hundred and forty! So, it was true. Encouraged, I pressed on.

"Do you know anything about Melungeons, Mr. Scu— er, Leats?"

The three geezers exchanged knowing glances. Then broke out laughing again.

"Know about them?" said Scump. "Damn, boy! I got Melungeon blood running through these tired old veins of mine. Three times removed on my grandmother's side, anyway." A nod toward his friends. "We all got a Ramp somewhere in our gene pool woodpiles."

"Sorry. I didn't mean to insult you. But you don't look . . ."

Scump raised his right arm.

"You mean our skin isn't dark enough for you? I didn't say we were purebloods like Hattie. Unlike her, our family trees have meandered over the years. It may have taken us several generations, but in time even the darkest of us lightened up right nicely." Scump donned a huge grin. Winked. "Nowadays we can even pass for human."

"Sorry if I said the wrong thing."

Scump nudged the geezer on his left.

"Nah. You didn't say no wrong thing. Just the usual thing."

Another glob of tobacco juice clanged into the spittoon. Wiping his lower lip on a sleeve, Scump settled back to rocking. His buddies followed suit.

"Now, Mr. John March, persactly what do you want to know about Melungeons?"

I pulled out my pad.

"Anything you're willing to tell me. Your ways, your customs, any habits or peculiarities my readers might find interesting. For instance, are Melungeons superstitious?"

This brought another round of laughter. I was batting a thousand.

"Are we superstitious?" said Scump, snorting a laugh. "Is the pope Catholic? Does a bear shit in the woods?"

Having asked the dumb-ass question, I had to laugh along.

"I'll take that as an unqualified yes. Could you give me some examples?"

Scump nodded at his buddy, who was slowly drawing his Bowie knife through a slab of butter, right to left, then left to right. An impressive twelve inches of polished steel, the knife gleamed in the dim light. After wiping the blade clean, he stuck it back into its sheath.

"I take it that's to preserve its shine?" I asked.

"Not hardly," said Scump. "The butter chases the devil away. Old Scratch is what you might call lactose intolerant." A wink at his buddy. "'Intolerant' is my word for tomorrow. A bit of butter on the blade prevents you from having accidents. Makes sure you don't cut yourself. I use some on my meat cleaver every day to keep from chopping off a finger. Fifty years of butchering." He held up both hands. Wiggled his fingers. "And as you can see, I ain't lost one yet. Still got all ten."

"Ah, butter on the blade," I said. Then wrote it down. "Sort of like throwing salt over your shoulder to ward off bad luck?"

Scump touched a finger to his forehead.

"The salt thing? That's one of ours, too. Broken mirrors, stepping on a crack, knocking on wood, walking under a ladder—just a few more you flatlanders hefted from us."

"Fascinating," I said. Third time I'd used the word in only one day.

TWENTY-TWO

"Over the years you flatlanders have copycatted a ton of our superstitions," continued Scump, "but not all. The important ones we've kept to ourselves. Like, when you peel an apple without breaking the skin and throw it on the ground, if it lands in the shape of a letter, that's the initial of the person you're going to get hitched to."

"Wow!" I said. "That's really elaborate."

"The ones that work real good usually are."

Señor Bowie Knife joined in. "How about dirt swept out the front door after sundown bringing bad luck?" he said.

Scump took another turn.

"Hold a sharpened ax to the darkened sky for ten seconds, then bring it down quick, black clouds will part within the hour. And everyone in the hills knows to collect the first snow of March to take the sting out of burns."

"Never heard of any of those," I said.

Geezer #2 leaned in to nudge Scump on the knee.

"Tell him about the preacher tree, Leats. He'll get a kick out of that one."

"Oh, yeah. That's a good'n," said Scump, tapping a finger to his nose. "When you chop down a tree on a slope, make sure it falls downhill. If it don't, a preacher man will be bound for heaven before sundown. Half a century I been tending this here store, and we're on our tenth reverend. Seems like every few years, some yahoo with an ax gets liquored up at Christmastime, goes out to cut his family a tree, and forgets the rules. Just like that, we're short one preacher."

"Amazing," I said.

Another nudge from Geezer #2.

"How about pig-slaughtering time, Leats? Can't forget that."

Scump slapped a thigh.

"Another good one. Hog killing is best done in the light of the moon. If you spill blood during daylight, the meat won't cure right. Your ham and bacon will taste funny. Might even make you sick."

It was Geezer #3's turn. "Then there's the cure for the wheezies."

"Even better." Scump nodded. "A lock of your hair stuck in the split branch of a willow tree will chase asthma away. I get a touch of it myself now and then. A quick snip, a trip to the willow out back, and I'm good to go."

"Slabbing?" said Geezer #2.

Scump waggled a finger at my notepad.

"Make sure you take this one down. Your friends will get a kick out of it. You can construct the framework of your house during the day, but always wait 'til the sun goes down before putting on the walls. They need the dark of the moon to keep from warping."

Scribbling furiously, I had trouble keeping up. By the time the four took their first breath, twenty minutes had flown by, and my gold Cross special had run out of lead. I'd lost sensation in three of my fingers but filled up ten pages of notes. My readers would love it. When I shook Scump's hand to thank him, I had a cramp in my wrist. Bollinger had been right about the Mercantile. You really can't tell a book by its cover.

I hated to leave my newfound friends in Mulberry Gap, but I had one more person to meet. One very important person. The real reason I'd come this far.

TWENTY-THREE

Outside in the fresh air again, Herkie calculated the angle of the sun. He looked at his watch, then leaned on the Studebaker's roof. Took off his cap and wiped his brow.

"Well, we'd better keep moving. Get enough in there for your article, John?"

"More than enough. I could have listened to those guys all day. I'm sure they had more stories to tell."

"No doubt about it. Those four will talk your ears off if you let them."

Herkie wiped the back of his neck with a handkerchief. I was reassured to see someone else affected by the heat. I was beginning to think I was the only one in Tennessee with active sweat glands.

"We don't want to keep Hattie waiting," he said.

When I opened my car door, it was like standing in front of a blast furnace.

"Damn!" I said. "You could fry an egg in there."

Herkie opened his door. Stepped aside.

"My fault for parking in the sun."

We moved back to the shade of the porch to wait for the car to cool down. With both of her doors open, Ginger looked like a giant bird of prey about to swoop in for a kill.

"That bit about the tree and the preacher," I said. "Do people up here actually believe such things?"

"That and more." Herkie tapped a finger to his chest. "Yours truly included. They may seem like a bunch of old wives' tales to most people, but to us they're a way of life. The old ways die hard up here. I've got a master's degree in English literature, and most times I like to think of myself as an educated man, but to this day, whenever I cut myself, I still quote scripture to stop the bleeding."

"Scripture?"

"Ezekiel 16:6, to be exact. 'I said unto thee, when thou wast in blood, live.'"

"And that helps?"

"Not sure how much, but it never hurts."

Herkie scanned the mountain ridge high above us.

"Strange things happen in these hills," he continued. "Things no educated mind can explain. Things like preachers dying suddenly, pork going bad, and houses warping. And that's just the tip of the iceberg."

I eyeballed the Studebaker's open doors.

"Speaking of icebergs, let's hope Ginger has cooled off enough by now."

TWENTY-FOUR

The second Ginger's eight cylinders sprang to life, Herkie cranked up her A/C full bore, then headed out of the clearing. Leaning in front of the dashboard vent, I savored the first whisper of cool air. Thank God for freon.

"How much farther to Hattie's place?" I asked.

"Two and a half miles, maybe three," said Herkie. "Of course, that's only as the crow flies."

"Unless you've made some alterations you haven't told me about, Ginger isn't equipped with wings."

Bollinger pulled a hard right up a steep incline, and the car's suspension groaned when we bounced into and out of a deep rut. A hard left thumped us over an embedded rock. My tailbone banged into the seat springs.

"Ground-bound, it's six miles to her cabin," said Herkie. He winked after a quick downshift. "Seven at the most. Sorry about that bump."

Back and forth, one climbing turn after another, we made our way up the mountain. Ten more minutes of jostling, and my guts felt like they'd been pureed in a Cuisinart blender. My arms ached from clutching the armrest, I had trouble breathing the light air, and thanks to an abrupt collision with the dashboard, I knew come morning I'd have a bruise on my knee the size of a softball. When we finally stopped in front of another small clearing, I had to blink twice to make sure my contacts were still in place.

Herkie puffed out a long breath. Leaned on the steering wheel and bent forward to look out the windshield.

"Well, here we are. Safe and sound."

I gently touched my throbbing knee. "You call this safe and

sound? I've got bruises over half my body and lost all feeling in my butt. My heart's pounding to beat the band, and I'm this close to urping breakfast all over Ginger's brand-new upholstery."

Herkie shot me a knowing grin. Reached over to open my door.

"You can thank your lucky stars it isn't the rainy season. Would have made the ride a whole lot rougher. This is as far as I go. The path to Hattie's cabin is over there."

"Path?" I said. "What path? I don't see any path."

In fact the clearing was a cul-de-sac. One that dead-ended into a forest.

"There's nothing here but trees," I added. "And those two boulders."

"That's Hattie's front gate," said Herkie. "Look closely. The path is between them. Just follow it for a mile or so, and it'll bring you to her place. As long as you don't stray too far, you should be okay. I'll be back to pick you up in ten hours. It shouldn't take you longer than that to gather her story."

My eyes shifted from one boulder to the other. Then back to Herkie.

"You can't be serious! You're dropping me off in the middle of nowhere?"

"Sorry, but I've got some business to conduct with Leats. Don't worry. You'll be safe. Hattie will see to that. She'll be watching you all the way. You may not see her, but she'll see you."

After a double sashay to and fro, Bollinger managed to turn the Studebaker around. As he came by, he leaned out the window.

"One more thing. Sunset comes cat quick around here. If I were you, I wouldn't lollygag. You don't want to get caught in these woods after dark."

My head swiveled toward the trees.

"After dark? Why not?"

"Strange critters live on this mountaintop. They come out when the sun goes down. And they have a tendency to be curious."

"Critters? What kind of critters?"

"Mostly of the hungry kind."

And with a wave, he drove off.

TWENTY-FIVE

I t's amazing how long a person will stare at an object that is no longer there. The Studebaker was long gone over the ridge, but there I stood like a simpleton, my mouth open, fixated on the spot where it had disappeared. It took me two heartbeats to realize I was now totally, irrevocably alone in the wilderness. A deep, dark, hungry-looking wilderness.

Get a grip, John, I tried telling myself. *Herkie said it's only a short walk to Hattie's place. You can handle this.*

Yeah, right! countered my pessimistic half. *"Over the river and through the woods"?*

A sudden flapping of wings startled me. Large wings, from the sound of it. Having a distinct aversion to bird droppings, I instinctively covered my head. As a kid I had a pet parakeet that delighted in flying around the house like a miniature B-52, targeting me with his 'keet bombs.

I looked up. Nothing in the sky. *Probably just a crow,* I thought, hoping that it wasn't something bigger, more aggressive. Or hungrier. Bollinger had warned me to be on the lookout for critters. I crossed my fingers that he hadn't meant the flying kind.

I noticed a sudden movement in the treetops. I ducked down, snapped my head around. Thankfully, it turned out to be nothing more than a clump of vines undulating in the breeze. It was then I realized how thick the overhead canopy was. Stretching from tree to tree like a thousand yards of live bunting, the green menace floated with the wind, rising and falling gently in the air currents. I swore the entire forest was breathing around me. As if I'd been inhaled into a giant green lung.

Another movement to my left swiveled me around. Had one of those boulders moved? I took another look. Rubbed my eyes.

"Of course it didn't move, John," I said to my shadow. "For chrissake, it's an inanimate object. Just a rock. And rocks don't move. Not unless they're being pushed by a bulldozer. And there's not a CAT of any kind in sight."

It had to be a dangling vine casting shadows across the boulders that was giving them facial features. For a fleeting moment it looked as if one of them winked at me. My active imagination had gone into overdrive. The way the two boulders were situated, they now looked like two tusks in a gaping green maw.

Passing between those granite sentinels, a tingle shimmied up my spine. Followed by the chilling sensation of being watched. Despite the ninety-plus-degree heat, I found myself shivering in my own sweat. I didn't look back until the path took a sharp bend into the forest. I was relieved to see that neither boulder had moved an inch. At least they weren't following me.

"Easy, John." Talking to myself again. "They're just two big rocks. They can't follow anybody."

But I still couldn't shake the feeling. The forest had a thousand eyes, and they all seemed to be trained on me.

Whistling in the dark, that's the ticket, I thought. Thinking "Yellow Brick Road," I puckered up and gave it my best shot. *"We're off to see the wizard."* Way off-key.

Something large rustled in the bushes to my left.

"W-who's there?" My voice two octaves higher than usual.

A branch snapped. Followed by a guttural snort. Fingers subconsciously crossed again, I prayed to whatever gods might be listening that it wasn't a grizzly, then quickened my pace. A high-pitched screech to the right shifted my canter into a quick trot. I switched from whistling to chanting.

"I do believe in spooks, I do believe in spooks. I do, I do, I do."

TWENTY-SIX

Five minutes later, somewhere overhead the sun had faded to a yellow-green blur, and I was totally disoriented. Draped now in shadows, the forest had taken on a sinister hue. Trees no longer had branches; they had arms. With clawlike hands. Their trunks wore hungry frowns, with eyes that glared down at me as if to say, "What the hell are you doing here, flatlander?"

Hanging vines had transformed into writhing snakes. A lopsided boulder in the distance looked like an ogre, ready to feast on my quivering flesh. Dust motes dancing in the few sunbeams able to penetrate the canopy looked like vampire fairies, darting ever closer, eager to suck my blood.

My heart began to pound. Panic overtook me, and I started to run. My lack of conditioning quickly caught up to me, leaving me panting like a runaway steam engine. Branches slapped me in the face as I careened through this jungle of imagined horrors. Glancing back to make sure those two boulders hadn't followed me, I tripped over a protruding root and tumbled into a bramble brush. I staggered and bent at the waist to catch my breath, sweat dripping from my nose. So much for the shower I'd taken back in Sneedville. I'd have to meet Hattie smelling like a pair of unwashed sweat socks. My lungs ached, and my legs felt like two strands of overcooked spaghetti.

What the hell were you thinking, John? Running pell-mell like that in this heat? It's a miracle you didn't give yourself a friggin' heart attack.

I took a moment to assess the damage my mad dash had done. My shirt was torn in three places, and I was covered with several nasty-looking burs. My face stung, and my forearms were crisscrossed with scratches. Mud had splattered my pants. I'd scuffed up my shoes something terrible. The only consolation was that I probably didn't look as bad as I felt. To make matters worse, the path was nowhere in sight. I was now hopelessly lost.

I was sure I was going to die out there, halfway between nowhere and anywhere. No one would ever find my body. My bones would be picked clean by animals I'd never heard of. I could see the front-page headline: SEMI-FAMOUS REPORTER LOST IN THE WILDERNESS.

Okay, maybe front-page coverage was a stretch. The best I could hope for was a few lines on the bottom of page three, far right. In the special interest section.

Before I could finish sketching out my obituary, another screech cut me off.

"What the hell was that?" I squeaked.

I looked up just in time to catch a huge shadow gliding overhead. Maybe a giant owl. It appeared to be circling me. It looked bigger than the Hindenburg, and suddenly I felt like lunch on the hoof.

"That can't be an owl," I tried to convince myself. "Owls are nocturnal. And that thing is way too big for an owl. It's got to be an eagle. Or, God forbid, maybe even a pterodactyl? Who knows what lost time zone you've stumbled into, John?" My high-octane imagination was shifting into fourth gear.

The dirigible with wings completed a low pass, and I made out two tufted horns.

"But it sure looks like an owl," I said to the tree I was crouching behind.

Then again, I know beans about birds. It could have been a giant Norwegian sewer rat with feathers.

Another branch snapped to my right. Something hopefully smaller was hustling through the underbrush toward me.

"Probably just a squirrel hunting for nuts," I said to the same tree. Hoping that said squirrel wasn't after my nuts.

The rustling became louder. Then another branch snapped. A much larger branch. Clearly it wasn't a squirrel. Twenty feet to my right, a shoulder-high bush began to shake back and forth, as if someone, or something, was digging at its roots.

BEAR!

My legs found a new source of strength—spelled "uncontrollable fear"—and my wind returned. Flying through the brush, I tripped over another root. I'll swear on a stack of Bibles the thing jumped up and bit me. After a face-first slide that would have done Pete Rose proud, I twisted around to face my attacker on my back, spitting out a mouthful of moldy leaves. I put up my arms and legs. Waved them around like a rabid turtle. At least I'd go out kicking and screaming.

Eat me if you must, Mr. Bear, but I'll make damn sure at least one of my bones sticks in your damn throat!

TWENTY-SEVEN

For all of five seconds, my life flashed before my eyes. My first day at school, my first bike, my first kiss (Becky Thompson). By the time I got to my college graduation, I realized the bush had stopped moving and nothing was happening.

No shadows were getting closer, and I hadn't been mauled by a bear. Nor even sniffed by one. I heard nothing but the susurrus of a gentle breeze whispering through the leaves. And except for my pounding heart, all had returned to normal in the enchanted forest. Whatever was after me—if anything had actually been after me—had given up the chase. I wasn't going to be eaten after all.

I gulped down a shallow breath. Then two deeper ones. I propped myself up on one elbow. Got to my feet. Looked cautiously to the left. To the right. Then brushed myself off.

"Now you've done it, birdbrain. From the frying pan into the fire. If you weren't lost before, you sure as hell are now."

My hair was matted with leaves, my clothes smeared with dirt. I looked and smelled like I'd slept in a compost pile. But it could have been worse. That hard fall I took? I could have broken an arm or a leg. Maybe both.

I ran my tongue over my lower lip. Tasted blood. Nothing serious, but the swelling below my left cheek told me I was in for a humdinger of a black eye. To top it all off, my ankle had begun to throb. On the positive side, when I glanced down, I realized that in my panicked retreat from the bouncing bush, I'd somehow stumbled back to the path.

Maybe I'd been herded there by that giant flying whatever-it-was. But were animals savvy enough to do that? There are herding dogs; maybe this had been a wild herding bird. I picked a twig out of my hair and headed down the path. He who hesitates is destined to get himself lost again.

Looking up, I noticed the green menace above me was getting thicker. Odd, the kudzu's long tendrils now seemed to be blowing north, as if pointing the way. Another quick glance over my shoulder reassured me nothing was following me yet, so I picked up the pace. I may have announced to the entire forest it was being invaded by a citified klutz, but it would take more than a few scrapes and bruises to keep John March from his Pulitzer.

Herkie had said it was only "a mile" to Hattie's place; however, my aching body suggested I'd already gone ten.

Twenty minutes after my tumble in the jungle, I was still on the path. With no cabin in sight, I began to question Herkie's sense of distance. Did he really mean as the crow flies or rather as a clumsy flatlander stumbles? There'd been no turnoffs, no forks in the road, just this damn two-foot-wide trickle through a never-ending sea of green. Frustrated, I promised myself if I ever made it out of these mountains alive—a fifty-fifty chance at that point—Abby's ficus on the back porch would be history. I now hated all things flora.

Is there no end to this damn green?

I picked up the sturdiest branch I could find to use as a crutch/ machete. Surging forward, swinging it back and forth to clear my way, I felt like Don Quixote sans his swift steed. Tired, hot, dirty, bruised, and scratched, I imagined myself with Pickett at Gettysburg, charging up toward Cemetery Ridge. If it was my fate to die in this godforsaken wilderness, I'd take a passel of blue bellies with me.

"Damn Yankees," I mumbled to what by now had to be an amused forest.

In my deluded state, I tripped again. After tumbling ass over teakettle down an embankment, I finally came to rest flat on my back on a patch of soft meadow grass. Staring up at a blue, blue sky. The green menace had miraculously parted, and I felt the warming rays of the sun again. In the distance, I saw a few gentle clouds. I heard birds singing. A wave of relief washed over me.

Sorry, General Lee, I apologized. *But we couldn't break through the Yankee line. There were just too many of the bastards.*

Relieved I was no longer destined to take a minié ball in the gut, I broke out laughing. "Well, John, it's now official. You've lost every last one of your marbles."

I rolled over and sat up. Spat out a wad of rancid moss I'd almost swallowed during my tumble. Then blinked twice. I found myself sitting at the edge of a perfectly round clearing, probably a hundred yards in diameter. It was as if the forest floor had burped out a gigantic circle. It couldn't have been more exact had it been laid out by the world's largest compass. My immediate thought was alien crop circle, forest version. But that was even more far-fetched than my imagined Gettysburg charge.

I scanned for signs of felled trees. Found none. The tree line had just abruptly stopped, held back by some mysterious power. Even more strange, the surrounding trees all slanted to form a perfectly curved wall. From a dense, vine-entangled jungle to an inviting, blue-green, grassy meadow, the transition had taken place in less than two yards. Forcing even the storm-trooper-like kudzu to back off.

"Fascinating," I mumbled.

Across the way, on the far side of the open circle and about five yards into the forest, stood what had to be Hattie's place.

TWENTY-EIGHT

Hattie's rustic log cabin blended seamlessly into its surroundings, looking like it had grown from the wilderness. Flanked by two huge poplars, its roof was topped with a greenish-brown moss, the perfect camouflage. A drooping porch ran across the cabin's entire front.

A huge horned owl perched on a mud-and-stone chimney—a thin wisp of smoke wafting from its flue—cast a wary eye my way. Behind the cabin, ten yards into the forest, stood a towering oak tree that dwarfed the poplars, its branches splayed out in all directions as if it had expanded solely to shade the cabin beneath it. Maybe even protect it. When I looked off in the distance, I spied an even larger oak, a true giant, one at least fifty feet taller than any of its surrounding brethren.

This can't be real, I thought. *I must be dreaming.*

A sudden deafening screech from the owl told me I wasn't. Anything that loud had to be real.

Could that be the same bird I saw circling over me in the forest? Probably.

I rose to my feet, my eyes fixated on the owl. Dusted myself off. Fat chance I'd looked halfway presentable now. Not after taking two flat-on-your-face tumbles in the dirt.

Well, John, this is what you've come a thousand miles for. Take your thumb out of your ass and knock on the woman's door.

But my feet had taken roots. It's amazing how sometimes the lower part of your body is smarter than your brain. I tried to whistle again, but my pucker had gone dry. All that came out was a pitiful rasp. I gave myself a mental kick in the butt. Forced my feet to take a few cautious steps forward.

When I got to within twenty feet of the porch, the owl flapped its wings and unleashed an even louder screech. It stopped me dead in my tracks. Palms up, I offered my most engaging smile.

"Easy, Mr. Owl, we're all friends here. I've been a bird lover all my life. And I'm a dues-paying member of the Audubon Society. Never owned a BB gun."

That last part was an outright lie, but it was the only thing I could think of. Like Ralphie from *Christmas Story*, my "Red Ryder, steel-barreled special" was the best present I ever received.

Perhaps it was my tone of my voice, or maybe all the trembling I was doing, but my pleas seemed to mollify the owl. Thinking it couldn't get any worse, I continued toward the cabin.

I was soon proved wrong. As if on cue, a monstrous boar came charging around one corner, its eyes red and ablaze. About the size of a refrigerator, its broad shoulders bristled with coarse black hair. It stopped to snort the air twice, drooling slobber and revealing two long, yellow tusks in the process. My clever feet promptly re-sank their roots.

"Thank you very much, John," they seemed to be telling me, "but this is as far as we'll be taking you."

Hands raised in a further gesture of peace, I turned to address the boar with a shaky voice. "Easy, Porky Pig. I never ate that much bacon. And I always passed on a second helping of sausage."

In desperation, I glanced at the chimney. No help there. The owl had taken to preening himself. I looked to the heavens. *Where's Jimmy Dean when you need him?*

A padded thumping came from the other porch corner. Adding insult to possible injury, a large mastiff burst onto the already overcrowded scene. I let out a half groan, half whimper.

"Great," I said. "Now I'm a giant bag of Kibbles."

Wondering which beastie would tear me apart first, I shrugged and mustered a pathetic attempt to smile.

"Can't we all just get along?" said I.

But the hungry trio would have none of it. The boar pawed the ground, then snorted loudly. Emitting a garbled bark, the mastiff exposed an impressive set of canines. Not wanting to be upstaged, Brother Owl flapped his wings again. Added an ear-splitting screech to the cacophony.

By then my foot roots had reached China. Baring my own inadequate chompers, I decided a bluff was called for. I tried to growl, but all that came out was a pitiful cough that wouldn't have scared my pet corgi, Jack. And Jack runs away at a soft sneeze. Clenching both fists, I braced for the inevitable. Closed my eyes. And uttered what had to be one of the world's most futile curses. Also one of the dumbest.

"May the fleas of a thousand camels infest your nether regions. I hope you all get food poisoning!"

TWENTY-NINE

"**W**yatt! Morgan! Virgil! You all hush up now! You're going to raise the dead with all this ruckus. Show our guest here some hospitality."

With the inexorable force of a tidal wave, Hattie Sexton's gravel voice silenced the trio in an instant. When she thumped her cane down, all three forgot about me, turned, and gave her their undivided attention.

"You get yourselves along," she said. "Haven't you got better things to do than scare this poor man half to death?"

The dog and the boar lowered their heads. Watching me all the way, they slinked back to their respective corners. They both circled twice to plop down on all fours, panting and shooting daggers in my direction. Hattie then looked toward the chimney.

"You too, Wyatt."

The owl shook out its feathers, folded its wings, bobbed its head three times, and resumed preening.

"That's better," said Hattie. "We can't have this fine-looking gentleman thinking we're unfriendly." A grin on her face, she turned to me. "Welcome, young feller. You can come up now."

I cast a wary eye at the dog. Then over at the pig.

"Um, are you sure it's safe?" I asked

"Safe as Daniel in the lion's den." Hattie shot a thumb toward her parked pets. "Them two ain't as mean as they look."

"That's a relief," I said.

"They're a lot worse," she added, her grin widening. "Tear your head off in half a heartbeat if I give them the nod. But they do as I say."

Grateful for my stay of execution, I crossed myself. Perhaps I'd live to see my grandchildren. One hand on my chest, I mustered up a weak smile.

"Then I guess I'd better stay on your good side."

"That be my way of thinking," said Hattie, stepping out of the shadows.

Two inches short of four feet tall, her spine was twisted to the right at a forty-five-degree angle, making her look even smaller than she actually was. Clutched in her arthritic, vein-streaked left hand was a knobby cane. From the way she was standing, it wasn't there for support. A sagging collage of nasty-looking tumors covered the left side of her face, tugging at the corner of her mouth and nearly covering a milky, akimbo eye. Patches of long white hair poked randomly up through the sides of her liver-spotted scalp. I tried not to stare.

Even from a distance Hattie Sexton smelled of old age. Of pain and the nearness of death. But also of wisdom and resolve. Despite the obvious passage of so many years, the woman radiated power. When she took my hand in a surprisingly firm grip, it felt like peeled snake skin.

"Quite an eyeful, ain't I?" she said. "But don't you fret none, sonny. Unlike Morgan and Virgil, I don't bite. Pleased to make your acquaintance, Mr. John March. I been waiting for you."

She nodded to the edge of the clearing, where I'd taken my last tumble. Winked her crystal-clear right eye. Green as the Mediterranean, it was an oasis of beauty in a sea of devastation.

"Nice entrance, by the way," she added.

For an awkward moment, words escaped me.

"Better get used to the way I look," she said finally. "'Cause it ain't gonna get any better. Not in my lifetime anyway."

"I'm sorry. I didn't mean to be rude. It's just—"

"No need to apologize, Mr. March. It's human nature to stare at all things ugly. Hell, I always do."

"You're not that . . ."

Hattie let out a soft chuckle.

"Mirrors don't lie, Mr. March. And this face of mine has broken more than a few in my lifetime. Look up 'ugly' in the dictionary, and you'll find my picture. I had this here bent backbone since birth. Pott's disease, the doctors called it back then.

"I was also infected with the tuberculosis bug the minute I popped out of my momma's womb. Born of triplets, I was the only one who survived. Charity, I suppose the luckiest of us three, was stillborn. Faith died six months later from a rat bite. Maybe the Lord in His infinite wisdom took pity on me and willed me their life spans. I changed my name as soon as I reached legal age. Never cottoned to the name Hope. Would have been too much of a cliché by my way of thinking."

She stood aside to snap open the screen door. Despite the cane, she was quick as a cat.

"Well, don't just stand there gawking, John March. I've got a story to tell, and we're wasting time. That is, if you're up to listening to it."

THIRTY

"Yes, ma'am, I sure am ready, willing, and able," I said. I looked up at the owl. Then over at the boar and the dog. "I don't mean to pry, but Wyatt, Morgan, and Virgil? Pretty unusual names for pets. If that's what you call them."

Hattie smacked her lips. Nodded.

"I named them after the Earp brothers. They were favorite lawmen of mine growing up. Real straight shooters, no-nonsense types. I remember like it was yesterday, them gunning the Clantons down at the OK Corral." A glance at the chimney. "Wyatt up there let me know you were coming. He also kept you from getting lost, by the way."

So, it had been an owl after all.

"That's amazing," I said. "You were actually alive for the most famous gunfight in history?"

"I heard about it growing up. But when you get down to brass tacks, it wasn't that great of a gunfight. I hear tell Ike never was much in the smarts department. Or much of a shot, either. And considering he and his brothers were all stumble-bum drunk, it wasn't much of a fair fight."

Hattie sighted down her cane as if it were a rifle. Pulled an imaginary trigger.

"The Earps were my heroes. 'Shoot first, ask questions later' kind of guys. Let the undertaker sort out what was left. Not like today where the police have to treat the bad guys with kid gloves. As if they had more rights than the victims. I blame it on all the lawyer types we got in Washington these days. Damn no-account liberals."

"I suppose there's a lot to be said for frontier justice," I said, making a note not to mention my wife's career. "It does make for fewer complications. Quicker and less expensive, too."

A faraway look swam into Hattie's good eye.

"Time was, I wanted to be a gunslinger myself. Bent over the way I am, I would have been a good one, too." Hattie made a quick-draw motion. "I'd have been closer to the holster. And faster on the quick draw. Then again, in my day women weren't supposed to be of the shooting kind."

I'd spent less than two minutes with the lady, and already I was smitten.

"What about Annie Oakley?" I asked.

"Annie was little more than a circus freak," snorted Hattie. "And hardly no gunslinger. A bit on the trashy side, I been told."

Hattie hung her bonnet on a hook next to the door. Gave it a pat.

"Wear a hat indoors, and there'll be bad news headin' your way by midnight."

Leaton Scump had failed to mention that particular superstition.

I followed her inside. My first step elicited a low groan from the floorboards, as if I'd trod on a vital organ. I had a chilling feeling Hattie's cabin saw me as an intruder. With visions of Amityville dancing through my brain, for a second I imagined the floor wanted to chew me up and spit me out.

The solitary window on the far log wall had been shuttered tight so the cabin's only illumination came from the glowing embers in the huge stone fireplace off to my right. Situated in the center of what appeared to be the kitchen area, its mantel was inlaid with dozens of flint arrowheads.

More shapes began to materialize out of the gloom as my eyes adjusted. To my left stood a neatly made single bed covered by a handmade quilt, with a set of dark drapes providing limited privacy. An old orange crate standing on end served as its nightstand. A rough-hewn plank table stretched from the kitchen into what I assumed was a living space, where a large grandfather clock ticked ominously in one corner. A strange addition to the room, its ornate craftsmanship was exquisite. I'd never seen one even remotely like it and was sure it was worth a small fortune. A bentwood rocker and a high-backed chair with one strut missing were the only other furniture.

Strange fragrances filled my nostrils. Pine and mortar to be sure, but also something more exotic. Pungent, yet mysteriously sweet—maybe ginger and something I couldn't put my finger on. A woodland herb maybe, one a flatlander like me wouldn't recognize. Somewhere between an opiate and ambergris, its smell was not of this world. My world, anyway.

Something on the wall moved. When my eyes finally adjusted to the lack of light, I saw a baby skunk, a baby raccoon, and a baby opossum curled up in large knotholes. All three watching me intently. Chittering softly amongst themselves, they seemed to be discussing what in the world I was doing there. *Good question.*

I heard a clacking above my head. Sitting on a rafter a foot from my left ear was a fledgling crow, bobbing its head up and down. Giving me a hairy eyeball. A scuttling of toenails off to my right diverted my attention. A herd (probably the wrong word) of mice hustled nose-to-butt along one log. My eyes followed them the entire length of the wall until they disappeared into a hole. Three feet below that hole lay a coiled rattlesnake, its body the thickness of my upper arm.

I have a thing about snakes. Even the harmless garden variety give me the willies.

Hattie noticed my jaw drop. Raised a calming hand.

"Those little ones on the wall are friends of mine. Orphans I rescued from the forest. Good conversationalists all. They keep me company."

I closed my mouth. Pointed a shaky finger at the serpent.

"Friends? What about . . . that?"

Hattie smiled. Scratched her right ear.

"That's just Doc Holliday. Also kinda friendly. No need to worry. He keeps the place free of bugs. It took me a few heart-to-hearts to convince ol' Doc not to eat the mice, but eventually he came around. Peaceful coexistence, some people call it. Between him and Ocho up there"—a nod toward a humongous wolf spider doing pushups on a web two feet above my head—"I ain't seen a cockroach in years."

I have an even larger thing about arachnids. Most of my nightmares involve critters with eight legs. Wimp that I am, whenever a daddy longlegs invades our bathroom, I have to call on Abby to do the honors.

After lighting a beeswax candle, Hattie dripped a few drops on the table, then nestled the shaft into the puddle. Its light added a green hue to the cabin. I now noticed a sink with an old-fashioned pump behind her. The kind normally attached to horse troughs in old Western movies. Above the sink were three sagging shelves chockablock with grimy Mason jars.

"Well," said Hattie, "we ain't got all day, so let's get to it. I do my best talking when I'm sitting."

With that, she pulled up the chair and started to rock.

THIRTY-ONE

After a quick glance to make sure ol' Doc wasn't heading my way, I headed for the kitchen. I still couldn't bring myself to look at the wolf spider.

"That's quite a spice collection you've got on those shelves, Mrs. Sexton," I said, trying to forget all about creepy-crawlies. Hanging on a peg a few inches below the shelf was a pitch-black cast iron kettle, and next to it the biggest meat cleaver I'd ever seen.

"They ain't spices. Them's my special remedies. I use them for butter and egg money. And the name's just Hattie, without the missus. Never had the time, nor the inclination, to ever get hitched. As if anyone would ask for my hand in marriage. Men can be stupid sometimes, but not that stupid."

Curious, I tapped a fingernail against the closest container, a foul-looking Mason jar with a hardened crust oozed from its top. When I picked it up, I detected dozens of purplish-brown globules suspended in goo. I held the jar up to the light, where it shimmered as if it were alive.

"Fascinating," I said. "If you don't mind my asking, what's this for?"

Hattie raised an eyebrow. Smiled, then set back to her rocking.

"Careful with that one, John. Get a drop of that stuff on your hands, and your horse will be out of the barn for a week. If you catch my drift."

With a hot face, I carefully replaced the jar. Hattie leaned forward to set her cane on the table.

"Now, I'm sure you didn't come all this way to ask me about my special medicines. First things first: are we agreed on the terms for me talking to you?"

"Connie told me you asked for two favors," I said, my eyes returning to the meat cleaver. Its shiny, clean condition indicated it had been polished often. And used recently.

"Two small favors. That's what it's going to cost you." Hattie crossed her arms. Ran her tongue across her gums. "Them's me terms. And there'll be no"—she seemed to be searching for the right word—"shenanigations. As the shysters say."

I assumed she meant negotiations. Somehow I liked her word better; it cut to the heart of the matter. No beating around the bush with some mumbo-jumbo legalese.

"Could you at least give me a hint what the two favors are?" I asked.

"They're nothing illegal or immoral, if that be your concern." Hattie narrowed her good eye to a sliver. Pulled at a tuft of chin hair. "Howsomever, one of the favors I'm asking is probably something you never even contemplated. What with you being a citified feller. But who knows? You might even like it. At least it'd be a tale you could tell your grandchildren."

THIRTY-TWO

I chanced another glance in Doc Holliday's direction. The snake still hadn't moved. Thank goodness.

"That's not exactly reassuring," I said. "Not to be impertinent, but how do I know your story will be worth these two unnamed favors?"

Hattie's belly laugh filled the cabin. In the glow of that one lonely candle, at least twenty sets of small eyes twinkled from the far wall. Apparently her critter housemates enjoyed a hefty laugh too. Rubbing at her good eye, Hattie slapped a knee.

"You're smarter than you look, Mr. John March. Tell you what, I'll spill half of my beans, then ask for my first favor. If at that point you think my story is not to your liking, or that your readers wouldn't be interested in what I have to say next, you can close up shop and walk away. No hard feelings, no questions asked. Of course, then you'll never get to hear the ending to my tale of woe."

Hattie puckered up, spit into her hand, and extended it to seal the deal.

"Fair enough?" she asked.

What choice did I have? I shook her tiny hand. It felt like a piece of brittle bark in my palm.

"Fair enough," I said.

Hattie's grin was a thing of beauty. So was the gleam in her eye.

"You're a man after me own heart, John March." She picked up her cane. Set it on the floor to lean forward, a gentle expression on her face. "Now, before we begin in earnest, is there anything else you want to ask me? Once my gums get to flapping, I won't be stopping for no interruptions. Interruptions tend to break my train of thought."

Made perfect sense to me. I pulled out my Sony recorder. Placed in on the table in front of her.

"Will this bother you?" I asked.

Hattie gave the small device a critical eye.

"Don't rightly know. What is it?"

"It's a machine to record what you say word for word. That way you can talk freely without me distracting . . . er, interrupting you by taking notes."

"Sounds doable. That thing able to hear well?"

"It can pick up a whisper from across the room."

"Good. 'Cause I ain't much for talking loud." She tapped the recorder with a finger. "Its label says, 'Made in China.'"

"Isn't just about everything these days?"

Hattie gave a derisive snort. "I don't like it none, but I guess that's where the world is heading. Pretty soon we'll all be speaking Mandarin. Thank goodness I won't be around to see it."

Exhaling slowly, she leaned back again. Placed her cane across her lap.

"Go ahead." She nodded. "You can ask your questions now."

I set the recorder equidistant between us. Turned it on, then spoke into it.

"September 8, 2019, around one o'clock in the afternoon. This is John March interviewing Ms. Hattie Sexton in her cabin, somewhere in the hills of eastern Tennessee."

When I glanced toward the corner, I saw that Doc Holliday had uncoiled himself and was now pointing directly at me. Two feet above me, Ocho the spider dangled down from his web. I tried hard not to look like a juicy bug.

"Hattie, according to the records, you're a mind-boggling one hundred and forty-three years old. I know it's trite, but I have to ask. What's the secret to your incredibly long life?"

Hattie rolled her good eye toward the ceiling. Scratched her cheek.

"Land sakes," she sniffed, "as if I never been asked that one before. I don't rightly know what trite means, but I'll take it to be a hair's breadth short of stupid."

Pondering her next words, she rocked for a few seconds.

"'Incredibly long life'?" she repeated. "You say that as if old age by itself is a good thing, a reward for following what some people might call the proper path. If there truly is such a thing in this topsy-turvy world.

"Well, Mr. March, I'm here to tell you that my path may have been long, but it never was anything close to proper. Despite this bent and broken body of mine, I done things in my lifetime that would make a sailor blush. Probably give an upstanding citizen like yourself a heart attack. Smoke, drink, cuss, carouse—you name it, I done it. This ain't no sweet little old lady you see sitting before you."

A grin swimming onto her face, Hattie spread her arms wide.

"Have a real good gander at me. Does this look like any kind of reward to you?"

"I'm sorry," I said. "I didn't mean to imply—"

She raised her hand to cut me off. I'd already forgotten she didn't like to be interrupted.

"A life that is merely long can be its own hell. Says so in the Bible. I think Job may be the proof. Something to do with patience being a virtue. Then again, at my age I tend to get my scriptures mixed up."

"Um, you make a good point about Job," I agreed.

Fumbling for direction, I backpedaled into already troubled waters. I knew I'd be risking Hattie's wrath, but as a reporter it was my duty.

"I know my next question is probably just as stupid as the first, but my readers will want to know. What's it like being almost a century and a half years old? To have breathed the air of three different centuries?"

A heavy silence settled over the cabin. Hattie squinted her good eye down to a narrow slit. Seeing her jaw muscles tighten, I braced myself.

THIRTY-THREE

"**F**eel like?" said Hattie, her eye narrowing even further. "Feel like, you ask?" A headshake followed. "Well, Mr. March, I've lived through twenty-five presidents. Twenty-six if you count Grover Cleveland twice. And at my age I've got more aches than I got places. There ain't a bone in this tired old body of mine that don't creak when I move. Half of which have been broken at one time or another. Some more than twice."

Holding up an arm, she waggled the folds of skin hanging from her bones.

"As any fool can see, everything on me sags, drags, or wheezes. I lost my last molar when I hit ninety, and now I have to gum just about all of my vittles. A few years after I lost my teeth, my stomach took a sour turn, and now I can't handle more than a few drops of liquor every other day. And without my daily three fingers of potato jack, I've been farting mostly dust. I got callouses on my callouses, and I can't remember the last time I felt anything in my right butt cheek. To top it all off, I haven't had a good night's sleep since Tricky Dick got caught with his hand in the cookie jar."

Hattie shifted her cane to her other hand. Scooched herself around in her chair to get comfortable for the long haul. Then set to rocking again.

"As for that flapdoodle about breathing three centuries' worth of air," she continued, "at this stage in my life, the only breath I'm concerned about is the one I'm about to take. And in case you haven't noticed, I probably ain't got too many of those left."

I felt like ten pounds of dolt stuffed into a five-pound bag. In all my years of conducting interviews, never had my ears been lowered so quickly, or so masterfully. At well over a hundred years old, she'd effortlessly put me in my place. Nailed me to the outhouse wall, as Leaton Scump might have said. I'd have hated to match wits with this woman in her prime.

"Okay," I finally managed, "time for a different tack. You're a Melungeon, are you not, Hattie?"

"Purebred, born, raised, and proud."

"Other than the hair and skin pigmentation, are there any other physical characteristics that distinguish your, uh, culture?"

"Culture?" said Hattie. "We Melungeons have been called many things over the years, but never a culture. Nice choice of words." Raising a hand, Hattie wriggled her fingers. "Count 'em. Is that enough of a 'distinguishing characteristic' for you?"

I took a quick count. "Six? I hadn't really noticed."

"Most people don't. They usually get hung up on the dark skin and green eyes. Guess it's too much to take in at a single gander. Not surprising, though. It's hard to tell what you're packing from a handshake. Especially if you've got a piss pot lot of other things wrong about you. Like I do."

"Fascinating," I said.

"You seem to fancy that word a lot, Mr. March."

A semi-successful writer being called to task for his lack of vocabulary by a woman over four times his age? How mortifying is that? My ears lowered yet another notch, I pressed on.

"Are there any other characteristics you want to tell me about?" Not too brilliant of a comeback, but it was the only thing I could come up with.

Hattie leaned forward to brush a long strand of white hair from her forehead.

"I got the ol' sleepy eye. Droopy eyelids runs in the family. My family, at least." She lowered her head. "So do these white patches on my scalp. Back at the turn of the century, when I still had a full head of hair, they weren't so noticeable."

She twisted to the right, turned her head to reveal the back of her neck.

"We also usually got these knots here. Mine aren't that big, thank goodness, but some get to be the size of crabapples."

She stuck out a tiny foot.

"Melungeons are also known for their small feet. Mine are a size two, I've been told."

"Fascina— Um, very interesting."

An ear-to-ear grin on her face, Hattie leaned back, rocking again.

"That be enough to satisfy your reader's curiosity about our . . . curiosities?"

"More than enough. No more questions, I promise."

"I can begin my story then?"

I pushed the recorder closer to her. Smiled and nodded.

"The floor is all yours, Hattie."

"Good. Then I have a question for you, Mr. March. Are you man enough to stare the devil in the eye without dropping a load in your britches?"

I was dumbfounded. Where had this come from? Struggling to recover from this unexpected broadside, I opted for humor.

"I've covered hot spots all over the world, Ms. Sexton. From the race riots in Los Angeles to the sands of Desert Storm. I like to think that I'm capable of mastering any crisis. Although my wife would beg to differ. Especially when it comes to dealing with creepie-crawlies of the eight-legged kind."

That gleam returned to Hattie's eye.

"I'll take that as a gussied-up yes. Then settle back and open up your ears, John March. We'll soon see how strong a stomach you really got."

THIRTY-FOUR

Meanwhile, unbeknownst to me, about the same time I turned my portable recorder back on down in Tennessee, my ever-inquisitive intern, Connie, was knocking on Helen Collette's door back up in Boston. As with most successful periodicals, Saturday is just another working day at *TIME* magazine.

"Mrs. Collette?"

"Come in, Connie," said Helen. "How'd it go with John? I take it he got off alright?"

"He left bright-eyed and bushy-tailed early today. Well, early anyway. It takes him a little while to get the juices flowing in the morning."

"I'm not much of a morning person myself. So, what can I do for you?"

"Sorry to bother you with this, and it's probably nothing, but while I was doing further research on Melungeons, I came across several facts you might find interesting. And perhaps a bit disturbing."

"Is it something in those books you've got in your arms?"

"One book in particular. It's a 1940 edition entitled *The Hawk's Done Gone*. And if I may, I'd like to read you one sobering passage. It begins on page three: 'Not Indians, not Negroes, Melungeons are a queer tribe of folks that live over there off Newman's Ridge and Blackwater Creek.'

"Later on it goes on to say that the Melungeons were snubbed by their fairer skinned neighbors and eventually pushed out of the valleys. Up into the snake-infested mountain gorges where they established a clannish way of life."

"That *is* interesting. Anything else?"

"What raised a red flag for me was something I discovered in this second book I have here, *A History of Tennessee and Tennesseeans*. Published in 1913, it's a bit dated, but on page 181, the author lists some personal impressions. And I quote: 'Whites left them alone because they were so wild and devil-fired. If a man was fool enough to go into Melungeon country and he came back without being shot, he was sure to wizzen and perish with some ailment nobody could name.'"

"Wizzen and perish, Connie?" said Helen. "Not exactly encouraging."

"My thoughts exactly. Until the early sixties, Melungeons were classified as Black for marriage, White for voting, and Indian for education. A curious mixture, to say the least. Maybe it's why they were generally looked down on by the rest of the populace. According to one lowland legend, the devil—they called him Old Horney back then—was expelled from hell by his harpy wife. He then traveled to the Smoky Mountains, where he took up residence with a Cherokee woman and fathered the Melungeons. A few pages later in the book, it gets even more ominous: 'Terrible things went on up in them hills. Blood drinking, and devil worship, and carryings on that would freeze a good Christian's spine bone.'

"It goes on to say there were rumors of human sacrifices, vampires, and even cannibalism. In 1915, a state senator went so far as to describe Melungeons as 'shiftless, idle, thieving, lawless, suspicious, cowardly, sneaky, exceedingly immoral, unforgiving, and a synonym for all that is doubtful, mysterious, and unclean. They aren't niggers, they aren't Indians, and they aren't white men. God only knows what they are.'"

"And this is where I sent John?" asked Helen.

"I'm afraid so, Mrs. Collette. Mr. Bollinger even mentioned Newman's Ridge specifically when I talked to him. And I'm sure he said Hattie Sexton's cabin was 'a stone's throw from it.' His exact words."

"What are our options, Connie?"

"Not much we can do now. Other than call out the National Guard. Which I'm pretty sure Tennessee's governor wouldn't appreciate."

"Do you think John can handle it?"

"John's been in tight situations before. I've seen him charm the horns off a bull with his gift of gab. But just to make sure, I'll mention him tonight in my prayers. He's the best boss I ever had, and I'd hate to lose him."

"Not a bad idea. I'm not the religious type, but I might do the same. Good reporters like him are hard to come by these days."

"Do you think I should call and tell him what I found? That is, if I can. So far I haven't been able to get through. Probably something to do with the bad reception in those mountains."

"At this stage of the game, it might not be wise, Connie. John's plate is full already. No sense in giving him something else to worry about."

At least somebody, somewhere, was concerned about my welfare. But Helen made the right decision. Adding blood-drinking sacrifices, devil-worshipping vampires, and cannibalism to the Earp brothers, Doc Holliday, and Ocho might have driven me over the edge.

THIRTY-FIVE

H attie tucked her shawl around her knees. Settled deeper into her bentwood and sucked a four-second breath through her nose. Then leaned back and began to rock in syncopation to the grandfather clock's ticking, as if the two were counting down to the story she was about to tell. While a hush fell over the rest of the cabin, I folded my arms and waited.

Outside, the birds had stopped chirping. The wind died down, and not a leaf stirred. As if the entire forest were holding its collective breath. A gallery of small heads on the far wall turned toward Hattie. Hardly a blink. All eyes riveted on her like children waiting for a bedtime story.

Hattie palmed her cane. Wet her lips. Looked me straight in the eye.

"Had I been born fair of face or straight of spine, this might have been a story about me. Although the good Lord in His infinite wisdom has seen fit to cram my life chockablock with enough twists and turns to fill a dozen of your highfalutin magazines, compared to the cursed existence and untold hardships He laid out for my dear sweet brother, my life has been a walk in the park. And it's his tale of misery I'm choosing to tell."

Nothing even halfway close to what I'd been expecting.

"Your brother? But I thought this was going to be about—"

"Patience is a virtue, John March. The race is not always to the swift."

I smiled an apology.

"You're trotting out Job on me again?" I asked.

"Job comes in handy around these parts."

Hattie resumed her rocking. Took a second to realign her thoughts.

"Now that I'm a step or two from death's door, I can finally close the chapter on my brother's torture. And since I'm the last of those close to the matter, there's no one left to hurt."

Her voice trailed off, and another faraway look filled her eye. When Hattie spoke again, her voice seemed to gather strength. Beneath the gravel in her words simmered the intensity of great orators. The stuff of Lincoln and Churchill. Of Kennedy before the Bay of Pigs, when he'd been at his best.

"I was born the year Alexander Graham Bell invented the telephone," she continued. "July of 1876 it was. Hottest summer in twenty years. My momma came down with the punies and took to her bed a full two months before she birthed me. Bless her kind heart, she was a large woman. Larger than any three hilltoppers put together. Some said that laying on her back for so long was the reason I came out with a crookified spine."

A wisp of a smile commandeered her face. She stroked her chin.

"But we mountain folk never pay much notice to things out of the ordinary. Over the years you get accustomed to people being . . . out of kilter, so to say. I was all of five before anyone even mentioned my tilt face-to-face. Willy Joe Butterfield, I think it was, brought it up first. We was down at the creek fishing when he turns to me and says, 'Hey, Hattie, why you always leanin' to the right?' 'Don't really know,' says I. 'Maybe I was born with a crick in my neck, and it just never went away.' Back then that was good enough for the both of us. Leastwise, Billy Joe never brought it up again."

Her smile turning wistful, Hattie gazed out the window. That faraway look wasn't long in returning. The seconds turned into a minute, maybe two. While her thoughts teleported to two centuries past, time seemed to stand still. I could only imagine the journey her mind was taking.

As long as I live, no matter what I do, the money I make, or the future awards I receive, none of it could ever compare to Hattie Sexton's amazing life span. The history she'd lived through, the people who had passed in and out of her life, the significant events that had come and gone. Names, dates, places, nearly a century and a half's worth. In comparison, my dreamed-for Pulitzer seemed mundane. Inconsequential.

Now two people in the cabin had that distant look. One was reliving an amazing past. The other could only project into what was waiting for him in a comparatively boring future. With a bob of her head, Hattie was the first to return from Vaporville.

"Sorry about that," she said, looking around. "Did I drift away a bit?"

No answer from me; I was still somewhere else, dazed and confused. Seeing my fogbound state, she reached out to nudge me with her cane.

"You still with me, Mr. March?" Then she clicked her tongue. Smiled. "Don't you go drifting off on me, now. I'm just getting started."

THIRTY-SIX

My cheeks were burning. "I apologize," I said. "I must have spaced out for a few seconds."

She thrummed her fingers on the armrest. Searching her memory banks added another row of wrinkles to her brow. The room's captive audience—furred, feathered, scaled, and citified—awaited patiently for what was to come. Hattie cleared her throat.

"It was a bright summer day, late in the afternoon. The year was 1881. Late that August, I think. Poppa had just finished building this very cabin we're sitting in. Brand spanking new it was. Tight and straight, and smelling of newly split logs, the porch didn't sag none yet, and the roof wasn't covered with moss and vines like it is today. It may not have been the biggest or the fanciest cabin on the mountain, but it was our home, and we Sextons were damn proud of it. Especially considering Poppa was never what you might call handy with a hammer and nail. God rest his soul, he always did his best. And for Momma and me, that was good enough."

Hattie's smile ran wide and deep with remembered sunshine. I love my own parents deeply, but not once in my yet young life had such a look overcome me when thinking of my childhood.

"I remember like it was just yesterday," she continued. "I was sitting out there, in front of our cabin. The grass was ankle high and soft as goose down. Sweet smelling as home-cooked apple pie. I was wearing my bibbed gingham dress, the one with the deep pockets in front. Its pockets were great for gathering special keepsakes from the forest. It may have been threadbare and ragged in places, but it was my favorite. My other dress was a calico. I liked it good enough, but it was my Sunday go-to-meeting dress. And it was kinda itchy. Good thing I only had to wear it once a week."

Hattie stopped to pat the dress she was wearing.

"To this day I still like deep pockets. You never know what you'll find in them."

Inhaling slowly, she wetted her lips.

"As I was saying, I was sitting out there on the grass, with a few of my woodland friends gathered around me. A full-grown raccoon was sitting on his haunches off to my right, cleaning his nose whiskers. He must have come from the creek, where he'd no doubt been snacking on some juicy mudbugs, a favorite meal of his. A pair of squirrels was curled up to my left, their cheeks full of acorns. In my lap I was holding a young rabbit, its left ear torn clear through."

After a slow nod in my direction, Hattie twinkled a smile.

"As far back as I can remember, critters seemed to be at ease when they came around. Fang, fur, and claw, they all took a shine to me. Mostly 'cause I always took the time to listen to them real good. And I liked all of them back. Never could explain how peaceful-like and open it got to be between us. It just happened somehow. I got along well enough with my own kind. I just got along better with the animals. Still do, in fact."

The longer Hattie spoke, the more captivated I became. Her voice no longer sounded like gravel rattling around an oaken bucket. And gone was the hesitation of old age, the traces of uncertainty that come with the passage of time. In their place was a calm clarity. Her voice transported me back to a happier era. Summoned up memories of favorite TV stars in my childhood.

As a six-year-old I used to prop myself up in front of our TV to listen to the golden throats of Winston Hibler and Rex Allen as they narrated Disney adventures. Later, in my early teens, I was captivated by the sonorous lilt of Burl Ives. At sixteen it was James Earl Jones's deep bass voice. When Darth Vader spoke—"No, I am your father"—I hung on his every word. And here in her cabin, Hattie Sexton's voice had that same effect on me. If I hadn't been hooked when I shook her hand, I was definitely hooked now.

THIRTY-SEVEN

With her cadenced delivery, Hattie took me back to the beginning.

❦

I cradled that fluff ball of a rabbit in the crook of my arm. Took a closer look at its torn ear. "What's this, Mr. Floppy?" says I.

Dried blood had matted his fur. Poor little guy. Some critter twice his size, no doubt a critter with a mouthful of sharper teeth, had also taken a bite out of his left leg. But I was no bleeding-heart fool. I knew that such things happened in the forest—that, for the most part, it was nature's way. Some critters eat grass, berries, or bugs. Others, those with fangs and claws, eat the critters that eat the grass, berries, and bugs. God's will, I suppose, but I didn't have to like the bloody results none. I held the bunny close, nuzzled his tiny pink nose. Cold as a well rock it was.

"Looks like you got yourself into a serious scrape of some sort," I says. "That mean old Mr. Fox been after you again?"

Of course, I got no answer. Except for a nose twitch or two, rabbits aren't much in the talking department. To soothe his hurt feelings, I stroked his good ear for a spell. Animals are right sensitive when it comes to being disrespected. Just like human beings.

"How'd you let him sneak up on you?" I asked him. "Number one law of the jungle, you should never let your guard down."

I cupped his feet in my palm. Though still a young'un, he had some powerful leg muscles on him. The Lord in His infinite wisdom never fails to even things out a bit. He may have given the fox a fearsome set of teeth, but he also gave the rabbit an impressive set of legs to escape those fearsome teeth. In the long run, it was only fair.

"Br'er Fox must have scared you near to death," I says to him. "Thank goodness you were on the quick side."

I still got no answer from him.

"I bet you kicked dirt into his face with those big feet of yours," says I. "Mr. Red Tail probably didn't know what hit him."

Enjoying that thought, I chuckled real soft. Rabbits tend to get spooked when you laugh too loud.

"Sure wish I'd been there to see it," I added.

However, I realized for every cottontail that got away, there were two who didn't. Bottom line, like every critter in the forest, foxes got the right to eat, to feed their young'uns, too. The Lord, also in His infinite wisdom, did not put any of his children on this good, green earth to starve. I guess when you get right down to it, there's only one rock-hard commandment in the wild. Eat or be eaten. I have to admit, though, it gave me pause every time Momma fried up a plate of her mouthwatering chicken. Made me think that maybe I, too, was part of God's all-knowing plan.

"Listen up, you three," says I to the others gathered around me. "Let this be a lesson to all of you. Never, ever, ever turn your back on Br'er Fox."

I have this habit of shaking my finger in an argument. Momma said it's not polite, but when I get excited, or feel real strong about something, I tend to forget.

Done with my finger wagging, I put my hands on my hips and scowled. I hear tell that's what schoolmarms do. Momma said a bit of the ham comes out of me at times, that I'd go overly "thee-hat-trick-all." Although at the time I had no idea what that word meant.

"Let a fox get too close," I continued, "and sure as shootin', he'll chomp down on you. He'd like nothing better than to wrap those big sharp teeth of his around a bowl of rabbit stew. Or maybe a heaping plate of coon fritters. Or a stack of squirrel flapjacks."

Br'er Raccoon pawed the air. Both squirrels crow-hopped back a couple steps. The one on the right choked on his acorn.

"If I were a hungry fox," I added, "I couldn't think of anything more delicious."

To drive my point home, I rubbed my stomach. Smacked my lips.

"Now," I said, "I want your solemn, cross-your-heart-and-hope-to-die promise that from now on you'll be more careful. I don't want any of you warming up the insides of no fox belly."

Chittering softly, all three lowered their eyes. Looked away.

"Good," says I. "I'll take that as a yes. And you'd better not go back on your word. Friends never break promises to friends."

THIRTY-EIGHT

A stir inside the cabin interrupted the palaver between me and my friends. Bless her good-as-gold heart, my mother, Mullie Moon Sexton, was clattering around in there. She was a mountain of a woman. At the time she weighed over six hundred pounds. Belly button to belly button she measured nigh three yards around. She was so heavy sometimes I thought our poor floorboards lay awake at night, fretting about when she'd come by next: "Lord, have mercy! She's heading our way again! Oh, my aching back! We're doomed!"

Momma always said I had a fertile imagination.

When she opened the door, my friends hightailed it back to where they came from. It's only natural for animals to be wary of something as big as Momma. T'weren't really her fault, though. Since she rarely left the cabin, they never got a chance to know her. And see how gentle she was.

Even though Momma was on the overly large side, she had the most beautiful face you'd ever hope to lay eyes on. Like an angel's it was. With a mile-wide smile always smack dab right in the middle of it. She had long, flowing hair the golden color of newly mown hay that reached down to her knees. She took great pride in the way it shined in the sunlight. Come rain or come shine, she always brushed it at least a hundred times a day. I know because I helped her count.

Between her face and her hair, one overlooked the fact that she was bigger'n a barn. At least, my poppa always did. Particularly when he sat himself down to dinner. The bestest, most scrumptious cook in five counties, Momma knew her way around a kitchen better'n anyone. At the Sexton table, there was no such thing as leftovers.

"Hattie," Momma called out. "Time to fetch your poppa. Supper's about ready."

When Momma let her wishes be known, you were wise to listen. She could pick up a newborn calf with one arm and carry the week's wash in the other. Stronger than any two fieldhands put together. Whenever my poppa—who was as skinny as Momma was fat—got to feeling cantankerous, she'd plop down on top of him, almost squash him flat. Then tickle him until he turned blue. Riding the rail, she called it. It never took Poppa long to see the error of his ways.

"What are we having, Momma?" I asked.

"Your favorite," says she. "Panfried chicken and grits, corn on the cob. With shoofly pie for dessert."

My taste buds watering up a storm, I was off in a flash. Well, maybe not a flash, persactly. But as fast as a six-year-old saddled with a crooked spine could manage. Even though it was a far piece, I knew the way to Poppa's still better'n the back of my hand. And bent over the way I am, I'd gotten to know the back of my hand pretty damn well.

We couldn't situate the family's livelihood close to our homestead. Not with all the government men snooping around. Once every few years the blue suits would get lucky and stumble across Poppa's works. Then they'd have themselves a fine old time with their axes, whacking it into little pieces. Oh, they'd pat themselves on the back, and Poppa would cuss a lot, but it never amounted to a hill of beans. Poppa would wait a week or so, move to a new location, and rebuild the still in less than a day. A cost of doing business, he liked to say.

You'd think them badges had better things to do than hassle poor country folk trying to make a living. It's not like we was doing anything wrong, really. Momma told me making moonshine was illegal only by the decree of some stuffed shirts in Washington. Back then I never understood what kind of logic they was using. But I took her word for it.

A slide down the mossy bank on the other side of the ridge, a rope swing across the creek—always my favorite part—and I was on my way. The rest I could have managed with my eyes closed. I tried it blindfolded once, just to see if I could do it, but forgot how things can change overnight in the forest. I hadn't counted on that fallen tree. Felt like a fool tumbling face-first into the mud like that. Cut myself on a rock. Still got the scar to this day. I guess it's there to remind me how stupid I was. As Momma always said, you should never take things for granted.

Anyhow, I stopped to rest a spell on the second rise. The trail could get pretty steep and slippery at times, especially after a rain, so I had to scramble on all fours. Being built so close to the ground, I'm pretty good at scrambling.

There's a flatiron boulder at the top of the ridge, a favorite sunning spot for half the snakes in the valley. I leaned on it to catch my breath. When I closed my eyes, sunbursts kept popping off, like my own personal fireworks. That happens a lot when I push myself too hard. Up ahead I saw a puny wisp of smoke, trickling upward. Poppa's still.

Puny smoke means puny fires. And a puny fire meant things hadn't gone well with Poppa's latest batch of moonshine.

THIRTY-NINE

"And it wasn't a surprise. God bless him, each time, Poppa gave it his all, but that mean-tempered still seemed to have a mind of its own." Hattie nodded. "That infernal contraption always got the best of him. He claimed to have been born under an unlucky star, so I guess it was to be expected. Snakebit, we mountain folk call it. If it weren't for Momma, I swear Poppa would have come to an untimely end before I was a twinkle in his eye. Some people are born for greatness. Poppa was born to stub his toes. Sometimes all ten of them at once."

⊶──⊰

I heard a popping sound in the distance. Not a good sign. Hoping to high heaven Poppa hadn't lost another finger—he was down two already—I crossed myself and picked up the pace. A quick hop and jump across Poker Creek, making sure to avoid that slippery third stone. The one that sneaky snapping turtle liked to hide under. Then it was a straight shot to Wild Boar Meadow.

After the heavy rains that spring, Wild Boar was more mud than meadow. By the by, the last of the wild boars in these hills vamoosed to higher ground the first time Poppa fired up his still. Couldn't blame them piggies none, though. Poppa's botched brews could empty an entire forest. One batch in particular stunk so godawful bad birds dropped dead out of the sky. Thank goodness our cabin wasn't downwind that day.

I stopped to sniff the air. I'd smelled worse. Poppa had built this particular still underneath a flat, overhanging rock that seemed to teeter in a fair to middlin' wind. The rock provided good draft for his fires, so he was willing to take the chance. Today, however, the rock wasn't providing much of anything. I'd seen bigger blazes in his corncob pipe. Poppa was bent over, trying his best to fan the fire with a flat piece of bark. So close I feared he'd set his beard on fire. And it wouldn't have been the first time.

"Not going so well, Poppa?" I asked.

Short and hawk nosed, Poppa was missing both eyebrows. Three or four times a year, like clockwork, he'd accidentally singe them off. After a while they didn't bother to grow back. He was thin as a sapling and one-fourth Momma's size, called Jack Spratt by those this side of Clingman's Dome. Behind his back, of course.

Coughing from the smoke, he was rubbing his good eye and cussing up a storm.

"Damn wet pine! What the hell was I thinking?"

I jumped up and down. Pointed at the piece of bark that had caught fire in his hand.

"Uh, Poppa?" I said. "Those flames are headed for your fingers."

He hopped around, trying to blow the flames out. Which, of course, only made the bark burn brighter.

"Throw it into the fire!" yells I.

And he did.

Watching that bark curl up into a blackened ball, Poppa let out with a mournful sigh. Shook his head, then looked up at the sky.

"Why me, Lord?" says he. "Why do these things keep happening to me? I must be a tomfool idiot."

Together we watched the fire wither and die. After a few seconds, he pulled up a crate and plopped himself down. My heart full of love, I laid a hand on his shoulder.

"Fires can have a mind of their own, Poppa."

"Ain't that the truth," says he.

"Maybe it was the kindling you used."

"Could've been," says he.

And we left it at that.

My poppa was a practical sort. Knew he wasn't the coordinated kind. Early on he'd learned to take things with a grain of salt. And truth be told, he'd tossed several shakers' worth over his left shoulder. But I could tell this mishap bothered him more than most. Thinking an encouraging word might help, I opened my mouth to say something. Then quickly closed it again. Sometimes it was best to let him be. So, together we watched the fire peter out. Although this fire wasn't up to snuff when it came to making moonshine, it would have been a respectable roasting fire. Had we something to roast.

"At least it's a beautiful day, Poppa," I said finally.

He tugged at his beard. Looked back to the sky.

"That it is, daughter," says he. "That it is."

"The Lord giveth, and the Lord taketh away," I said. "I guess that about covers it."

Just then, that damn still let out a raspy wheeze. Burped. Clanged twice, then blew its top. A coil sprang loose and began to twist about, spraying brown water all over the place. What was left of the fire hissed out. Half a dozen twitches, and the empty coil collapsed with a clatter. The rest of the still caved in a few seconds later.

Neither of us was much surprised. We'd seen it happen before. However, as Momma always said, "Every cloud has its silver lining." At least Poppa had been spared having to watch the government take axes to his still. This time, anyway.

FORTY

"Poor Poppa," continued Hattie, "he had this habit of turning silk purses into sows' ears. A couple of years prior to building his first still, he tried his hand at coining. Hard to believe, but he turned out to be a worse counterfeiter than a moonshiner. A year after he died, the revenoo'ers discovered the fake coins he made contained too much gold and silver. Turns out they cost Poppa more to make than what the government was putting out. Not a good business tactic, that."

I fanned away the smoke. Leaned forward to assess the damage.

"Your still shouldn't be hard to fix," said I. "Probably won't take more than a day and a half. I'm just thankful you didn't lose another finger."

Poppa grinned at that. Wiggled the stumps of his two missing fingers. "This time, anyway. Ah, well, it's no great loss. This last batch tasted like panther piss anyway."

"Then I guess you should count your blessings," said I.

Poppa slapped his thighs and rose to his full height. Which wasn't much taller than me. He stretched out his arms in a mighty yawn. Looked down at the pile of twisted metal that used to be a still. Sighed as he scratched an armpit.

"And leastwise it didn't explode like it did the last time."

"Amen to that, Poppa."

He touched his eye patch, a reminder of a previous accident. Turned real thoughtful.

"And I can't afford to lose another eye. There ain't much calling for a blind moonshiner. In this life, or the next."

Thumbs jammed into his overall pockets, he ambled over to the fire to nudge a dying ember with his boot.

"Your mother send you to fetch me, Hattie?" he asks.

"She says dinner'll be on the table by the time we get back."

Poppa puffed out his cheeks. "Seems I can't never do anything right. If it wasn't for Momma, I don't know how I'd get along. I'd probably just wither up and die."

I picked up a stone and chucked it into the ashes. Took his hand in mine.

"That's okay, Poppa. Someday you'll get the hang of this. It was a stupid still anyway. You'll build a better one next time." I gave him a gentle hug. "We'd better get a move on. Momma hates it when we're late for dinner."

I donned the biggest smile I could muster up. Patted my belly.

"Besides, I'm hungry as a bear. And Momma's made us shoofly pie for dessert."

FORTY-ONE

"**W**ith my cane crooked across an elbow and both hands holding tight to the rope," Hattie kept on, "I was making ready to swing across the creek when a familiar aroma wafted in on the breeze. The sweet smell of Momma's shoofly."

Poppa was wading halfway across the creek, his pants rolled up and his boots under his arm. Not partial to ropes of any kind, or ladders for that matter. He preferred to keep his feet planted firmly on the ground. Even if they were underwater. He was also deathly afraid of heights. Used to cross himself on anything higher than a barstool.

"Smell that, Poppa?" I say.

That stopped him midstream.

"Is that pie I smell?" he asks.

"I sure hope so," I say.

I gave the rope a quick yank, just to make sure. Definitely not strong enough to hold someone as heavy as Momma, but I had no doubt it would handle little light-as-a-feather me. And just like that, I was on the other side. I may have been awkward at a few things, but I was a whiz on that rope. Like a regular little bird, my poppa used to say. I tied the rope to its proper branch, then patted my dress down. Flying across creeks tends to fluff up one's feathers a bit.

"Hurry up, Poppa," I said. "Shoofly's a-waiting."

"Somewhere in the Good Book it says patience is a virtue," says he. "But not one of yours, I be thinking."

Suddenly, Poppa lets out with a high-pitched yelp. He drops both boots and begins to hop up and down on one foot.

Clamped onto his big toe was the biggest crawdad I'd ever seen. And from the looks of it, that stubborn critter wasn't about to let go anytime soon. Strange that it would be in the middle of the creek like that. Crawdads usually keep to the mudbank on the other side, where the current isn't so swift. Better hunting there, I suppose. Just Poppa's luck, he'd come across one who'd lost his way.

"Ee-yow!" yells Poppa, jumping about like a spider on a hot skillet.

When he grabbed for the crawdad, he lost his balance and tumbled into the water. Thank goodness it was only ankle deep. Any deeper, he might have drowned—water being just another on the long list of things Poppa was afraid of. About that same time, Mr. Crawdad decided to let go. Probably didn't care much for the taste of smelly feet. Not to badmouth my poppa none, but sometimes his feet got to stinking worse than his still.

For a few seconds he flailed his arms about like a tipped-over windmill. When he realized all he had to do was stand up, he stopped thrashing. Gasped for air, looked around.

"Sorta made a fool of myself, didn't I?" says he.

I puckered my mouth to hide a smile.

"It could have happened to anyone, Poppa. That was one *big* crawdad. Could have snapped your toe clean off."

"For a second there, I thought I'd bought the farm," he said.

"Could've been worse," says I. "Thank goodness your toe ain't bleeding bad."

With a shake of his head, Poppa tucked his boots under his arm again. Retrieved his hat when it floated by.

"I may be dumber than a rusty nail, but at least I ain't as bad as your great-granddaddy. Did I ever tell you about the time he turned into a preacher, Hattie?"

"No, Poppa," says I. "I don't think you ever told me about Gramps turning preacher." But of course, he had. I always liked listening to Poppa's stories, no matter how many times I'd heard them.

FORTY-TWO

"When it comes to doing the dumb," Poppa says, "ol' Hattler Sexton—in a roundabout way you was named after him, Hattie. Anyhow, he was in a class all by hisself. One fine Sunday morning our regular preacher was late in his arriving. So, fortified by a bit of the shine, Hattler took it upon himself to deliver a sermon of his own.

"Full of the spirit now, he hitched up his britches and ambled up to the pulpit as if he'd been preaching all his life. Your great-grandfather was never what you might call bashful. Especially when he had a few drinks under his belt. After wetting a finger, he opened the big Bible and thumbed to a random page.

"This, of course, set the entire congregation to snickering. They all knew Hattler couldn't read a lick. After pretending to decipher what chapter he was in, he rocked forward, burped, then proudly announced, 'Today's scripture would be from the book of Timothy, or some such tall grass.'"

Every time I heard that story, I'd get to laughing so hard I'd pee my pants. And that day was no exception.

"What happened when the preacher finally arrived?" I asked. Knowing full well the answer.

"Reverend Hubbleton was a patient man," says Poppa. "He let Hattler ramble on until grandpappy finally pitched forward, face down into that Bible. At least he had the good manners to mutter a final 'Amen' before he passed out."

"What happened then?" I asked, tears of laughter streaming down my face.

"It took half the choir to deposit Hattler's drunk ass in the last pew. They covered him with a blanket and went back to their singing.

There he stayed, sleeping it off for the rest of the service, snoring to beat the band."

With a slap of his thigh, Poppa laughed along with me. How he loved telling his stories. A good story is the best way to forget your troubles. But it didn't take him long to realize he was still standing in the middle of the creek. Now soaking wet. Scratching his head, he let out a groan.

"Look at me, Hattie. Why am I so damn clumsy? Your momma's gonna read me the riot act."

"Maybe," says I. "But we could say I bumped into you when I was swinging across the creek. That way she'd think it wasn't your fault."

"You'd do that for me?"

"I might be so inclined if someone I know would nudge his piece of shoofly my way at dinner."

Poppa scratched his beard. Stood there dripping water for a few seconds. He dearly loved his shoofly.

"You drive a hard bargain, Hattie Sexton. But you got yourself a deal."

And then we shook on it.

"You know, daughter," he said with a laugh, "there's a word for what you're pulling on me here. It's called blackmail."

I laughed along. Then winked.

"If'n it offends you so, maybe we should just tell Momma the truth."

"No, no," says he. "A deal's a deal. Damnation! How'd you get to be so all-fired tricky?"

"Momma taught me. She calls it being resourceful."

"It figures Mullie Moon would have a hand in this. Ah, well, we'd better get a move on. I gotta get out of these wet clothes. With my luck, I'll catch my death of cold."

"In that case, Poppa," I said, "you can keep your piece of pie. It ain't fittin' sending a person to the great beyond on a half-empty stomach."

"That's mighty thoughtful of you, daughter," he said. "You're all heart."

FORTY-THREE

Momma had this sixth sense about things, so she was waiting for us on the porch when we got home. Her keen eye zeroed in on Poppa's condition right away. Hard not to, what with the squishing his boots were doing and all the water dripping off him. Spatula in hand, she raised a slow eyebrow.

"Take another tumble in the creek, did you, Navarrah?" asks she.

Poppa was never much good at lying, especially to Momma, who always read his tells like a book. For a few seconds he just stood there, twisting in the wind.

"You see, it was this way, Mullie Moon. I, uh," he stammers, "er, had this little accident."

It was the start of teeny fib, hardly working up a decent sweat, but Poppa couldn't finish it. So, I had to step in.

"It was all my fault, Momma. I swung into Poppa. Hit him square in the back and knocked him into the water."

I put my hands behind my back and toed the dirt in front of me. Topped it off with a sorrowful puppy-dog eye. One of my best moves. It had taken me a couple of months to master it. But it worked real good. On most people.

"I sure am powerful sorry, Momma," says I. "Next time I'll be more careful."

Momma looked at me, then back at Poppa. He gave her that hangdog look of his. Similar to mine, but one he'd come by naturally.

"You're lucky you both didn't drown," said Momma. She sighed, then smiled. "Well, don't just stand there. Dinner's getting cold. Navarrah, hustle yourself out of those wet clothes. Hattie, you can help me set the table."

Thinking that our deal was working, Poppa actually whistled as he went inside. When I got close, Momma nudged me with her spatula.

"It was nice of you to speak up for your poppa like that, Hattie. Even though it was a load of hogwash. Tell me the truth, now. You didn't really bump into him, did you?"

I should have known better than to try to pull something on Momma.

"No, ma'am," says I, my eyes to the floor. "A crawdad latched onto Poppa's big toe and he lost his balance."

Only a fool would lie to Momma twice in one day.

"It figures," she said. "But let's not make a habit of telling tall tales in this house. No matter how much you love your poppa. Or how much trouble he gets himself into."

"No, ma'am," says I. "I won't."

"For now we'll keep the truth of the matter between us womenfolk. No need to embarrass your father any further."

"Agreed, Momma. Mum's the word."

"You hungry?"

"Horse-eating hungry."

"Then trot yourself over to the pump and wash up."

Nothing ever got by my momma.

Poor as we was, she always saw to it we had enough to eat. Even when times was rough. And since Poppa blew up his still on a regular basis, there were plenty of those. But our table always carried a full load come dinnertime.

Proof of what I'm saying, sitting beside a platter of chicken that night was a heaping bowl of mashed potatoes. Added to that, like chicks gathered around a mother hen, were dishes of creamed corn, yellow beans, bear's lettuce with chopped bacon, and a basket of warm corn bread. I, of course, had my eye on the deep-dish shoofly cooling on the windowsill.

After mumbling grace, Poppa reached over quicker'n a gnat's twitch to spear a chicken breast. Momma may have had the deadliest spatula in three counties, but nobody had a faster fork than my poppa. Especially when he was hungrier than a bear. Which he was anytime Momma put food on the table.

"Sure is good chicken, Mullie Moon," says he, his mouth dripping gravy. "Best ever."

After washing down his first bite, he leaned forward on his elbows. Inhaled slowly through his teeth. Then shook his head.

"I hate to tell you this, but things went haywire down at the still today."

"Not again, Navarrah," said Momma. "Don't tell me you lost another finger."

Poppa held up both hands.

"Nope, not this time. Knock on wood, I still got eight of these puppies left. I don't know what happened persactly. I'd ground up the corn, making sure it was double fine, just like you told me to. Then I poured it into the vat, real slow, also like you told me. But I had problems with the fire from the git-go. I'm thinking the wood might have been too wet. One minute I was stoking the flames, the next thing I know, the infernal contraption popped a gusset."

"Copper pipe costs money, Nav," says Momma. "Money we ain't got right now. How many coils have you gone through this year?"

Poppa tugged at his beard. Scratched his head.

"Two, I think."

"Just two?"

"Maybe three. I sure am powerful sorry, Mullie. It won't happen again. I promise."

"That's what you said last time."

FORTY-FOUR

"A slow smile inched its way onto Momma's face," said Hattie, keeping on point. "She never could stay mad at Poppa for long."

❦

For a few seconds, Grandfather's ticking was the only ballad being put forth in the room.

"Navarrah Samson Sexton," she said, "I dearly love your clumsy hide, but sometimes you can be a walking, talking calamity."

Going all sorry and sad, Poppa mumbled up his best get-out-of-jail card, the one that always tugged at Momma's heartstrings something fierce. No matter how bad he'd messed up.

"I just can't seem to do anything right, honey bunch. If I had a lick of sense, I'd shoot myself dead in the head. Then you wouldn't have to put up with all my miseries. But with my luck, I'd probably miss and just blast off an ear. Maybe another finger."

At that Momma stomped her foot. Hard enough to rattle every plate on the table. Scared me half to death. Poppa, too.

"I'll have none of that talk at my dinner table!" says she. "There will be no shooting in this house. Not today! Not ever! Is that clear?" She put a hand on Poppa's shoulder. "Lord knows, no one tries harder than you do, Navarrah Sexton. You give Hattie and me all you got. Each and every day. And in my book, that's good enough."

She sneaked a wink at me, then shot the old snake eye in Poppa's direction.

"Course, keep guzzling the shine on the job the way you been doing, and I just might shoot you myself."

Eyes fluttering down, Poppa reached for a second helping of chicken. Gave Momma a cautious peek.

"Um, I been thinking, Mullie. You're the brains in this here family, and that's a fact. Maybe you should take over the business. Hell, you make all the decisions anyway. Leastwise, all the important ones. You could run the still ten times better than me."

Momma took his hand in hers. Smiled.

"I appreciate the generous thought, Nav. I really do. It warms the cockles of my heart that you think so highly of me. But how, pray tell, in my condition am I to make it all the way to the still?"

She raised a slow eyebrow. Patted her hips.

"Even hauling these ham hocks of mine down the front steps is getting to be a chore. And the way I been piling on the pounds lately, soon I won't even be able to get through the front door."

"Me and Hattie could help you," says Poppa. "Couldn't we, Hattie?"

"You bet," says I, not sure it was the right answer.

"Besides," added Poppa, "you ain't that heavy, Mullie."

"Heavy?" laughed Momma. "Don't be sweet-talking me, Nav. Any fool with eyes can plainly see I'm fatter'n a cow. Two cows, in fact. And you well know it."

Poppa's smile basted the room with even more love.

"But you still look good to me, honey bunch."

"That's because you've only got one eye, and you're dumber than a mule." Bending over, Momma kissed him on his bald spot. "But you're my dumb mule."

Such was the life I had as a child. We Sextons may not have had much, but we had each other. And for the next two decades, that was more than enough for Poppa, Momma, and me. It took Poppa another year or so to master that cantankerous still of his, but eventually he got the hang of it.

It cost him another finger, half an ear, and most of a big toe, but by the turn of the century, he was cranking out some passable moonshine. It weren't no Jack Daniels, but at least it no longer tasted like panther piss. Most said if it didn't kill you outright goin' down, it would clean out your pipes slicker'n greased lightning. Thank God Poppa's customers weren't the picky kind.

Howsomever, John March, the real story I been hankering to tell begins in ought one, the year President McKinley got himself shot. In twenty years, my momma blossomed up to over eight hundred pounds. She got so big she couldn't leave the house no more. Nearly killed her, not being able to tend to her flowers like she used to.

When she got too heavy for the steps, I took care of her garden while she watched through the window, giving me tendin' advice on the roses. Roses was always her favorite. She still cooked and cleaned as much as she could, but as the years passed, it took her more and more time. Wasn't long before even baking a pie got to be a full day's chore.

Still, things were going good for us. That is, until that dark night late in June when Momma took real sick.

FORTY-FIVE

Without missing a beat, Hattie skipped ahead to early summer of 1901.

That year, the hot, sticky weather was still a month away. The days were comfortable, the nights cool. Quilt bundler-uppers, as we say in the hills. The grass had riz, and meadow bonnets were in full bloom. Over the years, the Sexton cabin hadn't changed much, but I sure had.

Anyway, it was several years after that bodacious shindig they held in Chicago. Or maybe it took place in Cleveland. All I know is it was in some big city far away. The World's Fair, I think they called it. Quite a goings-on, I hear tell. People from far and wide came to see all the newfangled contraptions the twentieth century was gonna deposit on our doorsteps. They even had a machine that talked back to you. If that didn't beat all. How they'd use such a thing was beyond me.

Twenty-six I was, and all growed up. Well, not so much up. More like sideways. I was still crooked in the spine, but I was getting around better'n some. I had no reason to complain. As if it would have done me any good.

That summer, it was Momma who gave Poppa and me a serious case of the concerns. Despite her proportions, she'd been healthy as a horse her entire life. That year, however, she took to her bed for three straight days, unable to keep anything down. Poppa was fit to be tied. Fretting and worrying up a storm, he never left her side the entire time. He was so shook up he almost sliced off another finger making her a ham sandwich.

"Hattie," he whispered to me after Momma fell into a fitful sleep that second night. "I've never been so scared in my life. I don't know what I'd do if your momma . . ." He turned away. Looked down at the floor. "I'd be plumb lost without her."

"Momma's gonna be alright, Poppa," said I. "She's just feeling a mite poorly; that's all."

"But she's never been this sick," he said. "I'm the one who always comes down with something. I'm the one who's breaking this, cutting off that. Your momma's been rock-solid healthy. She takes care of us. Not vice versa."

When he shifted in his seat, Momma opened her eyes.

"I'm sorry, honey bunch," says Poppa. "I didn't mean to wake you."

Momma's eyes were tired and pinched, but she still wore a smile.

"I wasn't asleep, Nav. Just resting my eyes a spell. I heard what you said about being lost without me, and I dearly appreciate the sentiment. But I have no intention of leaving anyone. Not just yet, anyway. A case of the sour stomach is all I got. It'll pass in its own good time. As it always does. Although, I must admit this one's lasting longer a mite longer than most."

Poppa poured her a glass of water. And of course accidentally spilled it on her.

"Do you think it was something you ate?"

"Not likely," says Momma. "I been eating the same as you and Hattie."

A twist to her face marked another sharp pain in her belly. She winced. Let out a soft groan. "Now, that was a right respectable hurt," she said. "Felt like our ol' mule kicked me in the gut."

"Maybe I should send for Doc Hickory," said Poppa.

"Over my dead body," says Momma. "And not even then. I'll not have that man in our house!"

"But, Mullie, it's been two days now. And you aren't getting any better. If the doc can help, I don't see why we don't—"

"No! Absolutely not! If and when I do need a doctor, we'll get someone else."

"But Hickory is the only doc this side of the ridge. The nearest other is down in Sneedville. And that's a hard two-day ride. Even if I lather up the mule."

Momma set her jaw tight. Crossed her arms.

"I've had my say on the matter, Navarrah. Doc Hickory's got a mean streak to him. I can see it in his eyes. And you can't trust no doctor with mean eyes. Especially one who collects animal bones on the sly. Human bones, too, I've been told."

Most days that would have been enough for Poppa. Never wanting to go against his chosen wifemate, he would have said, "Yes'm" to anything, then gone about his business. But these were dire circumstances, and he wasn't about to back down.

"Now, Hattie," he says, "you know those are only wag-tongue rumors."

"What about all the animal skeletons he's got nailed to his porch railing? Those aren't no rumors. Everyone this side of Newman's Ridge has seen them."

"A man's entitled to his hobbies, I suppose."

Momma took a drink of water. By herself this time. Then raised up on one elbow.

"Collecting dead things ain't a proper hobby for a respectable doctor," says she. "Hattie, please go to the kitchen and fetch me the third jar from the left. Top shelf."

"Yes'm. Right away," says I, hustling off to do her biding. From the kitchen I see Momma take Poppa's hand in hers.

"Navarrah, I'll not be ending up bone-naked on no country doctor's porch."

Oftentimes fear can give people a backbone. And for Poppa, the fear of losing the love of his life was more than enough. He'd never stood up to Momma before, but he sure as hell was standing up to her now.

"I mean no disrespect, Mullie Moon, but I'm sticking to my guns here. I say you need a doctor. And if that has to be Doc Hickory, then so be it. No offense to your considerable talents, but I think what you got is beyond even your medicines."

I could tell Momma was impressed. But she had a stubborn streak. More so than Poppa, anyway.

"And just who, pray tell," says Momma, "cured you when you came down with the grip last month?"

"You did," said Poppa.

"And what about last March, when you got the night sweats?"

"You cured me then too, Mullie Moon."

Momma snorted a laugh. "Darn tootin' I did! My medicines were good enough for you then, and they'll be good enough for me now."

"Here you go, Momma," I said, the asked-for jar in my hand. I didn't know what was in it and didn't want to know. Whatever it was, it was on the wrong side of appetizing. Downright disgusting, even.

"Thank you kindly," says she. She twisted off the lid.

It smelled so bad my eyes watered. She dished out a healthy portion, but before she could get the spoon to her mouth, she shot the cat. Made a real mess down her front. With that, Poppa snatched the jar from her hand. Dabbed a towel on her throw-up.

"That does it! I'm sending for Doc Hickory. And that's my final say-so on the matter."

FORTY-SIX

Too sick to muster up much of a tangle, Momma tried anyway.
"I told you I don't want Doc Hickory in—"

Poppa stomped his foot. "Not another word!"

Except for Grandfather ticking up a storm in the corner, you could have heard a pin drop. Momma blinked twice. So did I. Poppa never shouted. Hardly ever raised his voice.

"Hattie," says he, real forceful-like. "You take the mule and bring back the doc. Pronto! Tell him we got ourselves an emergency here. If he balks on you, prod him with your cane."

"Yes, sir," said I.

Out the door, down the porch steps, I hit the ground as fast as two legs and one cane could carry me.

"Move your boney ass!" I shouted at Mr. Jack as I tugged him from the barn. Good thing that ol' mule didn't give me his usual guff, or I'd have flailed his butt. I may be small, but I know how to wield a cane. Applied properly to one's backside, it stings like the dickens. Mr. Jack must have sensed something was up, because he came peaceably. Animals are like that, you know. Even the hardheaded ones.

Off at a trot, about as fast as Mr. Jack could muster, I headed down the mountain. A mile or so ahead, I'd have to cut through Devil's Ravine. One misstep, and my body would never be found. After that lay Hangman's Hollow. I hated that place. That's where all the snakes went after dark. And other than Doc Holliday, I sometimes have trouble communicating with snakes.

To top my fears off, ten years prior, Old Man Fipple hung himself on the dead oak tree at the Hollow's entrance. Got himself real depressed after his wife died and didn't want to live no more. They didn't come across his body until a year later. They say his ghost still haunts the Hollow. Maybe that's why nobody lived out that way no more. Except, of course, for Doc Hickory, who liked to keep the strange goings-on at his place private.

The ghosts and snakes didn't scare me as much as those goings-on did. Doc Hickory was something else you didn't want to meet after sundown. Thank goodness the moon was out full and bright that night.

Some thought the doc was already a ghost, what with his pale skin. Albinoism, you flatlanders call it. His skin wasn't so bothersome to me; it was those beady, close-set pink eyes of his. Always darting about, like a weasel tracking a mouse. I agreed with Momma. Hickory definitely had mean eyes. It may be un-Christian of me, but I did not like him. Not one bit. And there I was, on my way to ask him a favor.

As soon as Mr. Jack got an eyeful of Doc's house, he plopped down on his backside and refused to take another step. So, I had to tie him up at the tree line. If I'd been a mule, I'd have done the same thing myself. But Momma was depending on me. Standing in front of Doc's front porch steps, I took a deep breath. Then another for good measure. Seems my feet had turned into a pair of mules.

"Lord, give me strength," I half said, half prayed.

I climbed those steps as if they were eggshells. My heart turned a tumble when one let out a creak loud enough to wake the dead. Froze me in my tracks it did. With my cane hovered in midair, if you'd powdered me with flour, I could have been a statue.

Before I gulped down my second breath, a high-pitched "Who's there?" came from inside. Like fingernails on a chalkboard. Made me cringe up tight.

Get yourself out of there, Hattie! screamed a voice in my head. And my heart stopped altogether. I would have run like the wind had my feet not turned back into mules. I was about to whack them with my cane when the door flew open.

"Hattie? Hattie Sexton?" said Doc Hickory, grinning like a Cheshire on the quarter moon. Almost as short as me, he'd always taken an interest in my crooked spine. Probably wanted it for his collection. "What are you doing out this time of night?"

When he smiled at me, his gold front teeth, all four of them, glistened in the dim yellow light. Big and shiny they was, and so close I could see my reflection. It's downright scary, looking in someone's mouth and seeing yourself staring back.

I swallowed hard and closed my eyes. Thought real hard on Momma lying sick in her bed. She needed me, and I couldn't let her down. My knees were shaking so bad I had to take another breath. Then I narrowed my good eye at him. When push comes to shove, I can be pretty scary too.

"Come with me, Doc," said I, thumping my cane down for effect. "We need you."

The doc must not have liked my tone, 'cause he stopped smiling.

"See here, young lady," says he. "I'll not be talked to like that."

I leveled my cane at his throat.

"I've got no time for hurt feelings," I said. "Come NOW! I'll not be asking again."

And smart man that he was, he came.

FORTY-SEVEN

"**W**hat's taking him so long, Hattie?" asked Poppa. "The doc should know what's wrong with my Mullie Moon by now."

The minute Abel Hickory arrived, he pulled the curtain around Momma and went to work. I'm guessing he knew right off the bat she didn't have no stomachache.

The way Poppa was pacing, I was sure he was going to break something. And in Momma's sorry condition, the last thing she needed was hearing something shatter.

"Give the doc a chance," I says. "You don't want him to come up with the wrong . . . di-ag-no-sis, do you?"

I always had trouble pronouncing that word. Probably because I never used it much.

"But he's been with her for almost an hour," said Poppa, almost wailing.

I nodded toward Grandfather in the corner, whose tick-tocking seemed louder now.

"More like ten minutes," I says.

Leaned up against that clock was Doc's fancy cane. Carved out of mahogany in the shape of a snake, it was topped off with an ivory skull. A scary piece of nasty, he used that hunk of wood more as a weapon than a walking stick. And he was damn good with it, too. Doc could crack the shinbone of a man twice his size with a single tap. Just ask Haffney Coates. Hickory broke Haff's right leg in two places when Haff got liquored up one night and accidentally bumped into the doctor. Poor guy didn't apologize fast enough, and in the blink of an eye, Haff was saddled with a limp for the rest of his life.

The cane's skull was mean enough, but it was the eyes that crawled my skin. Two diamonds they was. Bigger'n a man's knuckle each, they must have cost a pretty penny. As rich as the doc was, though, he could afford them ten times over.

"Seems more like ten hours than ten minutes," says Poppa. "What's keeping him, anyway? I know it's bad, real bad. I can feel it in my bones. If anything happens to your Momma, I don't know what I'll do."

Poppa turned to his right. Bumped into Momma's favorite vase. Thank goodness I was quick enough to catch it before it hit the floor.

"Now, Poppa! You set yourself down!" I demanded. "Pacing about like a chicken with its head cut off ain't going to do Momma a lick of good. And to tell the truth, it's getting on my nerves."

"But—"

"Sit!"

Just then, Hickory yanked the curtain aside. He was covered with sweat and had a dazed look in his eyes. Poppa almost had a conniption fit.

"Well, Doc? How is she?" he asks. "She's going to be alright, isn't she?"

Hickory pursed his mouth into a tiny O. Sucked in a breath over his teeth. Rubbed a hand across his bald pate and leaned against the wall. Dabbed his forehead.

"Strangest damn thing I ever saw," he almost whispered. More to the floor than the two of us. "If I live to be a hundred I'll never . . ."

Doc wiped his mouth with a towel and cleared his throat. By now, Poppa was about to deposit a sizeable load in his britches.

"You better sit down for this, Navarrah," says the doc. "I've got some startling news."

Startling news? Those aren't two words you want to hear when you're worried sick about a loved one. Then again, Hickory wasn't known for his bedside manner. Poppa turned white as a sheet, and for a second or two I thought he was going to faint dead away. His legs went all wobbly, but somehow he managed himself into a chair. Then buried his face in his hands.

"It's not the . . . cancer, is it, Doc?" he asked.

To my mind, Hickory's answer was a mite long in coming. I saw the gleam in those beady little eyes of his. Doctors are supposed to cure pain, not enjoy it. So I stomped my cane to hurry him up.

"No, no, nothing like that," he says, waving the thought away with his hand. "You're wife's with child, Navarrah. She's going to have a baby."

FORTY-EIGHT

"**A** baby!" blurted Poppa.

He looked as if he'd been whacked upside the head with a fence post. In all my twenty-six years, I'd never seen such a discombobulated human being.

With child! Those two little words turned Poppa deaf, dumb, and blind. His eye began to twitch. His mouth drooped, and he started to drool. He tried to speak but only stuttered.

"A b-b-b . . . ?"

"A baby, Poppa," says I. "The doc says you're going to be a father." I had trouble with the concept myself. "Again, that is."

Then Poppa jumped up, real excited-like. He rolled the word around his mouth a few times, as if it were a hot pepper. "A baby. A . . . baby. A *baby*! A baby?"

He twisted his head to the right. Then back to the left. I don't know persactly why, but he began to count his fingers. When he got to four, it finally dawned on him.

"Hot damn! A baby!" Clear eyed now, he turned to me. "A father, Hattie! I'm going to be a father!"

"That's what I said, Poppa."

He looked over at Hickory.

"How can this be, Doc? I didn't even know she was p-pregnant." It wasn't a word he used often.

"Neither did she," says the doc, a bit on the smug side. "But it's not unusual for a woman her size to get into the advanced stages of pregnancy without knowing. No offense, but who's to notice a few extra pounds here and there?"

"Advanced stages?" says Poppa, scratching his head. "Just how advanced is she, Doc?"

"I'd say a day or two shy of nine months."

Another fence post to the head. Poppa crow-hopped back two steps. "Nine months! You mean she's due?"

"The way she's contracting, I'd say she's about to deliver any minute now. I can see the head already."

That was too much for Poppa. He collapsed back into the chair. Began to stutter again. He was cut short by a scream from behind the curtain. Momma was giving birth!

Hickory tossed his towel to me.

"Here," he says. "I'll need more of these. Lots more. Things are going to get messy in there, so I'll also need a pot of hot water. And bring me the sharpest kitchen knife you can find. Along with a slab of pig fat."

He darted back behind the curtain, and Poppa and me were left to stare at each other. I took a couple of seconds to snap out of it.

"I'll get the towels!" I said. "Poppa, you get the fire going! On second thought, I'd better handle boiling the water. I can't have you setting this place on fire."

Poppa just stood there, stupefied in spades.

"Kitchen knife? Pig fat?" he says. "What's he want them things for?"

"He's going to rub the blade with the fat, then put it under Momma's bed. Probably like she told him to. Maybe to help with the pain. Then maybe he'll use it to cut the birthing cord when the baby comes out. Just like what happened when I was born."

Poppa was still rooted to his spot.

"Towels, Poppa?" says I. "Momma's going to need them right quickly." To get him moving, I pointed to the pantry. "They're on the second shelf to the left."

By the time I got the water to boiling, Poppa had returned with two towels in one hand, a sorrowful look on his face.

"This is all I could find," he said.

"She's going to need a lot more than that, probably a dozen or so."

"I don't think we got that many."

"Yes, we do. Momma always keeps that shelf full. There was fifteen there by my last count."

Tears ran down Poppa's cheeks. Desperation filled his eyes.

"But I'm telling you they ain't there, Hattie. I searched that shelf three times."

"Second shelf on the left?"

"Left? I thought you said right."

"That's the to-do laundry side. The doc can't use no dirty towels. They'll infect the baby."

Poppa dropped his head. Began to moan. "Sweet Jesus, I can't do anything right."

"My fault," I said. "I probably told you wrong." Even though I knew I hadn't. "Go check again, Poppa."

In a flash, he returned with the towels. Together we approached the curtain. I cleared my throat.

"Uh, Doc? Where do you want these?"

Hickory yanked the curtain aside. Blood was on his hands, and he was covered with sweat, a stunned expression on his face. His shirt was all wrinkled. Over his shoulder, I saw Momma. She looked even worse.

"It's gotta be the biggest baby ever," says he. "Maybe the biggest baby in the whole damn world."

Poppa and I were dumbstruck. Him holding his towels, me holding that pot of hot water, with a kitchen knife and slab of pig fat tucked into my pockets.

"Um, Doc?" I managed. "Where do you want all this?"

Hickory pointed at the nightstand. "Put the water over there. I'll take those towels, Navarrah. Hattie can stay with me, but you'll have to wait outside."

When Poppa tried to move closer to Momma, Doc planted a firm hand in his chest.

"Outside," he said.

"But I'm the father," says Poppa, crestfallen. "Can't I at least—"

"We can't be having no accidents in here, Navarrah. Especially not at a critical time like this."

They were cruel words. Cruel, but true. Had I been in the doc's shoes, I'd have probably said the exact same thing. Maybe a little softer, though. Poppa took a step back. Then another. He put a slow hand to his missing eye. Then rubbed one of his finger stumps.

"Uh, I understand, Doc," he says. "If you need me, I'll be right outside the curtain."

FORTY-NINE

For the next five hours, Doc Hickory and I tended to Momma and her birthing. The size of the baby was causing her a great deal of pain. A considerable complication, the doc called it. Several times, he called out the Lord's name in vain. Along with a string of cuss words too nasty to mention—a few of which I'd never heard before.

Three times I thought the baby was about to come out, and three times it popped back in. Each time, Momma would cry out in frustration, causing Poppa to rush to the curtain, wringing his hands and mewing like a lost kitten. Maybe moaning out a prayer or two. After we calmed him down, he'd return to his pacing. Poor man, that night he must have prayed more than he had in ten years. Me too, I have to admit.

After the third hour, Poppa took to his moonshine heavy. Probably the smartest thing he'd done all day. By hour number four he'd fallen into a fitful sleep on the floor. At least it kept him out of our hair.

A few minutes before sunrise, my baby brother decided he'd had enough of all the folderol and fiddledeedee. Wriggling free of Momma, he let loose with an ear-splitting screech they must have heard all the way down in Sneedville. Woke Poppa right up it did.

And I couldn't believe my eyes. Doc Hickory had been right in his figuring. My baby brother was so big that I strained to lift him. Splotched all over and covered with afterbirth, he was still the most beautiful young'un I'd ever seen. And bless his not-so-little heart, the moment I picked him up, he stopped crying. Never saw that in no baby before. Human or critter.

Poppa knocked over the vase again trying to get to Momma. And with my hands full with a just-born babe, I wasn't able to save it this time. His eyes swimming with dread, Poppa gently pulled the curtain aside.

"Lord Almighty, Doc! Mullie Moon's not dying on us, is she?"

Hickory leaned against the bedpost to catch his breath. Wiped sweat from his brow. The man was exhausted.

"Your wife is just fine, Navarrah," he says. "Considering what she's just been through, she's in better shape than me."

Poppa looked down at the bundle in my arms. Then over at Momma.

"And the baby?" he asks.

"Hale and hearty," said the doc. "You've got yourself a brand-new, bouncing baby boy-child."

That brought another crowhop from Poppa. Stock still again, his head snapped back. Eyes wide as a Christmas dinner platter.

"Praise be!" he shouted. "I got meself a son! A *son*!"

The doc sagged against the far wall, queasy around the gills and looking even paler than he usually was. I have to give the man credit. He'd been through a lot in those five hours. I still didn't care much for him as a doctor, or as a human being, for that matter, but I don't know what we would have done without his help that night.

"Better set yourself down in that chair, Doc," says I. "You don't look so good."

When I shifted the bundle over to my right side, I felt just how heavy my newborn baby brother really was. I almost lost my balance.

"This young'un's a load and then some," I said.

To counter my stagger, I hoisted him to my crooked side, where he fit just fine. Seems the Lord in His infinite wisdom had provided me with a built-in shelf, perfect for handling a baby. Since I could never have one of my own, I figured this might have been what God had in mind when He made me all crookified. When I pushed the blanket to one side, two green eyes as bright as spring meadow grass stared up at me. Beneath them spread the most bodacious smile I'd ever seen. Needless to say, my tilted heart melted that very instant.

"Come, Poppa," I said. "Have a look for yourself. He's amazing."

Hands behind his back, a worried look on his face, Poppa took a slow step forward. Then stopped.

"Doc?" he says. "Is it alright if I touch him?"

Hickory nodded his okay.

"Don't worry, Poppa," says I. "He won't break. He's way too big for that."

Extending a cautious finger, Poppa inched closer again.

"I-I don't want to hurt him, Hattie," he said in a low voice. "You know how clumsy I am."

I pulled the blanket back, and my not-so-little baby brother reached up and grabbed Poppa's thumb. With that, Poppa's face lit up the room.

"Lord Almighty," he says. "He's got a right powerful grip on him."

I pushed the bundle toward him, but he shied away. I had to coax him.

"You're his father," I said. "You're going to have to handle him eventually. No getting around it."

"But what if I—"

"Don't fret none. You ain't going to drop him."

"But—"

"Babies' bones are soft as butter. Drop them and they only bounce."

And I forced him to take his son.

The moment Poppa cradled that newborn bundle of joy to his chest, his fearful look faded plumb away. So did his clumsiness. In their stead was the warm glow of love. Mixed in with a healthy dose of wonder. Wearing that goofy smile of his, Poppa looked for all the world like an addle-pated idiot. A look, I'm told, that's common to all new daddies. Bursting with pride, he turned to Hickory.

"Look at the size of him, Doc."

"Biggest baby I ever brought into the world," says Hickory.

"I ain't persactly sure," says Poppa, "but I think he has to weigh at least fifteen pounds."

"More like twenty," says Hickory. "Baby that big would have killed a lesser woman. No doubt about it, Navarrah. You've got a future giant on your hands. Got any idea what you'll call him? At first blush, the name Goliath comes to mind."

"Haven't had time to give it much thought," said Poppa. "Hell, until a few hours ago, the furthest thing on my mind was naming a son. You can bet your bottom dollar, though, his name won't be Goliath. No son of mine is gonna have a handle like that hung around his neck. Me and Mullie Moon will have to put some think time on the matter."

Poppa shifted the bundle. Almost dropped it.

"Here, Poppa," I says, taking him back. "In time you'll get the hang of it."

FIFTY

"I meant what I'd said to Poppa about babies bouncing," said Hattie. "But I wasn't about to put my new brother to the test. When I put him back on my sideways shelf, he looked up with relief in those big green eyes of his. I touched his little pink button nose, and what was left of my heart turned to cake batter."

"Imagine that," I said, mostly to myself. "I got me my own angel baby brother."

And that's when it hit me.

"How about we call him Micah, Poppa?" I asked.

"Micah?" says he.

"The name comes from the Bible. It means 'angel.'"

"Micah . . . Micah?" says Poppa, rolling the name over his tongue, testing it for grit. "Micah! I like it!"

Hickory came closer for a better look. With a clawlike finger, he pulled the blanket to one side.

"Yessiree," he said, "this one's going to grow up to be one *big* human being. Play your cards right, Navarrah, and he'll be a real moneymaker for you. Big-time, I'm telling you. You've got a gold mine under that blanket, and that's a bankable fact."

Micah scrunched up his nose, began to squirm. With a whimper, he turned away from Hickory. Covering him up again, I headed for the kitchen.

"You're scaring him, Doc," I said. "I better clean him up a bit before handing him back to his momma."

I heard Momma shift in her bed. After a soft groan, her voice came out from behind the curtain. Soft, but backbone firm.

"Thank you for all your help, Doctor Hickory," she said. When she coughed, I could tell it hurt her real bad. So bad she had to swallow twice before continuing. "But it's time for you to go now. Me and my family can take it from here. We'll settle up our account within the week."

She coughed again. Took a deep breath. Let it out slowly, then took another.

"Navarrah?" she says. "Please show the good doctor to the door."

Hickory turned to Poppa. Glanced over at the curtain.

"I meant no offense with my comment about the baby's size, Navarrah," he said. "I was only looking out for your family's best interests. Especially yours, considering how many, let's just say, physical mishaps you've had in the past. If young Micah there grows up to be as big as I think he will, people will pay money to see him. I sure as hell would."

Poppa may have been a bit dusty across the beam, but both he and I knew what Hickory was getting at.

"You probably would," said Poppa. Then he picked up Hickory's doctoring bag. "But no son of mine is going to end up in no damn freak show. Not yours, not anyone's."

Hickory's face turned a bright shade of red. His eyes darted about, agitated. He knew he'd played his hand wrong.

"I d-didn't mean it that way," he said.

"Oh, I know real well what you meant, Doc," said Poppa. "I may be slower than most, but I ain't completely dumb."

With a firm hand on his shoulder, Poppa angled Doc to the door. So quickly Hickory almost tripped.

"Just hear me out, Navarrah," says Hickory, struggling to keep up, hopping like a cricket. "Maybe I shouldn't bring it up just yet, but I'm willing to pay good money for, let's say, future considerations. You don't have to make up your mind this very minute. We can work out the details later."

"Thank you kindly for your service, Doctor Hickory," says Poppa. "Me and my family are much obliged, but the answer is no. And always will be no. As my missus said, we'll settle up with you by week's end. I don't know persactly how we'll find the money, but we will."

Hickory's eyes turned desperate. The man definitely did not want to leave.

"Forget what I said about considerations, Nav. What's important now is the health of your baby boy. And that of your wife. She's been through a hell of an ordeal, and it would be wise if I stayed on a bit longer. To make sure things are mending properly with her."

Poppa handed him his bag. Opened the door.

"That won't be necessary, Doc. Mullie Moon will be fine. She's strong as an ox. And as for the baby, Hattie and I will see to all his needs. Whatever they might be."

Hickory shot a pleading eye in my direction. But he got no help from me. The sooner he was out the door, the better.

"But can't I at least stop by tomorrow to check on—"

"Thanks again, Doc," said Poppa. "You've been most kind." Then he shoved Hickory through the door. Slammed it behind him.

Not trusting the man to leave peaceably, I pushed the window curtain aside. For a few seconds, Hickory just stood on the porch, his jaw to twitchin'. His pink eyes boring a hole through our front door. If looks could kill, the entire Sexton clan would have been sent to their graves that very moment.

Mumbling something into his chest, he finally picked up his bag and stormed off toward his buggy. After kicking at his horse, he grabbed the reins, then looked back at our cabin. For a heartbeat or two, I thought he saw me in the window. But with the moonlight staring him in the face, I realized it wasn't likely. *Thank God.*

Even from a distance, I could read his lips.

"So, Micah, is it?" he says. "Ha! An angel indeed!"

What shivered my spine was the laugh that followed. High pitched and wheezy, as if he were making a pact with the devil. I could still hear Hickory laughing as that black buggy of his dropped out of sight. I knew right then and there we hadn't seen the last of Doc Hickory. Not by a long shot.

FIFTY-ONE

After Poppa slammed that door in Hickory's face, Momma's voice sounded stronger.

"Has the doc left yet, Hattie?" Not a question. She meant he'd better be gone.

"Yes, ma'am," said I. "He's sure enough gone."

"Not to sound ungrateful," adds Momma, "but come hell or high water, that's the last time that man sets foot in this house."

She propped herself up against the headboard. Her jaw set tight, she inhaled once through her nose. Let it out slowly as she stuck out her arms wide.

"I'm ready for my little man now," says she.

Poppa handed the baby over. And like a duck to water, Micah settled into the soft round bosom of his mother. It was a toss-up who was wearing the bigger smile, him or Momma. If ever there was a match made in heaven, it was those two. Her eyes welled up with joy, and a small tear made its way down her cheek. A strong woman who cried once in a blue moon, she'd never looked happier. With one hand, she cupped Micah's head. She looked skyward, then with her other hand made the sign of the cross.

"Thank you, Lord," she says, "for this treasure You have bestowed on me and my family."

A hitch in both our hearts, Poppa and me nodded our amens.

"Isn't he something, Nav?" said Momma.

Poppa's smile turned sunbeam bright.

"An honest-to-God miracle, if you ask me," he says. "This young feller's going to be a strong one when he grows up. And that's a fact. He's already got a right powerful grip on him."

"He truly is a gift from heaven," I added.

With all that gushing going on, Micah looked up at Momma. Then over at Poppa. And finally at me. One by one, he reached out and touched our noses. I never saw a just-borned baby do that. Then he giggled the sweetest, purest, happiest little giggle you'd ever want to hear. As if a host of angels had been told a funny-up story. And bless his brand-spanking-new heart, he saved his broadest smile for me. I felt warm all over, like I been bathed in sunlight from the tip-top of my head down to my littlest toe.

"Poppa?" says I. "Do you think Micah's going to be a giant, like the doc said?"

Poppa scratched his head. Thought on it a bit.

"I don't rightly know. But coming into this world as big as he is, he probably ain't gonna grow up puny."

"Micah?" said Momma. "His name is Micah? So, while I was flat on my back, doing all the hard work, you two done gone and named my little boy? Don't I get any say-so in the matter?"

Momma forced a frown, but the twinkle in her eyes gave her away. At least to me. Poppa looked like he'd been whopped over the head with a skillet. Shuffling his feet, he stammered, "N-No, no, Mullie Moon," he said. "We were only trying on the name for size. You can name him anything you like."

"Micah was my idea, Momma," I said. "It comes from the Bible. Means angel."

Momma reached out to caress the good side of my face. Shot me a private wink.

"Micah's a great name, child," she says. Then turned to her newly born. "Angel it shall be."

Twenty-six years old, and I was still her child. I never felt so loved.

"Well, Micah," she says to her son, "as for being on the large side, there's nothing wrong with that. Lord knows I ain't what you might call dainty. They say good things come in little packages, but I'm here to tell you even better things come in big packages."

A joyful smile on his face, Micah reached out his hand for me again. Of course I took it. Bending down, I kissed his fingertips.

"Your big sister is here for you, baby brother," says I. "And I always will be."

Momma coughed again. Grimaced.

"Hattie, I seem to have worked up a powerful thirst. Would you kindly fetch me a glass of water? I'm parched."

"Coming right up," says I. I dashed off to the sink. While I was priming the pump, Momma motioned Poppa close.

"I hate to admit it, Nav, but birthing Micah wasn't as easy as it was with Hattie. Guess I ain't as young as I used to be."

"That was over twenty-five years ago," says Poppa. "And Hattie was only a smidgeon of Micah's size. Bringing a baby that big into the world? You could have busted your gut. It's a wonder you're still alive. Maybe the doc was right about staying a bit longer. Just to make sure you're on the proper mend."

Momma shot him a look that would have stopped a charging buffalo dead in its tracks.

"Not on your tintype! I'm much obliged for his help, but I don't want the doc on our property ever again. I've always had a bad feeling about him, and today only proved it. I heard what he said about Micah. That weren't no proper talk about a baby. No matter how big he is."

"I hear you," says Poppa. "Doc gives me the creeping jeebies too. Always has."

"Promise me," says Momma, "as God is your witness, you'll keep him away from our boy."

Poppa raised his right hand. Crossed his heart. "I swear it on a stack of Bibles."

"Me too, Momma," said I.

FIFTY-TWO

While the three of us were cooing about Micah, Doc Hickory headed back to his place, cursing to himself all the way. And getting madder by the minute. My animal friends always let me know about such things.

You'd be surprised how much a critter can convey with a simple chitter, a cock of the head, a twist of the body. And they always got more important things to talk about than most humans. Helpful things and not just a bunch of hot air.

The sun was still early in its rise, and mist hung heavy over the hills, draping our mountaintop in a cottony haze. Still in a foul mood, the doc was met by his two fumble-fingered hired hands when he got home.

The Butt brothers, Nosmo and Dewey, were a curious lot. Scarcely half a brain between the two, they were just as clumsy as Poppa but without a lick of common sense. Hickory was the only one in these parts who'd hire them.

A hook-nosed, stick-thin six-footer with no chin and a gaggle of cattywampus teeth, Nosmo was the talker, and the smarter of the two. If that meant anything. He moved like a splintered stepladder with a few bolts missing and spoke with a high-pitched whine that whistled through the spoon-sized gap in his front teeth.

Dewey, the quiet one, was a foot shorter than his brother and as wide as he was tall. A booger-eating mouth breather, he had a perfectly round head, three chins, and a pushed-in face too small for his body. He waddled more than walked and was always struggling to catch up. So, as usual, Nosmo got there first to take the reins from Hickory.

"It must have been a long night for you, Doc," says Nosmo. "How'd it go with the Sextons?"

"Mullie Moon gave birth to a boy," growls Hickory, still in a dither about being put off our property. "Fool woman didn't even know she was with child."

Coming around the corner, Dewey took a tumble in the dirt. He dusted off the pork chop he'd been carrying, an apologetic smile on his face. Dewey always had food in one hand or the other.

Nosmo tied the reins to a hitching rail. They promptly slipped off, so he had to tie them again.

"She didn't know she was pregnant?" he asks. "How could that be?"

"Have you ever seen her? The woman's big as a barn."

Nosmo wheezed in a lungful of air. Pulled on his chin.

"I never actually laid eyes on her. But I hear tell she can't leave the house no more."

Hickory shuddered, his face pinched as if he'd bitten into a rancid lemon.

"Disgusting cow can't even fit through her own front door. Touching all that blubber was disgusting."

Nosmo looked puzzled. "She gave birth to a baby boy, you say?"

"Biggest damn rug rat you ever did see. Twenty pounds' worth. Maybe more."

"Twenty pounds! That had to be one hell of a coming-out party. Surprised it didn't tear Missus Sexton apart."

"Damn near did. Hadn't been for me, she and her precious boy-child would have died on the spot. Saved both of their lives I did. And what thanks did I get? A goddamn door slammed in my face!"

Dewey dropped his pork chop again. Picked it up. Blew on it before he stuck it behind his back.

"Hear that, Dewey?" says Nosmo. "The Sextons had themselves a baby boy. Right big one, too."

Dewey cocked his head to one side, like a hound dog listening to his master.

"But don't worry," said Nosmo, "he may be the size of a bear cub, but the doc says he's healthy. Thank the Lord."

A slow smile spreading across his face, Dewey wiped pork grease from his lips.

"Thasss good," says he. His first words of the day. The shorter Butt brother had trouble with his *S*s.

Nosmo scratched his head. Scrunched up one eye.

"You know, maybe we should pay our respects to the happy couple. It's the neighborly thing to do. Besides, I'd like to catch a gander at that giant baby myself."

Hickory slapped the railing with his cane.

"You'll do no such thing! You two slackers are the last people they'd want to see. And they wouldn't let you within a mile of that baby anyway. I sure as hell wouldn't. Now, I don't pay you dimwits good money to stand around chewing the fat. Hustle your sorry asses into the kitchen and rustle me up some breakfast. After last night's ordeal I'm so hungry I could eat a horse. Maybe two."

Nosmo tripped as he backed away.

"Coming right up, Doc," he said.

Both brothers made a beeline for the kitchen.

"And don't you two get yourselves lost!" hollered Hickory. "I'll be sending you on another errand tonight."

Shaking his head, Nosmo bent down to whisper in his brother's ear.

"Not the graveyard again. I was hoping we were done with the digging this month. That place makes my skin creep."

"M-me too," said Dewey. Sunrise was still a couple of hours away, and he'd already used up his conversation quota for the day.

Beep . . .
Beep . . .
Beep . . .

For Hickory, the day would dawn on a new quest. A valuable prize had come into his world. One he vowed would not get away from him.

Beep . . .
Beep . . .
Beep . . .

He leaned on his cane. Turned back toward the mountain, a confident grin slithering onto his face. My bird friends heard what he said next. Every word, loud and clear.

"Giants never live that long. And I have all the patience in the world. Sooner or later, that boy will be mine."

Beep . . .
Beep . . .
Beep . . .

FIFTY-THREE

Beep, beep, beep.

Her tale-telling interrupted, Hattie turned toward the source of the faint beeping. My Sony. She raised an eyebrow. Leveled her good eye at me.

"I ain't rightly sure, Mr. John March, but I think that there fancy recorder of yours might be on the fritz."

I'd been so captivated by her words that I'd failed to notice my thumb drive had reached full capacity. Blushing furiously, I popped the sucker out. Fumbled through my pockets to find a new one. Quickly snapped it into place.

"Sorry about the interruption, Hattie. Please, continue with your story. Me and my machine are once again all ears."

Hattie leaned back to stretch out her arms. Inhaled slowly through one nostril. Squinted, then looked out the window. Mindless of what was transpiring in the cabin, the sun had continued on its daily trek across the heavens and was now full up in the sky. A quick glance at my watch told me two hours had already passed. It seemed more like ten minutes. And according to Hattie, she hadn't even gotten to the good part yet.

"Yessiree," she said with a sigh. "Micah was one big baby. Biggest ever seen in these parts. Ten days after he was born, we had him drink the blood milk, to protect him from the boll hives."

"Blood milk?" I asked. "Boll hives?"

"Boll hives is a kind of fever common to newborns in the mountains. Young'uns tend to come down with it during their first few weeks."

"What do you mean by blood milk?"

"It's a mixture of the baby's blood and the mother's milk. Helps ward off all kinds of things."

I donned my third stupid look of the day. It could have been my fourth.

"When a baby is ten days old," continued Hattie, "we nick a shallow cross in his back with a sharp razor, just below the neck. Micah never even felt it. Didn't let out a peep."

My expression turned to one of horror. Which Hattie ignored. As a flatlander, I couldn't be expected to understand their mountain ways.

"A sulfur match is struck, then placed in an empty blue quinine bottle," resumed Hattie. "When you place the mouth of that bottle over the nick, the burning match will draw out a few drops of the child's blood. You mix those with several drops of mother's milk in a silver spoon and feed it to the baby."

Hattie sat back. Rocked a twice.

"Works every time," she said. "Seven times a week, and twice on Sundays."

I was shocked. Appalled.

"You . . . *cut* a ten-day-old baby?!"

"What?" said Hattie, crinkling up her eyebrows. "You got a weak stomach or something? Your modern-day circumcision is much worse. Kinda barbaric, to my way of thinking. Some babies do raise a fuss when we nick them, but not our Micah. He just smiled up at me and grinned. As if he knew what we was doing."

Having been circumcised myself, who was I to pass judgment? I swallowed hard and pushed the Sony closer.

"And did Micah grow up to be a giant?" Changing the subject. "Like Hickory said he would?"

"Sprouted up to nearly eight feet tall. At ten, he had to duck going out our front door. At fifteen he could pull a branch off the roof flat-footed."

Hattie pulled out her pocket watch and clicked it open. Ran a loving finger over it. Handed it to me.

"That there is the only picture of me and my brother together."

A streaked photo, yellow and cracked with age, was nestled into the watch's cover.

"He looks to be three times your size," I said, carefully handing the watch back.

Hattie kissed the photo before snapping the timepiece closed. Rocked a few more times.

"Micah was strong as an ox. But gentle as a field mouse. Wouldn't harm hide nor hair of any living thing. Quiet as a field mouse, too. He never spoke much. Because of his size, people tended to shy away from him. A few would nod a howdy now and then, but most kept their distance. So, like me, Micah came to prefer the company of animals. By the time he was five, he knew his way around the forest as good as any critter. He had soft feet, like a cat. If he had a mind to, Micah could sneak up on anything or anybody."

FIFTY-FOUR

My mind swirled around Hattie's description of her brother, quickly conjuring up a cross between Steinbeck's Lenny and Shaquille O'Neal.

"Did Micah also have your gift with animals?" I asked.

"He was better with them than I ever was. Had a special link with bunny and bear alike. Critters of all kinds would tell him things, telepathically-like. No matter how far away they were. Things that had happened, and things that were going to happen. Like the weather, for instance. They would let him know when a storm was coming, when frost was headed for the pumpkin patch, or if we were in for a dry spell. Animals have a sixth sense about such things, you know.

"Many's the time Micah would wake up in the middle of the night and bolt off into the forest. I know because I followed him once to a clearing just this side of Newman's Ridge. Hiding behind a bush, I watched him pry loose this full-grown bobcat from a trap. Poor critter was half-dead, all covered with blood. But the minute that big cat saw my brother, he perked right up.

"My brother puts one hand under the bobcat's mangled foot and snapped that steel trap in two with the other. Easy as if it were a twig."

A trace of doubt slid across my face, and Hattie stopped rocking.

"And the bobcat didn't snap at him?" I asked. "Don't animals strike out at anything when they're injured?"

She looked me hard in the eye.

"What sense would that have made? The cat was the one who sent for Micah in the first place. When my brother cradled him in his arms, Mr. Bobcat purred like kitten. But that's not the amazing part of the story. Micah covered the wound with his right hand. Counted to ten, and just like that, it healed right over. Lickety-split, Bob's your uncle, cross my heart and hope to die. The bobcat licked my brother on the hand a few times, as if to say his thank-yous, then bounded off into the underbrush. Good as new he was."

That faraway look on her face again, Hattie glanced out the window. Except for Grandfather's ticking in the corner, the cabin had gone silent. A slow, pride-filled smile came to her face as she rocked back and forth.

"Damnedest bit of doctorin' I ever did see," she said. "Then again, my brother was always doing things like that. I once saw him sitting fifty feet up in a tree, on a branch thinner than my little finger, chatting with a golden eagle. At well over two hundred pounds, there's no way that branch should have supported Micah. But it sure enough did."

My mouth dropped.

"But how did he—"

"He must have flown up there somehow. Then hovered like a hummingbird. No doubt about it, Micah was blessed with special talents."

"You make him sound like some sort of mystic."

"Mystic, magician, forest wizard—call it what you will. I prefer the word gifted. He seemed to think things, and they just . . . happened. He never showed off or nothing. Only used his powers for good. Quiet-like, and not in the open. So's not to bring attention to himself."

"That's amazing! What about Doc Hickory? Did he ever bother your parents again? And could Micah—"

Hattie raised a finger to cut me off. Waved it a few times.

"So many questions, Mr. March. And I'll answer them all in due time. But first things first. It's time to pay the piper. I'll be needing that first favor from you now. That is, if you want to hear the rest of my brother's story."

Hattie knew I was hooked. There was no way I could back out of our deal now.

"You weave a mean tale, Hattie Sexton."

She laughed. Slapped her thighs. Grabbed her cane to stand up.

"I thought you might say that. Since you're a city feller, you probably have no idea what honey dipping is."

I scratched my head. "Never heard of it."

Hattie headed for the back door.

"Then you're in for a real treat, Mr. March. Let's get ourselves a breath of fresh air. Follow me. Micah's story will keep for a bit. It's time to educate you about another of our mountain ways."

FIFTY-FIVE

Sitting next to a mound of dirt thirty yards from Hattie's back porch was a small, weather-ravaged shed. The crescent moon on its door—combined with the eye-watering aroma wafting from inside—left no doubt about the structure's purpose. I may be a citified greenhorn who, spoiled by indoor plumbing, had never used an outhouse in his life. But I knew what one looked and smelled like.

My imagination quickly filled in the dots concerning what Hattie meant by honey dipping. In the midday sun, the stench was overwhelming. Sweating profusely, I held my nose. Tried to smile.

"Ho-boy," I groaned. "I'm not liking the looks of this."

"You ever done any, let's just say, manual plumbing, Mr. March?" she asked.

"Other than opening a bottle of Drano? Can't say that I have. Although I do have the local plumber on speed dial. But something tells me that's not what we're talking about here."

"Well, here in the mountains we folks don't have the luxury of flushing. And that means every so often, we have to remove what you might call the 'sweetness of our labors.'"

I groaned again. "As a writer, I've manhandled a few euphemisms in my day, but that one's a real doozy."

"You catch on real quick for a rookie," said Hattie.

"So, what does this . . . for the lack of a better word, evolution entail?" I asked.

Hattie nodded at a nearby rust-covered tin bucket.

"You've got two options. You could scoop out the honey with yonder bucket." She thumbed toward the shovel propped against the outhouse. "Or you could dig a new hole."

I pondered the bucket. Then the shovel. The devil or the deep blue sea. This was going to be a shitty detail no matter which I chose. The decision more or less made for me, I grimaced. Then took it like a man.

"I, John March, intrepid flatlander that I am, hereby cast one vote for digging a new hole."

"Good thinking," chuckled Hattie. "That would be the smarter choice."

She pointed to where she wanted the new hole dug.

"Over there would be a good spot. Two feet in diameter, round, four feet deep should do right nicely. I don't see much muscle on those scrawny arms of yours, but it shouldn't take you more than an hour. *If* you put your back into it and don't mind working up some elbow grease. Once you're done digging, you can nudge the crapper over the new hole and fill in the old one. To complete the flush, so to speak. It's only a one-holer, and it's on skids, so it should slide real easy. If'n it gives you any trouble, I'll have Morgan lend you a hand."

It had been years since I'd seen a shovel, much less attempted to use one. Trying to look like I knew what I was doing, I held the thing out in one hand, then gave Hattie a thumbs-up. Radiating more bluster than confidence.

"It's got a nice balance to it," I said. As if I knew what I was talking about. "Piece of cake. I should be able to knock this out in no time flat."

Watching Hattie head back to the cabin, I vowed to never again take copper pipes for granted. Suddenly I missed my super-quiet, low-flush, water-saving Elger back home. And its padded seat. I took off my shirt. Set it aside.

"Well, John," I told myself, "this hole isn't going to dig itself. So, as they say in these hills, better get crackin."

A pleasant surprise: when I jammed foot to shovel, it sliced through the pungent soil like a hot knife through butter. After a few minutes of effort, I'd worked up a respectable sweat, and my hole was starting to take shape. Even more surprising was the simple joy I felt in doing something so menial. Moving a hundred pounds of dirt from point A to point B shouldn't have been that satisfying, especially for someone who pushes papers around for a living. But somehow it was. Leaning on the shovel to take my first break, I found myself grinning ear to ear.

"Four years of college, and I'm digging holes in the boondocks," I confided to the nearest tree. Who didn't give a hoot what I was talking about. "If my classmates could only see me now."

Whistling an off-key rendition of Sam Cook's "Chain Gang," I really "put my back into it," and within ten minutes my hole had doubled in size. Damned if I wasn't getting good at it. Maybe there was a future for me in the waste-removal business.

A bucket of sweat later, my digging was interrupted by an old man walking down the path off to my right. Slightly stooped but still moving at a sprightly clip, he wore bib overalls and thigh-length wader boots. On his head sat a multicolored sombrero, the kind tourists in Tijuana gobble up for ten bucks a pop. Strapped to his shoulders was an empty backpack. Oddest of all, he was pushing a power-driven lawn mower in front of him. Well, not so much pushing as following it. Even though it wasn't running, it seemed to be pulling him downhill. When Lawn Mower Man tipped his hat to me, I donned my fourth stupefied look of the day. Maybe my fifth.

"Howdy, young feller," he says. "Beautiful weather we're having, don't you think?"

"That we are," I said.

He nodded at my shovel. Smiled.

"I see you're digging a new hole for Hattie's crapper."

"That I am."

Another nod, and he picked up his pace. Just before he got to the ridge, he looked back over his shoulder.

"Sure is a nice day for it," he said. And with a wave, he dropped out of sight.

Unsure if I was hallucinating, my expression grew too heavy for my face.

"What in the hell was *that* all about?" I asked that same uncaring tree. Mumbling, "Curiouser and curiouser," I resumed my digging with renewed vigor and some serious dirt began to fly.

FIFTY-SIX

After another thirty minutes, and now completely drenched in sweat, I stood back to admire my handiwork. Hattie would be pleased. In my mind I ranked myself right up there with de Lesseps. Although I hadn't moved as much dirt as he had at the Suez Canal, I'd been just as efficient.

Climbing out of my hole, I heard the chug of a small gasoline engine. The old man had returned. This time his lawn mower was going full bore, and his backpack now bulged at the seams. Moving half a step slower than a trot, when he got closer, he tipped his sombrero to me again.

"I see you finished the hole!" he shouted over the lawn mower's roar.

"That I did!" I shouted back.

"Should make Hattie right happy!" says he.

"That it should!" says I.

Around a bend, up over another rise, and just like that, he was gone, the rumble of his lawn mower fading to a mild hum.

Other than the fact that I'd probably been out in the sun too long, there wasn't a good explanation for what I'd just witnessed. So all I did was lean forward on my shovel. After all the sweat I'd shed, it was my shovel now. We'd sort of bonded. *Even this far up in the hills, isn't possession nine-tenths of the law?* I smiled up at my still uncaring tree. Laughed at myself.

"Of cabbages and kings," I said. "And whether pigs have wings."

I'd finally had that conversation with a walrus I'd always yearned for.

A sudden wind change told me I wasn't finished with my assigned chores. I still had to fill in the old hole and manhandle the outhouse over to its new one. Semi-intelligent sort that I am, I saw a problem.

The outhouse may have been on skids, but it looked heavier than sin. One misstep, and I'd fall into the old hole. And taking a tumble into all that you-know-what was not a workable option.

However, after a few careful back-and-forths, I was able to clear the poop. Without stepping in any of it, thank God. From there it was an easy slide over to my masterpiece. And wonder of wonders, it fit perfectly. Maybe I'd missed my calling. I'd started to shovel in the old hole when Hattie called out from the porch.

"Looks like you're about finished, John March. You didn't take as long as I expected."

"I still have to fill the old hole in, but that shouldn't take more than a few minutes," I said. To show off, I heaved in an especially large shovelful. It's pathetic what men will do to impress the female of the species. Even one who's 143 years old. Women may be the weaker sex, but we're definitely the dumber of the two.

Hattie nodded twice. Waved for me to come in.

"You can let that go for now. I've made a pitcher of lemonade."

Lemonade! Instantly I was dying from thirst.

"That sounds great! The only thing better would be an ice-cold beer."

"If'n beer be more to your liking, I got that too. I stash a few bottles underneath the floorboards to keep 'em cool."

"God bless you, Hattie Sexton. You're a woman after my own heart."

I stopped at the first step to wipe my brow. Glanced back at the ridge. I could no longer hear the lawn mower.

"Um, you wouldn't happen to know anything about a tall, elderly gentleman in a sombrero and wearing wading boots, would you?" I asked. "I know it sounds crazy, but I swear he was walking behind a lawn mower."

A knowing smile on her face, Hattie nodded slowly.

"You must have run across Stratton Briggs. Biggest ears in three counties. The sombrero is the only thing wide enough to cover both, or they'd burn up like two slices of bacon left too long on the grill. Today's his shopping day. Once a month, regular as clockwork, he drives to town to pick up groceries. The waders are for the two creeks he has to cross along the way."

I wasn't sure I'd heard her right.

"Did you say 'drives'? But he wasn't in a car. He was walking. Behind a lawn mower."

"Ol' Strat can't tolerate automobiles. Too confining for his long legs. In tight places, they cramp up on him something fierce. He's rich enough to afford a dozen cars, expensive ones, too, but he prefers lawn mowers. Likes to be outside his vehicles. Besides, he never saw fit to get a driver's license. Says it's a waste of time learning the rules of the road when there ain't no roads up where he lives."

My face was getting used to wearing a stupid look.

"Um, if it's transportation"—finger quotes—"he's looking for, why doesn't he buy himself a riding lawn mower?"

"He prefers to walk. Says it's good for his ticker."

"Then why bother with . . ."

I felt as if I'd slipped into an Abbot and Costello "Who's on First?" routine.

"His mower is one of those fancy self-propelled jobs," continued Hattie. "The kind that go by themselves. Since Strat ain't got no lawn, he took the blades off. To keep him from hitting rocks. He doesn't fire the thing up until he's ready to make the return trip. Then he uses it to pull him back up the mountain. Strat's knees ain't what they used to be, and he needs a little extra kick on the upside."

I looked off in the direction the old man had gone. Scratched my chin. Hattie's explanation made perfect sense.

"Fascinating," I said.

"Necessity is the mother of invention," said Hattie. "Even way up here in the hills."

"Another Melungeon proverb?" I asked.

"Just one of many, Mr. John March. One of many."

FIFTY-SEVEN

The temperature drop inside Hattie's cabin was refreshing. As if I were standing in front of my open refrigerator back in Boston. Poor man's air-conditioning, I call it. I straddled the kitchen chair backward. Checked out one of the blisters on my hands. I had at least three. *Badges of courage*, I decided. Hattie bent down to pull up a floorboard.

"Can I help you with that?" I asked.

"I got everything under control," she said. "I may be older than the hills and bent double, but I can still fend for myself."

She set the floorboard to one side. Extracted two long-necked bottles from a battered Styrofoam cooler. After wiping one off, she handed it to me.

"Need a glass?" she asked.

"No thanks. I prefer my beer raw."

"Good man. So do I."

She did the honors with a church key—I didn't know they still used those things—and we clinked bottles.

"Cheers!" she said. "Over the lips, under the gums, look out stomach, here she comes."

My first swallow was pure heaven. And before I blinked twice, I'd drained half the bottle.

"There's nothing like a cold beer on a hot day," I said. I searched the bottle for a label. Found none. When I looked up, I saw that Hattie's bottle was empty. I'd been out-chugged by a little old lady.

"What's the brand name of this beauty?" I asked.

"It's a local brew. Some of Stratton Brigg's private stock. He mixes it up in a shed out back of his place. Adds a few special ingredients to give it extra pizzaz."

"Special ingredients?"

"You don't want to know."

I held my bottle up to the light. Hesitated, but only for a second. As thirsty as I was, I dead-soldiered it. The beer could have been brewed out of mouse turds for all I cared. It was that good.

"Slap a designer label on this stuff, and he's got himself a gold mine," I said. "It would sell like liquid hotcakes in Boston's trendy bistros."

"I'd offer you another," said Hattie, "but I don't think you could handle it. It tends to sneak up on a person. Two beers, and you start seeing things. Three, you skip and go naked."

Two seconds after I set the bottle down, the room tilted sharply to the right. Then back to the left. My arms and legs felt warm and fuzzy. My fingertips tingled. I heard faint strains of "Hey Jude" being played on the bagpipes. I had trouble focusing.

"Wow! You weren't kidding, Hattie. What's the alcohol content of this stuff?"

"That's something else you don't want to know."

I wasn't tipsy, just feeling no pain. Pleasantly happy, as social drinkers like to say. Closing my eyes was out of the question, so I shrugged.

"Then from here on, temperance shall be the word of the day," I said.

Hattie nodded a grin. Settled back into her chair to rearrange her skirt. She set her cane on the table in front of her. Leaned forward to look me square in the eye again.

"Think you're ready for the rest of Micah's story, Mr. March?"

I shoved the Sony front and center.

"We're all ears, Hattie. Doc Holliday, Ocho, and me and my trusty recorder."

Before she could pick up her story, there was a knock at the door. Hattie frowned, looked over at Grandfather, then back at me.

"Who in the world could that be? I ain't expecting anybody. Never am, come to think of it."

Standing on her front porch was a man with a floppy hat in his right hand. He was missing his left arm at the shoulder, his limp sleeve pinned to his shirt. He was missing his left leg, too, and when he shifted his weight, his peg leg thumped on the floorboards. His body language screamed nervous. Bald like a monk, head lowered, he boasted thin blond hairs that sprouted from his temples to tumble down below his shoulders. When he finally spoke, his words came out a mumble above a whisper.

"Sorry to bother you, Miss Hattie, but my brother's taken to feelin' poorly again. I was wonderin' if you'd be so kind as to, um . . ."

"Spike needs another poultice, does he, Ike?" asked Hattie.

Eyes on the floor and blushing beet red, Ike prodded a knothole with his peg leg.

"Yes'm, he does."

"His fingers acting up again?" said Hattie.

"Yes'm, they are."

Hattie nodded. Smiled her sympathies.

"Considering how they got whacked off, I can't say I'm much surprised. You're a menace with a hoe, Ike Goins. And that be the honest-to-God's truth."

Ike's shoulders sagged.

"I swear it was an accident, Miss Hattie. I never saw him reaching for that clump of weeds."

Pursing her lips, Hattie let out a sigh.

"At the rate you two are whittling away at each other, there won't be much of you Goins left to bury. I suppose it's my Christian duty to pick up the pieces whenever I can. You wait right there, Ike, while I tend to my mixing. I don't want you traipsing none of your bad luck into my house."

Ike took a crowhop back. Bowed slightly, hat still in hand.

"Thank you kindly, Miss Hattie."

FIFTY-EIGHT

With the speed of a professional pharmacist, Hattie mixed up her poultice in the kitchen. A pinch of this, a dab of that. A dollop here, a spoonful there, and in less than three minutes she had ground up a foul-looking mixture in a porcelain dish. She added two more ingredients, and the smell of sulfur filled the room. Rolling her eyes, she looked over at me.

"That's Ike 'Stumpy' Goins out there," she whispered. "He and his brother, Spike, are two of the three clumsiest human beings ever to stumble across the Smoky Mountains. The third being my dearly departed poppa. May he rest in peace."

Hattie retrieved a jar from the first shelf.

"Spike started it ten years ago by slicing off Ike's left hand. Said his ax slipped while he was chopping wood."

I took another look at Ike through the window by the door.

"But he's missing his whole left arm."

"Spike finished the job a year later in a hunting accident. Dropped his shotgun and blew what was left of Ike's arm off at the shoulder. Poor Ike nearly bled to death."

"Amazing," I said.

Hattie looked up at the ceiling. Pulled at her chin.

"If'n I recollect rightly, about six months later it was Spike's turn. Ike was clearing brush with a chain saw out back of their cabin, not the smartest thing in the world to do. The chain caught on a branch, snapped, and hit Spike on the forearm. Chewed his right hand off above the wrist. Made a messy job of it, too."

Hattie looked down. Tapped her nose twice.

"Lessee, it was two, maybe three months after that, Ike was knocking clumps from Spike's plow on the move. Again, not a smart thing to do. He got his foot caught, and the plow twisted it off at the shinbone. Spike didn't have time to rein in the horse. Another messy one, that."

Back in the '40s and '50s, Al Capp, the world-famous cartoonist, popularized a down-on-his-luck character named Joe Btfsplk. Joe was followed around by a private black cloud. Same with the Goins brothers, apparently.

"Talk about rotten luck," I said. "Are you sure they were all accidents?"

"They was all accidents, sure enough. The Goins may be sharp as marbles and all thumbs, but there never was a closer pair."

I took another peek at Ike.

"From the looks of him, he's fast running out of appendages."

Finished with her mixing, Hattie poured the concoction onto a gauze-like cloth, folded it twice, then headed for the door. Winked as she passed me. The stench was overpowering.

"One loses a finger," she said, "the other loses a toe. Things sort of even themselves out."

She opened the door. Gave the poultice to Ike.

"Here," she said. "This should ease Spike's pain. Check it out every hour to make sure it isn't drying out." She handed him a small jar. "If it is, dab some of this on it. The swelling should go down by the day after tomorrow, but you'll need to replace the cloth come morning. Make sure it's clean, though. Can't have Spike coming down with an infection. Other than the one he's already got."

Ike backed off the porch. Almost tripped on the first step.

"Me and my brother are eternally grateful, Miss Hattie."

He donned his hat. Hobbled away. I didn't know a man with a peg leg could move that fast.

"You and Spike steer clear of any sharp implements for a while!" Hattie called out after him. "No sense in tempting eternity!"

She watched Goins until he disappeared over the ridge, a wistful smile shadowing her face. Her good deed done, she tightened her shawl and closed the door. Then turned to me.

"They's good people, them Goins brothers. Dumb as a pair of rocks and poor as church mice, but good people. Both would give you the shirts off their backs. If'n they had any."

Hattie retook her seat. Smoothed out her skirt and began to rock again.

"Now, where were we?"

FIFTY-NINE

I switched the recorder back on. Checked the levels. Turned to Hattie.

"Um, you left off with Micah healing that bobcat."

"Oh, yeah," said Hattie. "Mr. Bobcat. Well, neat as you please, that critter licked my brother in the face, then bounded off into the brush. Good as new."

A wistful grin trembled her lips, and Hattie had to rock a few times before continuing.

"Yep. That was Micah, alright. Him and his many gifts. And how that boy did grow! Never saw anything like it, the way he shot up. By the time he turned five, he was taller than me. At eight, he was a full head taller than Poppa. Good times they was, back then. Those were the days when Poppa finally mastered that peevish still of his. Make no mistake, it would blow up now and then, only not as often. And with Momma's help, our moonshining business was finally bringing in some money. Not great, but halfway good at least."

Hattie looked out the window. Her smile now gone, a heavy weight seemed to settle on her shoulders.

"Then came 1910," she sighed. "The year ol' Sam Longhorn died."

"Samuel Longhorn Clemens?" I asked. "As in Mark Twain?"

"The very same." Hattie puffed out her cheeks. "The year started out goodly enough but turned sour real quick for the Sexton clan. The trouble began around the end of March, with spring just around the corner. We'd been having an early hot spell. Buds were straining at their seams, and the green was getting ready to bust out all over. Poppa was making some late-night deliveries at the graveyard, and Micah and me were helping him out."

I wasn't sure I'd heard correctly.

"Graveyard deliveries?" I asked.

"Another of Momma's ideas. Anyhow, it was close to midnight, and we was just finishing up . . ."

SIXTY

"It was early June," elaborated Hattie. "I was in my mid-thirties, I think, and Micah was about ten. A full moon hung lazy in the late-evening sky, peeking half an eyeball around a meandering cloud. Hound-dog shadows stretched across the forest, turning the graveyard brown-your-trouser spooky. A small wooden house, just one of many in the yard, sat atop the tallest tombstone in the cemetery. Those little houses are another Melungeon custom. Intended to provide safe haven for dearly departed souls on their journey to heaven. They served our purposes right nicely."

"I'm afraid I can't reach this one, Micah," I said.

"I'll get it for you," he says.

Now over six and a half feet tall, it weren't no stretch for him to retrieve the three coins from the house's small front door.

I stashed the coins in my pocket. Handed him a Mason jar full of moonshine. Which he promptly put in the house.

"That's the last of them," I said. "Good thing you're so tall."

Micah just smiled that sweet smile of his. Never one to waste words, he put his arms behind his back. An owl hooted in the distance, and he cocked his head toward the breeze. Listened real hard. That's when Poppa returned from the bushes. Not to tell tales on anyone, but he had this bad habit of watering the grass whenever he'd had a few too many.

"Pretty smart of your momma," he said. "I never would have thought of using them houses to hide our shine. We all done here?"

I patted my pockets, and the coins jingled like Christmas bells.

"All delivered and paid for," says I. I spotted Poppa's half-empty jar. Shot him a look. "Now, Poppa, you know what Momma said about drinking on the job."

His hand caught in the cookie jar, he hid the Mason behind his back.

"Yeah, I know," says he. "But this was my best batch ever. Smooooth as cornsilk. You ain't gonna tell on me, are you, Hattie?"

I never could stay mad at Poppa. Not for long, anyway. Especially not when he laid them big puppy-dog eyes on me. Or rather, his puppy-dog eye.

"I suppose not," says I. "But only if you put away the booze."

Poppa took a last swig from his jar. Winked as he twisted the cap tight. "Just one for the road."

I tried to look stern, but my heart wasn't in it. Since Poppa was two sheets to the wind, the horse was already out of the barn, and scolding him then would have been like peeing up a rope. I picked up our lantern and turned it up a notch. We needed more light on the way home. Especially with Poppa so tipsy.

"I'll lead, you follow me, Poppa," says I. "I can't have you staggering off into the woods again. And you needn't worry. I won't tell Momma. I won't have to. Any fool with eyes can see you've been sampling your wares."

A chuckle gurgling around in his throat, Poppa put a sloppy finger to his lips. Winked again.

"Shh," says he. "Mum's the word."

With a shake of my head, I turned to my brother, who was still listening to that owl.

"It's time we headed back, Micah," I said.

"One of Missus Owl's eggs just hatched," he whispered. "And the second's on the way."

"How about the third?" I asked.

He tilted his head to the right. Listened more intently for a few seconds.

"Third 'un should be out by daybreak."

What happened next was my fault. I should have noticed Poppa wandering off. As he often did when into his scuppers. But I was so intent on what was happening with that owl I neglected my own. First I knew he was gone was when I heard a high-pitched "Whoops!" It meant Poppa had had himself another accident. Lantern held high, I charged off, Micah hot on my heels.

"Poppa!" I called out. "Are you alright?"

SIXTY-ONE

"Not far, I came to an open hole," continued Hattie, "no doubt dug for tomorrow's funeral. Old Man Tucker had passed away two days prior, and it was probably for him. I saw Poppa laying at the bottom, his neck twisted around almost backwards. The smile on his face told me he must have died instantly, felt no pain. I sagged to my knees. Almost dropped the lantern. I felt dizzy. Sick to my stomach. For the longest time, I could only stare at what had once been my father."

"Oh, Poppa," I finally managed. "Just when things were going so well, you go and do something so all-fired stupid like this."

I thought back to all the times he'd cheated death, tinkering with this brew and that. At least it wasn't his damn still that had done him in.

Micah knelt down beside me. Soft as an angel wing, he put a giant arm around me. A single tear trickled down his cheek.

"Poppa's gone, isn't he?" he asks.

"Yes, Micah. I'm afraid so."

"Gone to a better place?"

"I'm sure of it."

He held me tighter, and I felt his chest heave.

"At least he went quick," says he.

We buried Poppa three days later. Fitting the mood, it rained all day. But that didn't stop half the county from showing up for his funeral. My poppa may have been clumsy as a newborn calf, but he was well liked. Well respected, too.

Poor Momma. Because she'd gotten so big, she couldn't be at the graveside. Tore her up something fierce. In her condition it was all she could do to haul herself from the bedroom to the kitchen. Managing eight hundred pounds around our tight-as-a-mouse-hole cabin wasn't easy, but she was waiting for Micah and me when we got back. Had a pot of stew simmering on the stove for us.

At first none of us could find the words. We just stood there, looking at each other, expecting Poppa to burst through the door any second, yelping about how he'd lost another finger down at the still. Momma was the first to break through the awkward.

"So, Hattie, how was the service?"

"Right respectable," says I. "The minister did Poppa proud with some nice words. Sent him off in fine style, he did."

Momma managed a thin smile. Wiped away a tear.

"That's good to hear. Lots of people there?"

"Too many to count. The usual friends and relatives came. Just about all of his customers, too. They all send their regrets, by the way. Said they'd miss Poppa and his moonshine."

"Nav would have appreciated that," said Momma, nodding. "He always took great pride in his work. I just wish he wouldn't have sampled it so much. Maybe he'd still be with us today."

I hung up my coat. Took Momma's hand. I didn't want to upset her more than she already was, but she had a right to know.

"I hate to worry you, Momma, but Doc Hickory was there, too. He came up to me afterwards to tell me how sorry he was about Poppa. Extended his personal regrets."

Momma's eyes turned stone hard real quick.

"Personal regrets? That's a laugh and a half."

"He also said that if there was anything he could do to help, we should call on him. Said if we needed money, he'd be willing to—"

Momma thumped her cane so hard the floor shook.

"Damn that man's hide! At a time like this, he's still after my son's bones. He'll give us money, alright. But only if we sign that blood paper of his. I hope you told him what he could do with his offer, Hattie."

"Where the sun don't shine, Momma."

"Good girl."

Her jaw tight, Momma motioned Micah and me closer. She took our hands in hers. Looked us both in the eye.

"This family don't need him, or any of his kind. As long as we have each other, we'll do just fine."

SIXTY-TWO

"**A**nd Momma was right," said Hattie. "We missed Poppa real bad, but we survived. Micah and me tended to the still. Momma kept the house and saw over the books. We never got anywhere halfway close to rich, but we weren't starving either. Come July 4 that year, we had enough money left over to buy our own fireworks. First time ever we'd been able to do that. Ever the cautious one, Momma sent us to the first clearing over the ridge to try one out."

"You two be careful now," she said. "Light the firecracker, then hightail it to a safe distance. I don't want you losing no fingers like Poppa used to."

I was all atingle, holding that firecracker in my hand as we set off. Micah wasn't so sure about the whole exploding thing. Casting a nervous glance back at our cabin, he shook his head.

"We ain't gonna start a fire, are we, Hattie? I worry about burning any of our animal friends."

"We're only going to test one firecracker," says I. "What's the danger in that?"

"Will it be loud?" he asks. "You know I don't like big noises. And neither do the animals."

"It's the Fourth of July, Micah. You're supposed to make big noise on the Fourth. Otherwise it wouldn't be much of a celebration."

I mounded up some dirt. Stuck the firecracker into it. Snapped a match aflame.

"Are you ready?" says I.

Micah covered his ears.

"Ready as I'll ever be."

I put flame to the fuse. Then stood up.

"We'd better back up a bit," I said. "Just in case something goes haywire."

We both hid behind the nearest wide tree. The fuse sputtered for a few seconds until the firecracker went off with a pitiful fizz. Talk about a letdown. Hell, I'd heard louder bangs from Poppa's accidents down at the still. I felt three parts disappointed, one part embarrassed.

"See, Micah," I said. "You had nothing to worry about. There weren't no fire."

I smoothed down my skirt. Walked over to the so-called blast site and nudged the shredded firecracker with the toe of my boot.

"Weren't much of a crack, either," I said. "But there's no time to get another batch."

"That's okay," said Micah. "It was loud enough for me."

A distant commotion from our cabin startled both of us. Momma was shouting over two male voices. After exchanging knowing glances, Micah and I took off running.

"Tarnation!" I groaned. "Those damn government men are back!"

"Think they'll hurt Momma?" asked Micah.

"It's not Momma I'm worried about. She can handle her own, and then some. I just hope she don't skin them alive."

A jet-black horse was tied to our porch, hitched to one of them two-wheeled buggies, the kind that's useless for hauling things. I heard Momma's voice raise an octave. Riled up, there was no stopping her. And today she was in rare form. It was clear the government men had bitten off more than they could chew.

"Shouldn't we help Momma?" asked Micah.

"No need," says I. "Sounds as she's doing just fine all by her lonesome. Let's just stand back and see what develops."

"But what if—"

"Shh, Micah. I want to listen."

From inside the cabin came a male voice. Deep, and trying to sound important.

"But, ma'am, what you're doing is illegal."

"Not by me, it ain't," said Momma. "I'm just a poor business woman trying to eke out a living in these hard times. I supply my faithful customers with what they want. What's the harm in that?"

Momma always got right to the point.

"That may be," replied the voice, "but moonshining is against the law."

Comes back Momma: "And persactly who's law are you talking about?"

"Why, the people's law, of course," said a second male voice. "Says so in the Constitution of these United States of America."

Ganging up on Momma was never a good idea, and she was having none of what those blue-suiters were dishing out.

"Prove it," she said.

"You'll just have to take our word for it, ma'am," said the deeper voice. Sounding more flustered than important now.

I pictured Momma's jaw jutting out at that. When needs be, she could jut a jaw farther than just about anyone.

"Until I see it in writing, I ain't budging from this here house!" she said, laying down her own law.

"I'm sorry, Missus Sexton," said the second voice, "but we've got a warrant for your arrest. I'm afraid we'll have to take you in."

SIXTY-THREE

Momma's next words came out slow, deliberate, and hard as rocks.

"Then go ahead and do what you think you have to. But you'll be getting no help from me on that score. I'll not be moving a solitary inch from this chair."

That brought a grin to my face.

"What did I tell you, Micah?" I said. "Momma's got them right where she wants them."

The cabin fell silent. After a minute or two, the government fellers came out onto the porch. All red in the face and perplexed. The tall skinny one shook his head. The shorter, pudgy one scratched his chin. Caught between a rock and a hard place, they didn't pay Micah and me no mind. Probably didn't even see us. The tall one took off his hat. Wiped his brow.

"Well, she's definitely catchable," he said. "But fetchable? That's a horse of a different color. I never did see a bigger woman."

The short one shook his head.

"Did you see the size of her arms?" he says. "They're bigger than my damn waist. She has to weigh at least seven hundred pounds."

"More like eight," said the tall one. "What are we going to do? For sure we can't pick her up."

"Not with my bad back we can't," says Shorty. "Even if we somehow manage to move her, how do we get her down the mountain? Our buggy barely handles the two of us. She'd snap the axle like a toothpick. And I ain't about to walk back just so she can ride. Not in this blasted heat, anyway. Hate to say it, partner, but she's got us by the short hairs."

"I agree," said Mr. Tall. "Besides, even if we did somehow manage to take her in, half the county would be up in arms. I say we leave this case for the higher-ups. Let them bust their humps."

I could tell from the pained looks on their faces that some serious thinking was going on in their government-issued brains. Running a hand through his thinning hair, the short one finally mumbled something.

"We're damned if we do and damned if we don't. Missus Sexton has us buggered and far from home. And she jolly well knows it."

"What do we tell the captain?" asks Mr. Tall.

"To hell with the captain. If Hattie Sexton is that important to him, he can bring her in himself. Damn stupid, sending us out the day before a holiday like this."

The two climbed back into their buggy. His hands on the reins, the tall one took a long last look at our cabin.

"Yes, sir," says he, "that's one hell of a woman in there."

Shorty leaned forward with a smile to pat the horse on its rump.

"You can thank your lucky stars, Midnight. You dodged a heavy bullet today."

When they were gone, Micah and I rushed up the porch steps and into the cabin. Momma was sitting in her chair, cool as a cucumber, rocking and tending to her knitting. Poppa had that chair made special for her. Bolted several two-by-fours together to handle her considerable weight.

"Are you okay, Momma?" I asked.

"Fit as a fiddle, daughter. Them two weren't nothing to worry about."

"They were more polite than the last bunch," I said. "How long ago was that, anyway?"

Momma counted off on her fingers.

"Six, maybe seven months?"

"You'd think those government types would wise up by now."

Momma set her needles aside. Laughed from the belly. Then: "Wisdom has nothing to do with it, child. That's why those two work for Uncle Sam. Now, you and your brother wash up. Dinner's almost ready."

SIXTY-FOUR

T hinking back on how her mother had bested those two government men, Hattie donned a lazy grin. She nodded twice, lost the grin, then continued her story.

❧

It all fell apart later that fall, a few days before Thanksgiving. A hard chill trickled in on a hefty breeze one morning to lay the trees pretty much bare. Micah and me went down to the meadow on the other side of Parson's Ridge to pick the last of that year's blueberries. Late on the vine was always best for pies, and Momma made the most scrumptious blueberry pie in the whole state. Midafternoon it was, and we had just about picked the patch clean. I dumped my berries into Micah's basket.

"Here," says I. "Take these back to Momma and ask if they're enough."

Momma always made an extra pie or two, just in case company dropped by. As they sometimes did when she got to baking. One eye on his basket, Micah scratched his head.

"This doesn't seem nearly enough," says he. "You know me. I can eat one whole pie all by my lonesome."

I stood to stretch out my back. When the weather turns suddenly cold, like it did that day, the crick in my back gets to aching something fierce. Nothing I can't handle, but it slows me down a step or two.

"You and that giant-sized appetite of yours!" I laughed. "Not even a teenager yet, and already you're outeating a plow horse."

Micah slapped on that shy grin of his.

"I guess God must have borned me hungry."

"Ain't that the truth! You'll probably eat us out of house and home when you're full growed. Get along, now. I'll keep on picking until you come back. Don't dawdle none."

"Maybe this time Momma should make four pies."

"Why in the world would we need four pies for the three of us?"

"One for you and Momma. One for company. And two for me."

That got me to laughing real hard.

"Lord! Would you listen to this young whelp? Two whole pies for himself! Do you know what a glutton is, Micah?" I asked him.

"Can't say that I do," says he.

"Well, as soon as you get home, take a gander in the mirror. A first-class glutton will be staring back at you."

His breath kicking up vapor clouds, Micah glided into the forest. As big as he was, he still moved like a cat. I bunched my wrap around my shoulders and settled back to my picking, a happy feeling in my belly.

In less than ten minutes, Micah was back. And as usual I didn't hear him coming. His face was bright red, his breath coming in gulps.

"Hattie! Hattie!" he shouts. "Come quick! Something's wrong with Momma! She ain't moving!"

He yanked me by the hand so hard I dropped my basket. Half pulled, half carried, I never moved so fast in my life. Before I could catch my breath, we were clattering up our porch steps. Shivering all over, Micah hid behind me. As if someone that big could hide behind little old me. Head down, a look of terror on his face, he did not want to go in first.

"Momma?" I called out. Then once more. But I got no answer.

Edging through the door, I saw Momma's head. My heart dropped out of my chest. I felt dizzy, almost fainted. It took me a few breaths to figure out what had happened.

The old floorboards in the kitchen had finally given way to Momma's weight. She had plunged down to her neck and was wedged between two splintered planks. Her face blue as a winter sky.

Eyes rolled up in the back of her head. No doubt about it: our mother was dead. I felt a huge, pillow-soft hand settle on my shoulder, gently, like a butterfly's kiss.

"She's gonna be alright, isn't she, Hattie?" Micah whispers in my ear. "Tell me she's just sleeping."

I'd never felt so tired, so drained, so old, in my life. Fighting back tears for Micah's sake, I knelt down to smooth out Momma's tangled hair. It was caught up in a fan of splinters. Momma was always real proud of her long hair. The way it sparkled in the sunlight. She didn't like to have anyone see it messed up. I reached down to close her eyes.

"No, Micah," I said. "I'm afraid she's not sleeping. She's gone to her reward."

I felt more than heard Micah's sigh on the back of my neck. Shaking his head, he sat beside me. Crossed his legs and began to stroke the top of Momma's head. Grandfather ticked through a minute or two before either of us could say anything more. Finally, Micah nodded three times.

"When she gets to heaven, will Poppa be there?"

"Yes, Micah," I said. "He'll welcome her with open arms."

More silence from Micah. Then a long, drawn-out sigh.

"At least she'll be happy again."

SIXTY-FIVE

It took six strapping workmen half a day to get Momma out of our cabin. They had to take down the front door and knock a hole in the wall to fit her through. Sandwith Yass, our local minister at the time, was kind enough to handle the arrangements. Six men and a four-horse freight wagon might seem a bit much to some, but you have to remember, Momma weighed over eight hundred pounds. And that was a lot to handle.

Through the entire ordeal, Reverend Yass, bless his heart, stood by my side.

"Easy, men," he said when the workers almost dropped Momma. Using our detached door as a stretcher, they were having a dickens of a time getting her through that hole.

"Jesus Christ," I heard one of them mutter. "She's gotta weigh a damn ton."

"Try two," grunted a second. "How the hell she get to be so big, anyway?"

The reverend raised his right hand in a fist. Scowled down at them.

"Keep a civil tongue in your head, you two. There's a young'un present."

"Sorry, Reverend," says one, a sheepish look on his face.

They had to sashay Momma back and forth a few times before they finally managed her out onto the porch. Twice they froze when the steps groaned in protest. At the wagon, it took all six of them four tries to get the door high enough to slide her into the back. When she was safely on board, four of them leaned forward on their knees, drenched in sweat and exhausted. Two sagged to the ground, panting like a pair of horses rode hard and put away wet.

"Oh, my aching back," mumbled one. "I think I broke it."

"I might have given myself a hernia," whispered the other. "I pity the poor fools who have to dig a grave for this one. I wonder what they'll use for a coffin."

The other looked over his shoulder. Momma's stomach stretched above the sides of the wagon by a foot.

"Whatever they use," he says, "it better be bigger than this damn wagon."

"Enough!" said the reverend. "It's time to get this poor woman down the mountain."

Tails tucked firmly between their legs, the two scrambled up into the wagon's front seat. A snap on the reins got the horses to straining, and with a creak and a groan, the wagon inched forward. There being too much weight on the axles, the other four workmen had to walk behind. As they went by, I heard some grumbling but couldn't make out the words. Just as well, I suppose.

I watched that wagon until it dropped out of sight, sagging as it went. We all had serious doubts about whether it would make it down the mountain in one piece.

"Don't you worry, Hattie," said the reverend. "I'll take care of everything. Your momma was a fine woman. I'll see to it she gets a proper send-off."

"You'll notify everyone?"

"You can rest assured the entire county will be at her service. You got my word on it."

His eyes on the ridge, Micah clutched Momma's shawl to his chest. He hadn't let loose of it since she was pulled out of the floor. A question on his face, he bent down to whisper into the reverend's ear.

"Reverend Yass, are you gonna make sure my momma gets into heaven?"

The reverend beheld the gaping hole where our front door used to be. Let out a soft sigh as he took my brother's hand in his.

"I'll do my best, Micah. My very best."

SIXTY-SIX

"We laid Momma to rest the day after Thanksgiving," said Hattie. "She wouldn't fit in a regular-sized coffin, so Reverend Yass had a special crate built for her. A carpenter fancied it up a bit, but it was still a crate. They dug a hole twice normal size and had to set up a block-and-tackle thingamabob hanging from three timbers to swing that crate over her grave."

Despite the sadness in the air, the day had turned out bright and sunny. And as the reverend promised, people came from far and wide to pay their respects to Momma. Truth be told, he might have twisted a few arms.

Micah and me appreciated his kind and thankfully short words at the service. At the end, he raised his Bible to the heavens: "Lord, we commend our beloved sister, your faithful servant Mullie Moon Sexton, to Your infinite care. May You see fit to guide her on her journey to everlasting peace. She will be missed here on earth."

"Almost as much as her moonshine," someone muttered in the back row.

"You got that right, brother," said the guy next to him.

A stern look from the reverend silenced those two rumpots, and they quickly bowed their heads. No one with a lick of sense interrupted Reverend Yass in the middle of his preaching. Clutching the Bible to his bosom, he adjusted his robes, then continued with his good words.

"We who remain behind take heart in knowing that this good woman has gone to a better place."

Then, ever so slowly, with his eyes closed, he made the sign of the cross over us all.

"In the name of the Father, and the Son, and the Holy Ghost, I pray. Amen."

"Amen!" said the crowd.

That thingamabob holding Momma let out a groan, and I crossed my fingers. It took eight strongish men tugging at four ropes to get Momma's crate airborne. Another two to maneuver it over the hole. When one of the timbers jerked a few inches to the right, I was sure the whole contraption would collapse, taking all ten men with it into Momma's grave. I held my breath as they put their backs into it. Once she was lowered into her grave, and there was no danger of anyone else dying, the choir broke into a chorus of "Rock of Ages," Momma's favorite hymn.

When they were done, a sea of sad faces streamed by to offer their sympathies. Micah held my hand, Momma's shawl clutched to his chest, his eyes fixated on the gaping hole in front of us.

After the first dozen faces, their voices blurred into a mass of I'm-so-sorries, if-there's-anything-I-can-dos. It was more than I could take, so I tuned out everything. I never cared much for funerals. Still don't. Funerals can't help the dead none. They only make the living sadder. First Poppa, now Momma. Such was life on the mountain.

When the sea of mourners finally parted, Micah moved to the other side of the grave, where a mound of dirt tall as a good-sized man was waiting. I was about to join him when bony fingers pulled me aside. Took my hand.

"Words cannot express the sorrow I'm feeling in my heart for you and young Micah, Miss Hattie," says Doc Hickory. I politely, but firmly, took my hand back.

"Thank you, Doctor," I says.

"If there's anything you need," he adds, "please feel free to call on me anytime." Working way too hard at sounding sincere. Something he was never good at.

Fighting back a tear, I looked over at Micah. The last thing I wanted was for Hickory to see me cry.

"That's mighty kind of you," I said, avoiding his pink eyes. "But Micah and me will manage just fine. It's gonna take him awhile getting used to not having Momma near, what with him being so sensitive, but he'll come around. He's got more backbone than most people think."

With a slow shake of his head, Hickory peered into the grave. A crocodile-sad look came to his face, as if he'd lost his best friend.

"Such a huge loss," says he. "A tragedy like this oftentimes tears a family apart. And Lord knows, you two have had more than your fair share of grief this past year. I don't know what I'd do if I were in your shoes, Hattie. What with both your momma and poppa gone."

SIXTY-SEVEN

"**I** should have put an end to Doc Hickory's nonsense right then and there," said Hattie. "But I didn't. Maybe it wasn't the time or place. Maybe I was just too damn tired."

"I know this may be inappropriate, given the present circumstances," says he, "but I'd like to make you an offer. The same one I made to you and your momma when Navarrah passed away. Only considerably more, shall we say, substantial."

My first eyeball-to-eyeball with the doctor was razor sharp.

"I think you've said enough!"

"Please, hear me out," he said. "If only for Micah's sake."

After a quick glance over his shoulder at Micah, he bent close to whisper.

"May the Lord forgive my boldness, but we live in a harsh world. Now that both your parents are in the everlasting yonder, you and your dear brother will be facing harder times. Times that will sorely test your mettle."

He tried hard to look sympathetic, but any tomfool idiot could see through his snake skin.

"My words may seem harsh," he adds, "but as much as it pains me to say them, there's going to come a time in the not too distant future when you might find it difficult to make ends meet. What with both the breadwinners in your family gone."

I couldn't believe my ears. The nerve of the man! I was about to say something unladylike, but I remembered where I was. You shouldn't cuss at a funeral, so I kept my thoughts to myself.

"I don't have time to listen to this," I said, and turned away.

Not taking the hint, Hickory grabbed me by the arm.

"You've got to be realistic, Miss Sexton. Taking care of yourself will be hard enough. But you've also got a strapping young'un to feed and clothe. And with his appetite, well, that's going to be nigh unto impossible without some help."

I had half a mind to whack the son of a bitch upside the head with my cane.

But instead I said, "We'll get along just fine without any help from the likes of you. In case you haven't noticed, my young'un brother is stronger than any two men, including those lamebrain goons you got on your payroll. I have no doubt Micah will carry whatever load the future has in store for him."

Hickory must have seen the fire in my eyes, because he stepped back. Clasped his hands to his chest, preacher-like.

"I hear what you're saying, Hattie, but there's no sense in making it hard on him. Think of the strain you'll be putting on the young man's mind. First his poppa, now this. It could be so much easier for him. I'm willing to pay you handsomely for, let's say, future considerations. Considerations that will have absolutely no effect on Micah during his lifetime. Or yours, for that matter."

I'd heard enough. I stepped forward to point a finger right between his beady little eyes.

"Stop right there! Not another word! I know what you want, and it has nothing to do with helping either of us. You're no good Samaritan. And certainly not a well-meaning neighbor. You're a greedy little man who wants Micah's bones for his damn collection!"

I'd lost my temper. Something I told myself I would never do. Especially not at Momma's funeral. But once I get my hackles up, there's no holding me back. I spat on the ground. Raised my cane high over my head. Ready to strike that poor excuse for a human being dead on the spot.

"Shame on you, Doctor Abel Hickory!" I growled. "And curse that tar pit you call a heart!"

SIXTY-EIGHT

"My outburst stopped the doc in his tracks," said Hattie. "Fear swimming from his eyes, he looked around to see if anyone heard my outburst. Especially Micah. Who could've torn Hickory in half."

"My apologies, Hattie," said the doc, both hands raised. "I can see I've upset you. This probably isn't the time or place to discuss Micah's future with you. Again, my condolences for your loss. We can talk later."

"Not if I have a say-so in the matter!" says I.

And off he hurried, like the singed rat that he was.

Hearing the commotion, Reverend Yass came over. Jabbed a thumb toward Hickory's rapidly departing backside.

"Has the doc been bothering you, Hattie?"

"That man won't leave us alone, Reverend. He's been after my brother since the day Micah was born. Every time Micah sees him coming, he gets all wound up inside. Sets him off his feed something fierce. I wish there was something I could do. Doc's got him scared half to death."

The reverend followed the black buggy with his eyes until it turned out of the graveyard. The frown on his face told me he was thinking un-reverend-like thoughts. Much like I was contemplating.

"Most of us on this side of the ridge feel the same way, Hattie," he says. "It ain't no secret that the doc's been collecting bones, or how he goes about it. But he's got some powerful men in those deep pockets of his. Including our sheriff."

"He's bought out the sheriff?"

"Lock, stock, and barrel, I'm afraid. How else can he get away with those midnight raids of his? As sure as I'm standing here, he pays the sheriff to look the other way. May the good Lord forgive me for saying this, but if ever there was a man who needs some serious redirection, it's Abel Hickory."

The reverend looked over at my brother. Bunched in Micah's left hand was Momma's shawl. In his right were two shiny, silver-green stones.

"What you got there, Micah?" asked the reverend.

Micah nodded at the mound of dirt besides Momma's grave, where two workers were still shoveling. Then held out his hand.

"Just these two pretty pebbles. I took them off Momma's ground. They remind me of her eyes. Um, has Doc Hickory been at it again, Hattie?"

I took his hand in mine. Cupped my fingers around the two stones. They felt both cool and hot to the touch at the same time.

"Don't you worry yourself none, Micah," I said. "Come need be, I'll take care of the doc."

Micah gave my hand a gentle squeeze. With his other hand, he rubbed Momma's shawl against his cheek. Looked down at the green stones. Let out a soft sigh.

"It ain't gonna be much of a Christmas, now that both Momma and Poppa are gone."

I put my arm around his waist. Dug down deep to find a stiff upper lip.

"We'll make our own Christmas this year, Micah. Just you and me."

Knock, knock.

"You and me," he says. "I guess that's all we got left now." He looked at Momma's grave. Then up toward the ridge. "Promise me you won't let the doc come around no more, Hattie."

"I give you my solemn word," says I.

Knock, knock, knock.

SIXTY-NINE

*K*nock, knock, KNOCK!
And back to the present Hattie and I both went. Someone was knocking at the cabin door.

Exasperated at having her story interrupted again, she puffed out a sigh.

"Land sakes!" she said. "It's getting to be a regular Grand Central Station around here. At this rate I won't finish my yarn before midnight. And that means you might miss your flight back to Boston, Mr. John March."

The last thing on my mind at that point was missing any plane. No matter where it might be going. In fact, I'd forgotten about all things Boston. My boss, my deadline, and even my family.

At the door stood another grand lady. Just another in a long list of surprises today. Nowhere near as old as Hattie, maybe in her late eighties, but, and I kid you not, she wasn't wearing a stitch of clothing. Nada! Zip, squat, diddley!

To top it off, she was covered from head to toe in what looked to be plastic wrap. After the sombrero-wearing lawn mower man and a slowly dissipating Goin brother, I shouldn't have been shocked. But I was. Hattie, however, took the woman's nakedness in stride. Plastic wrap or not, she seemed to be glad to see the visitor.

"Florence Hogjaw!" she exclaimed. "What a pleasant surprise. Come on in!"

Without a hint of self-consciousness, Her Nakedness gave me the quick once-over.

"I don't want to intrude," said she. "I see you've got company."

She then nodded toward the swaybacked horse she'd tied to the front porch. A glue-factory reject, its belly sagged to within a foot of the ground.

"Ol' Cervantes has been dragging his prance again, Hattie. And I was hoping you might have some more of that elixir left. The kind you mixed up for him last time. Worked like a charm, it did. Put some real pep back into his step. Mine, too." Wink, wink. "If you catch my drift."

Hattie pulled at her chin. Gave the nag a critical eye.

"He does seem a mite under the weather, Flo. Probably something from your back forty didn't agree with him. As it just so happens, I do have a leftover batch in the back. Give me a minute, and I'll fetch it for you."

While Hattie was gone, I couldn't keep my eyes off the woman. It's not every day you come across a naked octogenarian. Missus Hogjaw shot me another wink. When she smiled, she revealed three yellow and crooked teeth. The only teeth in her mouth.

"Like what you see, Sonny?" she said. "Come closer. I won't bite."

I dropped my eyes. Blushed a beet red.

"Sorry. I didn't mean to be rude. It's just that I never . . ."

Never what? I thought. *Never made a bigger fool of myself?*

Coming to my rescue, Hattie returned with an open jar filled with a dark-brown fluid. It smelled worse than it looked.

"Here you are, Flo," she said, tightening the lid. "Give Cervantes half with his feed in the morning. The other half when you bed him down for the night. That should do the trick. If you want to take a snort for yourself again, you might want to water it down a bit. Too much of the stuff can play tricks on your mind."

"Much obliged, Hattie," said Flo.

Looking over her shoulder at me, Flo bent down to whisper in Hattie's ear.

"He's kinda cute," she said. "Wanna share?"

Hattie rolled her eye. Then laughed from the belly.

"Later, maybe. At the moment, I'm in the middle of telling him my story."

Blushing even hotter, I watched Flo mount Cervantes sidesaddle. After gathering her long hair to one side, she nodded down to Hattie. Then urged her trusty steed forward. A gentle giddyap, and he plodded off at a ridiculous trot, his belly swaying back and forth. I'd seen dog food in better shape.

Chuckling softly, Hattie waved her goodbyes. Shut the door, then took her seat. After smoothing out her skirt, she turned to me.

"Now, where were we?" she said. Seemingly prepared to ignore the confused expression on my face.

"Um, that woman was naked as a jaybird!" I said.

"Nothing unusual in that," said Hattie. "Granny Hogjaw's always naked. Has been that way ever since that box of sweets showed up in the mail, special delivery ten years ago."

At a loss for words, I found myself staring again. This time at the door.

"Sweets?" I managed.

"Godiva chocolates they was," said Hattie. "Most expensive chocolates you can buy, I'm told. They were sent to the wrong address, but there was no telling Florence that. First express mail she'd ever received. She thought they were from her long-dead husband. Flo took the name to heart and hasn't worn a stitch of clothing since."

Some distance in her eyes, Hattie pulled at an ear. Smiled as she remembered.

"Folks around these parts took a while getting used to Flo's, er, lack of clothing. But now we don't pay her no never-you-mind."

"Godiva chocolates?" I said. "But she was covered with at least five yards of plastic wrap."

"Nothing odd in the plastic wrap," said Hattie. "It gets a bit nippy when you're buck naked, even in the summertime. A few years back, some smart-ass nicknamed Flo 'the Queen of Saran.' Not to her face, of course. She may be getting up in years, but she still packs a mean wallop in that riding crop of hers. And Cervantes has been known to take a nip out of anyone who looks at her sideways."

Florence Hogjaw was at least fifty years younger than Hattie, and yet she'd referred to the woman as "getting up in years." I guess when it comes to aging, perspective is key. To keep from smiling, I shuddered instead.

"In nothing but plastic wrap? I'd hate to see what Flo looks like in the dead of winter."

Hattie raised an eyebrow. Smiled herself.

"It's not a pretty sight. I can assure you that."

SEVENTY

"**S**peaking of odd, er, eccentric characters," I said, "that reminds me of a question I wanted to ask you. Several years back, *TIME* sent a reporter here to do a story on you and your people."

A look of recognition on her face, Hattie cupped her chin.

"So, that was you folks?"

"You remember him?"

"Remember him? Hell! I was the one who shot him. Feisty, loud-mouthed bantam rooster with a mushed-in face?"

"That's Bulldog alright. I take it you didn't welcome him with open arms."

Hattie slapped her thigh. Chuckled.

"I peppered his backside, if that's what you're getting at. Kinda unneighborly of me, but he was too pushy for my tastes. Said he wanted to hear what I had to say but never shut up. I couldn't get a word in edgewise. What kind of reporting is that?"

Her description of Bulldog was spot-on.

"Bulldog can be like that," I said, "especially after a few beers. He showed me his scar at a bar late one night. Said he almost bled to death from it."

"I think he must have been funnin' with you, John. Nobody dies from bird shot. It may dimple your butt cheeks a bit, but a few hen pecks with the tweezers, and you're good to go. Just shows how some folks can get the story wrong. Hate to say it, but your friend seems better at making up stories than reporting them."

"I wouldn't call Bulldog a friend, exactly. More like a tolerated acquaintance. He was a hell of a reporter, one that usually never let go of a juicy lead. But he was also known to exaggerate now and then. Especially when he had one too many."

I switched my recorder back on. Pushed it closer to Hattie.

"Sorry for the interruption. I'll hold off on the questions until you're finished."

Hattie raised a finger. Opened the door again.

"Before I pick up on my yarn, I'd better make sure we're not further disturbed."

She let out a shrill whistle, and Virgil, the mastiff, bounded up the steps. Panting eagerly, his bright eyes quickly fixated on his master. He barked twice as if to say, "Here I am," then plopped down on his haunches. A puddle of drool formed between his massive front paws. Hattie scritched him between his ears, and his tail pounded out a backbeat. It sounded like ten pounds of sausage slapping the floorboards.

"Good boy," said Hattie. "I got a chore for you, Virgil. Think you can handle it?"

Virgil's response was two strong tail thumps. Translation: "You bet I can!"

"Park yourself at the top of our porch steps. I want to make sure my guest and I aren't disturbed again. Come hell or high water, don't let anyone near our front door."

I swear that dog did a perfect Scooby Doo imitation. "Yeah, yeah, yeah!" he seemed to chuff.

Hattie cupped Virgil's jowls in both hands. Looked him long in the eye.

"Anyone gives you trouble, you have my permission to take a chunk out of his leg." She winked, then kissed him on the nose. "On second thought, better make that a nip instead of a chunk."

Virgil sneezed twice. Nodded, then pranced over to the steps, a determined look in his eyes. He circled twice and plopped down with a grunt. Facing the woods, he let out a slow, rumbling growl, on official guard duty now. He looked back over his broad shoulders at Hattie. "Have no fear, Virgil is here," he seemed to be telling her.

"That's some watchdog you got there," I said.

"Best in the business," said Hattie. "You can rest assured we won't be interrupted again. People see him sitting on the porch, they know not to bother me."

For the umpteenth time that day, Hattie smoothed out her skirt, set aside her cane, and returned to her rocking. I was getting familiar with the routine.

"Anyhow," she said, "back to Micah's tale."

Looking out the window, she turned thoughtful. I noticed that Doc Holliday and Ocho had also resumed their positions.

"As you can well imagine," began Hattie, "Doc Hickory was none too pleased with me."

And once more I was transported back to the turn of a century, over a hundred years ago.

SEVENTY-ONE

A rattlesnake named after a gunslinging dentist, the biggest, hairiest arachnid this side of Knoxville, and a citified reporter a long, long way from Fenway Park—and totally out of his element. All three of us leaned forward to once more hang on Hattie's every word.

"I'd rode to Hickory's place just that once," said Hattie, "but that was more than enough to keep me from ever wanting to go back. Raven's Lair, he called it. Black as pitch from weathering too many winters, it was a huge, festering sore, something like a bottomless pit you might fall into after wandering around a week lost in the forest, half-starved and mindless. Rusted iron fence out front, dead vines on the chimney, stuffed animals in the windows, it gave me the creeps. Hickory inherited the land and the home from his father, along with two coal mines on the other side of the mountain."

Rumor has it he got tired of waiting for the family fortune to legally fall into his hands, so he pushed the old man down a mine shaft one night. Some say the senior Hickory ended up in his son's bone collection, kept away from prying eyes in a back closet on the second floor. Those foolhardy enough to venture close to the Lair swore they could hear Daddy's ghost roaming the grounds. Supposedly looking for his body.

Nobody ever called Hickory to task about offing his father, but he never out-and-out denied it. Probably kept the rumors alive to keep people away from his place. The doc didn't cotton much to visitors. Or to his few patients, either. When Yowler Cabb complained about the crooked way his broken arm was healing, Hickory sloughed him off. Said if Yowler didn't like the way he was doctorin', he could take his business elsewhere. Yowler was kind of crabby himself. Lived all by himself, the other side of Hognose Hollow.

Trouble was, there weren't too many "elsewhere" doctors in these hills. So, for the rest of his life, poor Yowler was saddled with an arm that was bent in places it shouldn't have been. Kinda like me and my backbone.

Although I'd never gotten past the front door when I went to fetch the doc, I knew the Lair was even more spooky on the inside. My feathered friends kept close tabs on Hickory through the windows. They saw firsthand what was going on in that workshop of his, where he worked on his collection. They told me what he did in there.

They was watching one night when his two bumblers returned from one of his midnight errands. Hawks and crows got good eyes, a hundred times better than we humans, and they didn't miss a thing. They saw Hickory standing at the back door, watching Nosmo and Dewey struggling to unload a wagon an hour or so before daybreak.

"If'n you drop that bundle," said the doc, rapping Dewey across the shoulders with his cane, "I'll skin your worthless hide. Put it over there on that workbench. And be quick about it!"

Hung over the bench was a small oil lantern, the only light in the room. As I said, Hickory's eyes were pink and sensitive. He liked keeping things in the dark.

Sweating like stuck pigs, the Butt brothers were having a rough time with that bundle. Not the most coordinated human beings on the planet. When one pushed, the other pulled. After several tries, they finally managed that bundle up and onto the bench.

"Are you sure you weren't followed?" asks the doc.

Exhausted and out of breath, Nosmo leaned against the bench. Took a few deep breaths. Stick thin and with a weak back, he was never much in the strength department.

"I kept looking over my shoulder all the way back," says he, "and I never saw nobody."

Twice as strong as his brother but half as smart, Dewey only nodded. His clothes were covered with dirt and his face smudged up. He was always a mess, but that night he was messier than usual.

"Have any trouble at the graveyard?" asked Hickory.

"Except for Dewey tumbling headfirst into the grave," said Nosmo, "things went slicker'n silk."

"Did you do as I asked?"

"We sure did. We put that dead raccoon and those heavy rocks into the coffin after we took the body out. Then covered the hole back up with dirt. I get that the rocks was for weight, but what was the raccoon for?"

"For the smell, stupid. Rocks don't stink. Someone comes nosing around, they're gonna be suspicious if the grave don't stink a bit. You sure you two yahoos got the right one this time?"

On two prior occasions, the Butt brothers had brought back the wrong body. And there'd been hell to pay.

"This time I double-checked," said Nosmo.

"You better have," said the doc.

SEVENTY-TWO

Doc Hickory pulled aside a corner of the blanket to make sure, revealing the body of a small child with a monstrous head. All four of Doc's gold front teeth glittered in his serpent smile.

"That's the Babblejack girl, alright," he said. "Good thing, too. Or your asses would have been grass."

A pinched look overtook Nosmo's face. Dewey, he of the weaker stomach, had to turn away.

"She's not a very pretty sight," said Nosmo. He may not have been much as human beings go, but unlike Hickory, somewhere deep down he must have had the remnants of a heart. A heart that sometimes skipped a beat at the things he was forced to do.

Hickory poked at the dead girl's abdomen with a bony finger.

"On the contrary, Nosmo," he said. "Miss Babblejack here is actually quite beautiful. Just ripe enough. She's perfect for my collection."

Next to one wall stood a huge tin vat—over six feet long, at least three feet wide, and over two feet deep. From inside the vat came an eerie buzz-clicking sound. Hung on the wall above the vat were a variety of shiny instruments, all sharp and mean looking.

"My lovelies are going to feast well tonight," said the doc. "Come morning, little Anna will be as shiny as a brand-new silver dollar."

After rolling up his sleeves, he pulled a scalpel from under the bench. Began to cut away the young girl's clothes. As he did, a putrefied smell swirled around the room. Nosmo blanched. Covering his mouth with both hands, Dewey gagged, his face turning a pale shade of green. When Hickory was finished, the last of poor Anna's clothing lay in a heap on the floor.

"That should do it," he said. "She's ready now."

"I hate this p-p-p-part," Dewey whispered to his brother. Dewey also had trouble with his *P*s.

"Well," grumbled Hickory, "what are you two slack-abouts waiting for? Put her in the vat!"

The two brothers inched forward to take up positions at each end of the bench. Then, ever so slowly, they grabbed the corners of the blanket wrapped around Anna. Hickory waved his hands to stop them.

"No, no! Without the blanket! You don't know where it's been. My hungry friends have delicate constitutions."

After removing the blanket, a shuddering Dewey grabbed the girl's ankles. Nosmo grabbed her shoulders. By that time, the stench was so bad they had to hold their breaths. Arms extended and heads turned away, they hustled the body toward the vat.

"Careful, you idiots!" shouted Hickory. "Damage a single hair on her head, and I'll dock you a week's pay!"

Into the vat went Anna's body. The buzzing intensified, and before Dewey was able to let loose of her ankles, a single black beetle ran up his arm. Bleating like a terrified lamb, he raised a hand to smash the huge insect and was whacked on the shin by Hickory's cane.

"Don't you dare!" says the doc. "Hurt him and it will be your turn in the vat."

Dewey turned white as a just-washed dinner plate. His knees began to knock together. Then he wet himself. Hickory picked the beetle off Dewey's arm with two fingers. The size of a large man's thumb, the bug seemed to relax in his grasp, as if it knew it was in good hands.

"There, there, my little coleoptera," said the doc. "Did the clumsy fat man frighten you?"

For a second, it looked as if Hickory was going to kiss the disgusting thing on the lips. As if beetles had lips.

"Back you go," says he. Then lowered it into the vat.

Both Butts backed all the way to the far wall. Nosmo looked as if he'd bitten into a lemon. Dewey was clutching his wet crotch, mumbling the Lord's name. In vain, I might add.

When Hickory turned, he noticed the yellow puddle on the floor. He pounded his cane, disgust on his face.

"That mess better be cleaned up by the time I get back!"

With that, he stormed off into the house. Slamming the door behind him.

SEVENTY-THREE

"**F**or nigh unto six years," continued Hattie, "I kept my word. With a little bit of luck and a smidgeon of ginger, I made sure Micah never crossed paths with Doc Hickory. It took the help of all my forest friends, but somehow we managed it. Finally, Micah was in his sixteenth year. Close to shadowing eight feet, he was pretty near the biggest thing to walk the woods."

One day, on a Saturday, I think, he was down on the grassy knoll just this side of Parson's meadow, talking with two of his animal buddies. I know because they told me. Animals are the truest friends you can have in this world, but they ain't much for keeping secrets. If'n I remember correctly, it was a young black bear and a full-grown raccoon he was talking to. As always, Micah was sitting cross-legged, with Momma's shawl draped across his lap, her two shiny green stones nestled in a crease.

"Look, fellers," he says to them, "I know Ol' Man Whizzlehut's trash is mighty enticing. Downright scrumptious, you're probably thinking. But from now on, it's off limits to both of you. A little bird told me he's plumb run out of patience with your midnight raids. Madder'n a wet hen at egg-laying time, in fact. And your tramping through his poke patch was the final straw. Very next day he went out and bought himself a brand-new shotgun. A twelve-gauge is a wicked piece of work. Blow a barn-size hole in you quicker'n you can spit."

Hearing those words, the bear pawed the air. Let out a half whimper, half groan. The raccoon began to chitter up a storm.

"My feelings exactly." Micah nodded. "And for certain Mr.

Whizzlehut didn't buy a bodacious gun like that to plink no tin cans. I'm here to tell you he's aiming to nail your pelts to his outhouse wall. He's a crack shot, and his wife's just as good. If not better."

Micah paused for a second or two. Then turned real serious. Put on his most understanding face.

"Now, I know how much you two love to snoot around in their garbage. Especially when Mrs. Whizzlehut gets to baking. Lord knows I'm kinda partial to her apple pies myself. But for your own good, I'm asking you to steer clear of their place. At least until things calm down a bit."

Both critters hung their heads. To give up their midnight raids was asking a lot. They dearly loved what the Whizzlehuts threw away. It was like asking a kid to give up chocolate chip cookies. Seeing them hesitate, Micah sighed.

"Tell you what," he says. "Anytime you get the urge for some after-hours snacking, you come by our place. Me and Hattie will fix up something special for you. It might not be as tasty as one of Mrs. Whizzlehut's apple pies, but it'll stick to your ribs right nicely. And you won't have to stare down the barrel of no shotgun. Who knows? Now and then Hattie might even see fit to whip up an apple pie or two for you on her own."

His deal on the table, Micah leaned forward, a giant smile on his face.

"How about it?" says he. "We got ourselves a deal?"

The bear wiggled his nose. Let out an excited snort. The raccoon jumped up and down. The deal signed, sealed, and delivered, Micah slapped his thighs. Nodded twice.

"Alright then! My nose tells me Hattie's putting dinner on the table. Remember, now, you two gave me your solemn word, and I'll be holding you to it. If I hear you been messing with the Whizzlehuts' garbage again, I'll be roundly upset. Might even have to do something . . . drastic."

Big bad bears and wily raccoons aren't supposed to look sheepish.

It's not in their nature. But those two did a pretty good job of it.

"Okay," says Micah, "off with you two. And give my best to your families."

SEVENTY-FOUR

"As big as my brother was," noted Hattie, "his heart was even bigger."

—⊶—⊰—

That night at the dinner table, I noticed something downright disturbing. When Micah stuck out his arm to hold hands for the grace giving, I saw two purple bruises on his inner forearm, halfway between his elbow and his wrist. Each was the size of a small punkin'. Yellow around the edges and mottled at the center, they were nasty-looking things. Made me wonder why I hadn't seen them before.

After crossing himself, Micah noticed me staring.

"This is the first I've noticed those bruises," I said. "How long have they been there?"

Micah covered up his arm. Looked away. He never liked to make a fuss about being hurt or sickly.

"A week," he says. "Maybe two."

"How'd they come about?" I asks.

"I tripped in the forest. Banged my arm on a stump. You know how clumsy I can sometimes be. Just like Poppa always was."

I knew he was hiding something. Micah was nimble as a cat. He never tripped on anything.

"They hurt a bit at first," he added. "But not anymore."

"You've had those bruises for two weeks, and you didn't tell me?"

Always with the big appetite, Micah reached for the mashed potatoes.

"I didn't want to worry you none, Hattie. Besides, they were a lot bigger last week. Um, could you pass the fried chicken, please? I sure am powerfully hungry."

"How much bigger?" I asks.

"An inch, maybe."

I pulled his sleeve up to take another look.

"They still look pretty big to me. And their dark color tells me they ain't gonna be quick in saying their goodbyes."

His mouth full of fried chicken, Micah offered up what he probably hoped was an appeasing smile.

"There's nothing to worry about, Hattie. They are getting smaller, I swear. And I promise you, I'll be more careful. Could you pass me the biscuits, please? They sure look tasty."

Eventually, the bruises did go away, but they took their good time in the going. A whole month, if I recollect right. And it wasn't the last purpling I saw on Micah. During the next year, the bruises came more often. Lasted longer each time. And they sure as hell didn't come from no tripping in the forest. I watched my brother like a hawk the rest of the year, and not once did I see him trip on anything.

By the time I figured out what was really wrong, it was too late. That's the way cancer works. Eating at you from the inside. Taking its time while you go about your business all fat, dumb, and happy.

I guess I was just fooling myself. Maybe deep down I didn't want to know. That maybe the cancer would go away by itself. But once the big *C*'s got you in its clutches, it's not about to let you go. Not much I could have done about it anyway. I just wish it had been me and not Micah. Wishes and fishes, they all swim upstream in the end.

Well, by nineteen Micah was full grown. At a hair's breadth under eight feet tall, he was quite a sight. Taller'n some young trees. For all I know, he could have been the biggest human being in these United States. Maybe the entire world.

Sometimes I'd find people—and not just mountain folks, mind you—standing outside our fence, trying to catch a glimpse of my brother. One day I even had a carny man knock on our door. He wanted to pay us a goodly sum to have Micah sit in his sideshow tent for a few hours each day. The nerve of the man!

Of course, I shooed him off. My little brother wasn't gonna end up in no freak show. Not while I was still drawing breath. Bless his heart, through it all Micah was good natured about the attention. Whenever he was up to it, he'd give the lookie-loo's a wave and smile. There wasn't a mean bone in that boy's body. Too bad he never lived to see his twentieth birthday.

Nineteen and twenty it was, the year President Wilson thought up that League of Nations nonsense. Sitting a bunch of palm-pressers around a table is never a good idea. About as worthless as teats on a bull. Hell, those mealymouths in that so-called League didn't even speak the same language. On the plus side, we women got the vote that year. As if it did us much good. The lamebrains in Washington also voted the country dry. So, liquor became illegal. For some folks, that is.

SEVENTY-FIVE

"**I**t was late October that year, a Saturday again," said Hattie. "Then again, it might have been a Sunday. The morning broke sunny and bright, with a crisp, nose-nipping feel in the air. The few stubborn leaves still hanging to their chilled branches were being rattled around by a kick-up breeze from the north. That meant winter wasn't far off. Another week or so, and a white slumber from above would cover the ground. I could feel it coming in my bones. And my bones never lied."

Against my better judgment, I let Micah come with me down to the store in Mulberry Gap. It had been two months since I'd gone shopping, and our pantry was looking on the middlin' to sparse side. Lately my brother's get-along had been slowing down. He hunched over a lot and tended to limp, his eyes sometimes pinched in pain. Mostly when he thought I wasn't looking. Mind you, he never complained, but I could tell he was not well. And getting worse. His skin had taken on a pale shade of gray. Weathered looking, like our front porch. His face seemed drawn, and he was always short of breath.

I told him I could make the trip all by my lonesome, that I could handle the shopping, but he begged to come along. Said he needed a breath of fresh air. I should have put my foot down and told him to stay home. But when he laid those puppy-dog eyes on me, I always turned to mush. By the time we reached the Mercantile, however, he didn't look so good. His wheezing had gotten worse, and his face was sunken, kinda yellow-like.

"I knew this was a bad idea, Micah," says I when we arrived. "This cold weather can't be good for you."

"Give me a second to catch my breath," says he. "My pipes are a bit chilled, that's all."

"You should be home in bed, where it's warm."

Micah tried to sit up straight, and I could tell it pained him. Still, he managed a wink.

"Being stuck inside so long, I've developed a serious case of cabin fever," he said. "A person can go stir crazy cooped up all the time."

"But if'n you'd just—"

"If if'ns and buts were sweets and nuts," says he, trying hard to smile, "we'd all have a Merry Christmas." To make his point, he squared his shoulders. Stood to his full height. "We're here now, so let's get on with the shopping, dear sister. No sense in jabbering over things that's already done. You know what Momma used to say about crying over spilled milk."

Micah could be rock-headed. Especially when it came to helping people. So, he climbed right down out of the buggy and headed for the store. On the third porch step, he winced and had to grab a rail. I rushed to his side.

"You've always been a stubborn whelp," says I.

"And I probably always will be," he said, pushing out a laugh. "I guess I come by it naturally. Runs in the family, I've been told."

Leaning against the railing, he took in a long, deep breath. Then exhaled through his mouth, something he'd been doing a lot that month. Taking his arm by the elbow, I nudged him toward the sturdier of the two rocking chairs on the store's front porch.

"Set yourself down and rest for a spell, Micah," I said. "The buggy ride must have tuckered you out."

He opened his mouth to object, but I would have none of it.

"Not another word!" says I. "You watch over the buggy while I gather our supplies. Shouldn't take me but a few minutes. You can visit with your animal friends while I'm inside. Call them if you'd like. I know they'd be eager to chat for a spell."

SEVENTY-SIX

"I knew the critters wouldn't be long in coming," Hattie confided. "They always knew where Micah was. Arguing time over, it took him a few back-and-forths, but he finally managed to set himself down, his knees jutting out at awkward angles. Size-wise, chairs never fit my brother. And he wouldn't let on, but his eyes told me it was a relief to sit again."

$\rightleftharpoons$

"Well, you might be right, Hattie," he admitted. "Maybe I'll just rest my bones a bit. And see what comes down the road."

I took off my wrap and tucked it around his knees. Then adjusted Momma's shawl around his shoulders.

"If you need anything, just give a holler," I said. "I promise I won't be long."

"Take your time," he says. "It's a beautiful day, and I'm sure there'll be lots out here to keep me busy."

His chair let out a fearful creak when he set to rocking.

"Now, don't you get too rambunctious," I said. "If that rocker collapses, you'll probably break a leg. And Lord knows you're too heavy to pick up. Heaven forbid, I'd have to shoot you on the spot."

"Shoot me like a horse?"

"Hell yes." I winked. "You're big as one. And eating like two."

But in fact, Micah had lost his appetite lately. In the past month, he'd eaten less than me. More like a bird than a horse.

"Give my regards to Br'er Raccoon when he shows up," says I. "As I'm sure he will."

Not wanting my brother to see me go teary eyed, I hustled into the store.

Going about my business inside, I kept peeking through the window to check on Micah. Sure enough, it didn't take long for half the forest to gather around him. A blue jay showed up first, then a crow. They were followed by a horned owl, who swooped down onto the porch railing with a great flapping of wings. A big one he was, too. Fine ears, perked straight up. After him came a raccoon, two rabbits, a groundhog, and a ma possum with three young'uns clutched to her belly. Sitting at Micah's feet, they were having themselves a grand old time, chirping and chittering away to beat the band.

Satisfied my brother was in good hands, I returned to my shopping. What I didn't see was the black buggy coming around the corner.

SEVENTY-SEVEN

With a flurry of rustled feathers and raised hackles, Micah's friends scattered to the four winds. Critters hated that damn black buggy even more than we Sextons did. Hickory pulled the buggy to a sliding stop in front of the porch. Then leaned forward, his gold teeth gleaming in the morning sun.

"Top of the morning to you, Micah," says he, all cheery. "It warms the cockles of my heart to see you up and about this fine autumn day."

One foot on the kickboard, he lit up his pipe, his pink, beady eyes steady on my brother. He blew out a smoke ring. Then another.

"I truly am sorry to hear about your . . . condition," he adds. "How are you feeling today?"

Micah gathered Momma's shawl tighter around his neck. Ill wind and all that.

"Better," says my brother. "Mighty kind of you to ask."

Hickory cracked a one-corner smile. Rested a hand on his cane as he blew out another smoke ring.

"That's good to hear. Your sister with you?"

Micah tried to stand, but his right foot slipped sideways a bit.

"She's inside the store, gathering groceries. If you want to talk to her—"

"Don't bother getting up, Micah," says the doc. "Actually, it's you I'd rather talk to. Just between the two of us, I'm concerned about her welfare."

Micah had a good head on his shoulders. He knew damn well Hickory was lying through his teeth. It had been years since Momma had passed, and the doc hadn't changed one damn bit.

"What do you mean by her welfare?" asks Micah.

Hickory shifted the pipe to his other hand. Slapped on a real serious look. The best he could muster up. Sucking a lungful of air through his nose, he bent forward.

"Man-to-man, Micah, there's no sense in beating around the bush. You and I are smart people. We both know you might not be around much long— Um, well, let's just say, as mere mortals, our days on this earth are limited. We're all destined to meet our maker in the end. Some quicker'n others, sad to say. But as caring human beings, we have an obligation to provide for the loved ones we leave behind."

"I couldn't agree with you more," said Micah. "And your point is?"

"Ah." The doc smiled. "I can see you're the no-nonsense type. I like that in a man."

Leaning closer, he stole a glance at the store, no doubt to make sure I wasn't listening.

"I'm worried about what will happen to Hattie if you, heaven forbid, should pass away sooner than later. It pains me to bring this up, but she's not getting any younger, you know. And given her, um, unfortunate physical condition, what with both your parents dead and in their graves, who would be left to take care of her?"

Micah tightened Momma's shawl around his neck. Went stone faced. Something he never, ever did.

"Hattie does fine all by her lonesome. Always has, always will. Done right fine by me, I might add."

"I'm sure she does," says the doc. "But what happens when she gets up in years? When her bones get to creaking and her memory starts to fade? Time takes its toll on all of us, Micah. It's a hard fact of life. Sad, but true. Lord willing and the creek don't rise, I'm sure your sister is destined to live a long and meaningful life. But will she be happy?"

The doc nodded toward the store. Folded his arms across his chest.

"And where will she get the money she needs to buy groceries? It doesn't grow on trees, my friend. I can provide all the money she could possibly need, Micah. You know how rich I am, so it's well within my means. All I'm asking in return is one little signed piece of paper. A simple piece of paper that will see to her wants for the rest of her life."

Breathing hard, Micah glanced toward the forest. Then at the store.

"I know what you're talking about, Doc. And Hattie would never sign such a thing. Never in a million years."

"She doesn't need to, my boy. You're of legal age now, so she wouldn't have to know anything about it. We could keep it between you and me. Our special agreement, so to speak. I'd keep it short and sweet, and it would cover all her future needs."

SEVENTY-EIGHT

"**I** was paying for my groceries," said Hattie, "when I saw Micah gasping for breath. That did it! I dropped my bags and rushed onto the porch and to his side."

"Get away from my brother, Doc!" I shouted. "You're upsetting him!"

I cradled Micah's chin in my hands. Brought his face close to mine.

"Look me in the eye, Micah," I said softly. "Take slow, deep breaths."

I breathed along with him. After a few seconds, he calmed down, his air coming easier. His forehead felt cold as a well-digger's backside. So I took off my scarf and wrapped it around his neck. I kissed him on the cheek, then turned to face Doc Hickory. I was so mad I was shaking. For a second, I could only glare at that snake with legs. Gritting my teeth, I hawked up a big one.

Spitting may not be ladylike, but then again, nobody ever called me a lady. At least I'm accurate. I hit him square between the eyes, I did. The way the doc squawked, you'd have thought I whacked him with a pickax. I raised my right hand to the heavens.

"As God is my witness, if you ever, *ever* come near Micah again, I'll rip your heart out and feed it to the crows!"

The doc went wide eyed. Almost fell out of his buggy.

"I-I was just being neighborly," he said in a whine.

"I know what you're doing, and I'll have none of it! Now git! Or I'll lay a spell on you this very second!"

Hickory jerked back so hard he scared his horse.

"You can't protect him forever, Hattie Sexton," he almost hissed.

"Sooner or later, your brother will be mine!"

Likely fearful that I was about to unleash the screaming beasties on him, he applied the whip. In a flash, he and his buggy were bouncing over the ridge, a bad memory on the run. Still shaking, I took a moment to calm myself, then turned to my brother.

"You ready to go home now, Micah?"

Micah looked anxiously down the road.

"Is he gone?" he asked.

"Long gone," says I. "He'll not be bothering you no more. On that you've got my solemn word."

SEVENTY-NINE

I was still madder'n a cut snake when we got home. My hands were shaking so bad I dropped a bag of flour. Busted wide open when it hit the kitchen floor. What a mess!

The nerve of that man! And him calling himself a doctor. I know the Good Book says you should turn the other cheek, but you can bet your bottom dollar the Lord didn't have Abel Hickory in mind when He wrote that bit of heavenly advice. As I was sweeping up the spilled flour, I noticed Micah standing at the back door, his ear cocked to the wind.

"You hear something out there, Micah?" I asked.

Micah raised a finger. Sniffed the wind.

"My animal friends are calling for me," says he. "They say something important has come up."

"Your friends can wait for now," I said. "You need to get yourself back to bed. It's time to rest. Warm yourself up a bit."

Micah twinkled that big smile of his at me.

"I suppose that would be the smart thing to do," he said. "Too bad I've never been what you might call the brainy type."

"You're acting like our mule," I say. "You've both got stubborn streaks a mile wide and ten feet deep. But I know there's no keeping you from your critter friends. Do me a favor, though, and keep within hollering distance. Please don't stay gone too long. And bundle up tight. I can't have you catching cold on me."

He bent down to kiss me on the forehead. Raised his right hand.

"I promise I'll be careful. You know"—he winked—"sometimes you sound a lot like Momma used to."

"At times like these, someone has to," I said.

Something must have blown into my eyes, 'cause I felt a sudden attack of the misties coming on. I turned back to my groceries. Started to bustle them away.

"You go along now," I said. "I'll have dinner ready by the time you're done jawing with your friends."

Watching him head off into the forest, a little piece of my heart dropped in my chest. My brother used to glide over the ground like a whisper on the wind. Now he looked like an old man, all hunched over, every step a pain. I knew he should have been in bed, but his friends were calling him. They needed him, and that was that. Never was a bigger heart than Micah's.

For the next hour, I busied myself in the cabin. A regular whirlwind, I plucked a chicken clean for dinner, snapped a bowl of green beans, set a pie to baking—apple, Micah's favorite—and even scrubbed the cabin floor. All to keep my mind occupied. I knew the forest was my brother's second home, but something didn't feel up to snuff. I felt it in those crooked old bones of mine.

Even though it was freezing out, I decided to hang our quilts on the line. Not that they needed it, mind you. I'd aired them out just last week. Anyhow, I was snapping the last pin in place when a familiar-looking crow swooped in to land on the line, no more than two feet from my head. It shuffled to the right to gain its balance, then bobbed up and down three times. Ruffling its feathers, it cocked its head to one side. Stared down at me with one black eye. It clacked its beak twice and let out a soft chitter, almost a coo.

"Come for a little visit, Br'er Crow?" I asked.

He bobbed two more times. Then took off with a loud flapping of wings. Left a pin feather floating in the breeze. He circled me once before heading off into the woods. Right away I knew something wasn't right.

"Wait for me!" I shouted.

I may be pint-sized and crooked in the spine, but when needs be, I can motor with the best of them. Cane in one hand and my skirts in the other, I flew through the forest as fast as my bandy little legs could carry me. In less time than it took to work up a decent sweat, I found myself standing in front of Micah's favorite meadow. His friendly place, he called it.

Tuckered out from all that running, I took a few seconds to catch my breath, hands on my knees. I cast a quick look around. About twenty yards to the right, across a patch of matted-down timothy grass and beneath a tall pine, sat my brother. His face was tilted up at the sky, as if in prayer. His legs splayed out in front of him formed a large V. A congregation of small critters had gathered motionless at his feet.

A sense of dread churned up like a storm cloud in the pit of my stomach as I made my way slowly toward him. That messenger crow sat on branch a foot above Micah, his head cocked at a downward angle, as if he was searching for something. Hush quiet, the rest of the animals didn't stir when I came close.

For the longest time, I only stood there, my heart in my throat. I'd been through it before, knew all the signs, but didn't want to believe my eyes. For the past year, I'd been dreading that very moment. Seems like every morning I'd wake up with the same prayer on my lips. "Please, God, just give me one more day with my brother." Apparently, that day God saw fit not to hear my plea.

With a sigh, I bent down to kiss Micah's eyes closed. Never in my life had I felt such a crushing loss. Not when Momma died. Not Poppa either. Overcome by sorrow, a single question popped into my mind.

"Why so soon, Lord? Why take someone so sweet, so kind, so quickly?"

For the second time in my life, the Lord had no answer for me. The first time had concerned my affliction. And He'd eventually given me the strength to live with that. But this? If the Almighty could turn His back on someone as good as my Micah, what hope was there for the rest of us?

My dear, sweet brother was dead. And that vile serpent of a man, Doctor Abel Hickory, was still alive. Walking around free as a bird. It didn't make no sense to me. Still doesn't.

Never again would I feel so alone, so helpless. Doubt raised its ugly head, and a curse began to ferment in my broken heart. But before I could utter something unthinkable, blasphemous even, that crow let out a wailing caw. Thankfully, it brought me back to what was left of my senses.

I struggled to stand. For a minute, maybe a year, I stared up at that crow, a dumbified look on my face. That crow stared back at me for a few seconds. Ruffled his feathers as he let out a mournful cry. Then it dawned on me.

"I hear you, Br'er Crow," I said at last. "I guess it was just his time."

Hot tears on my cheek, I bent down to brush a stray lock of hair from Micah's face. The one that was always drooping down into his eyes.

"God's will, I suppose," I muttered to no one in particular. "And who am I to question His purpose?"

But try as I might, I couldn't fathom a reason for Micah's dying so young. There hadn't been a hateful bone in that boy's body. But now there sure as hell was more than one in mine.

EIGHTY

Hattie took in a pain-filled breath. Her loss as painful today as it was a century ago. Locked her eyes on the rafters for a few seconds to gather her thoughts before maintaining her course.

"As word of Micah's death spread," she said finally, "it became something of a pilgrimage to attend his funeral. Hundreds of people from all over the state showed up to pay their respects to the giant man-child with a heart as big as all outdoors. People came who'd never even seen my brother but had heard the good word from others."

When we laid Micah to his final rest, the crowd overflowed the graveyard's rail fence, all the way down the hill and halfway to the creek. It did my heart proud to see people think so kindly of him. Granted, there were more than a few curiosity seekers in the bunch, but I didn't hold that against them. At least they were respectful about it.

Micah didn't fit into a regular casket, so we had to break two apart and nudge them back together. We buried him next to Momma and Poppa, of course. One normal-sized plot, one extra wide, now one extra long. All that remained was a small one to the right of Momma's. The one that was waiting patiently for me. The way I was feeling that day, I was sure the four of us would soon be together again beneath that there patch of grass. Sooner better than later, I might have been hoping.

Hattie looked off, a sad twist to her face. Several seconds passed before she saw fit to continue her story.

"Who'd have ever thought I'd live this long?" she said to me. "Just shows how poorly I was at calculating time. Past, present, and especially the future.

"Truth be told," she continued, "I don't remember much about Micah's service. My mind kept wandering this way and that. Back to happier times when the entire Sexton clan was alive and well. We may have been poor, but we had been happy.

"I recall Momma's and Poppa's faces around the dinner table. And Micah's, of course. Poppa reaching for the taters, Momma with her all-powerful spatula at the ready. Micah grinning up a storm. Momma laughing when she listened to Poppa's latest mishap at the still. Hearing Micah go on about one of his forest friends.

"It all seemed like yesterday. I know the Reverend Yass must have said some fine words over Micah, but for the life of me, I can't remember a single one."

Next thing I knew, the crowd was breaking up and heading home. Still in a daze, I felt the reverend's soft hand on my arm, then saw a puzzled look on his face. He nodded at the pile of cement bags off to the left, and the two workmen I had standing by with shovels.

"Do you really think all that is necessary, Hattie?" he asked.

"I don't trust Doc Hickory as far as I can throw him," I said. "And with my bad back, that ain't very far."

I motioned the workmen forward.

"I'm seeing to it that my brother rests properly in peace for all eternity," I said to the reverend. "And I sure as hell don't want Doc Hickory digging up his grave."

"I understand your concern, Hattie," he said, "but I don't think Hickory would be so foolish. They'd boil him in oil if he tried any shenanigans here. What's more, I've heard some folks are planning on patrolling the graveyard to keep his goons away."

"All well and good, Reverend. But Hickory's never been caught before. He's a tricky bastard, that one. And I'm sure he's already conjured up a blackhearted plan of some sort."

I had to look away when the workmen dumped that first load of cement into Micah's grave. It made a hollow thump when it hit his casket. As sickening a sound as I'd ever heard.

Bless his heart, Reverend Yass stayed with me for twenty minutes. Finally, he nodded at the remaining bags of cement.

"From the looks of it, this is going to take some time," says he. "Maybe we should all head on home, Hattie. Nothing's going to happen today."

"I have to make sure this is done right," I say. "I gave Micah my word that Hickory would never bother him again. Not in this life, and not in the next."

The reverend looked at his pocket watch. Then up the hill.

"I'm powerful sorry, Hattie, but I've got a commitment at the church. If there's anything you need, anything at all, you know where to find me."

"Thank you for everything, Reverend. You've been a comfort to me and Micah. I'm grateful for your kindness." I stretched up to kiss him on the cheek. "I know others are depending on you. I'll be fine."

I watched him struggle up into his buggy. The reverend's bum knee was giving him trouble that day. Leaning forward, he took off his hat and made the sign of the cross. I nodded in return, thankful for his blessing. He snapped the reins to the right, and I followed his buggy's progress until it dropped out of sight over the ridge.

My workmen took the better part of an hour to finish the job. When they were done, my brother's casket was safely wrapped in a cocoon of cement, hopefully impenetrable for any grave robber. With a sliver of relief, I took heart at the gray mound that had become Micah's final resting place.

Leaning on his shovel, one workman wiped his brow with a handkerchief.

"We're finished, Miss Hattie," says he. "There's about two tons of cement in there. That should be more than enough. Is there anything else we can do for you?"

"No, that will be all, thank you kindly." I handed over the two shiny new silver dollars I'd promised them. Fair wages for an honest day's work. "You can go now."

After they left, I just stood there, fogbound for I don't know how long. Could have been a year or two. So there was no telling when Micah's furry friends began to arrive. But there was a steady stream of them.

One by one, they made their way to the graveyard fence. The smaller animals came first. Raccoons, rabbits, squirrels, mice, birds, and the like. They was followed by several elk, a dozen or so deer, two bobcat families, and finally three full-grown bears. Even from a distance, I could feel the pain in their hearts.

One well-fed raccoon, the bravest of the lot, ducked under the fence and waddled over to Micah's grave. Nose to the newly churned dirt, he took a sniff. Jumped back, pawed the air. With a low growl, he stamped the ground, then beelined it for the woods, his tail puffed out like a hairy balloon. The rest of the animals turned and followed him in unison.

Realizing what had happened, I fell stunned to one knee. Felt all my air rushing out as if I'd been sucker punched in the gut.

"Damn it to hell!" I groaned. "I was too late. Hickory already has him."

EIGHTY-ONE

The weather turned bitter cold that night, dropping the temperature to well below freezing in some places. In wind-protected valleys, ponds crusted over with a thin sheet of ice. The few leaves left on the trees stiffened up and dropped dead away. And just like that, with a shudder and a shiver, winter was upon us.

Way up here, near the tip-top of the mountain, we call it the dying season. 'Cause all things green tend to wither away, forcing fur, feather, and claw alike to snuggle deep into their burrows and nests. But we hill folk are used to having frost barge in on us unannounced, so it came as no surprise. This side of Newman's Ridge, Old Man Winter never bothers to knock.

Unbeknownst to me at the time, however, that very same night, Nosmo and Dewey Butts were up to no good. Despite the nip in the air, both were sweating up a storm in manhandling a heavy bundle back to Doc Hickory's place. When they finally got there, it took them three grunts and a groan to haul their burden onto his back porch. Dewey sagged against the wall after setting the bundle down, panting like a steam engine.

"I got a b-bad feeling," Dewey says to his brother.

A wary eye on the whitening forest, Nosmo was breathing heavy himself.

"What else is new, Dew?" he says. "You get a bad feeling for just about everything." Puffing out a vapor cloud, he nudged the bundle with his boot. "My back is killing me! I never saw a taller drink of water. Damn hard getting a grip. Might've strained something."

Real nervous-like, Dewey glanced down the road.

"T-think anyone saw us, Nosmo?"

"Not likely. The entire town was at his funeral. Damn fools!"

"B-but what if—"

"You worry too much, brother."

Dewey tugged at one of his chins. Peered down the road again. Then into the forest.

"They say Miss Hattie's g-got eyes in the forest."

"Aw, that's nothing but a wag-tongue rumor."

"W-what about her . . . b-black magic?"

"Little good it'll do her or her brother now," said Nosmo. "You saw with your own eyes all the cement they dumped into Micah's grave. Day late and a dollar short, I tell you. Now help me with this body before it stiffens up in the cold. Doc'll have our hides if it goes brittle on us."

That's when my crow friend landed in a nearby tree, no more than twenty feet from them. He fluttered his wings, then clacked his bill three times, loud enough to wake the entire forest. Turning his head to one side, he leveled an eye at the Butts.

"S-see?" said Dewey, shaking in his boots. "I told you! Hattie sent that crow to spy on us. She knows! S-she knows!"

Nosmo scowled. Then cuffed his brother upside his head.

"Calm down, Dew. You're gonna piss yourself again. Stop being such a chucklehead. It's just a big, ugly bird."

Dewey buried his face in his hands. Turned to the wall and began to whimper. Nosmo thumped him on the head again.

"You blubbering tub of lard! It's nothing but a damn crow. It can't hurt you. Watch!"

Nosmo jumped down from the porch. Flapped his arms at the crow.

"Get out of here, you flea-bitten bag of feathers!" he shouted.

But that crow didn't budge. Not even an inch. Cocking his head back to the right, he clacked his beak three more times. Then let out a soft clucking sound. As if to mock the taller brother.

No critter, winged or not, had ever done that to Nosmo Butt before. So, it pissed him off something fierce. At first he didn't know what to do. He just stood there with his thumb up his ass. Finally, he charged forward a few steps. Waving his arms and yelling like a banshee.

"Git! You uppity son of a bitch!" he roars out.

And still, Br'er Crow didn't budge.

Frustrated, Nosmo picked up a rock and hurled it at him. Missed by a scant half foot. Expecting to be swooped down on, Nosmo covered his head with his arms. But Br'er Crow just sat there, neat as you please. Didn't even bat an eyelash. If crows had eyelashes. And a pregnant silence settled over the forest.

The taller Butt brother gulped air for a few seconds. The short one peed his pants.

Finally, that crow flapped his wings. Tilted forward to crap out a big juicy one in Nosmo's direction. Point made, his shrill caw brought the forest back to life. When a brother crow flew up to resume the vigil from a safer distance, he flew off over the ridge, disappearing behind the moon's shadow.

EIGHTY-TWO

Nosmo could only blink and stare. He eventually gulped down another big breath.

"See, Dewey?" he said. "I told you it was nothing but a mangy crow. Damn bird shows up again, he'll be facing the business end of my shotgun!"

"Is it g-gone?" asks Dewey, his face still planted to the wall.

"Gone, and forgotten," says Nosmo. "So shut up and give me a hand here. We gotta get this body inside. The doc's waiting for it."

Speak of the devil, at that point the door opened.

"What's all the commotion about?" asks Hickory. He spies the bundle. Breaks into a jig. "At last! Don't just stand there. Bring him in! Bring him in!"

The doc slammed the door behind the brothers, then double-bolted it.

"Good work, boys," he says. "There'll be something extra in your pay this month. Put him up on the workbench."

When the doc blew out one of the two oil lamps, shadows filled the room. He shuttered the only window with a loud bang, and Dewey almost dropped his end of the bundle.

"Clumsy oaf!" said Hickory. "Damage that boy any and I'll have your liver for breakfast. Lay him down gently. And stomach up."

"Don't you want him in the vat like all the others?" asks Nosmo. After counting to three, he and his brother swung that bundle onto the workbench. No easy task, given the size of my brother.

Hickory came over, laid his right hand on Micah's chest.

"Can't put him in just yet. He won't fit without some serious . . . alterations."

The doc pulled two nasty-looking knives from a drawer beneath the bench. The first was wider than a man's wrist, with a serrated blade. Straight and two feet long with an inch-wide prong at the tip, it was for cutting bones and prying them apart. The second knife was thinner, curved and shiny, a foot shorter, and sharp enough to slice through a silk scarf floating in the breeze. It could part flesh like a finely stropped razor. Cradling its shaft in one hand, Hickory admired his reflection in the blade.

"My favorite," says he. "I do my best work with this one."

When he whipped the blade back and forth, it made a whistling sound. Well aware of what it could do in the hands of their master, Dewey and Nosmo both cringed.

"Uh, Doc?" says Nosmo. "Will you be needing us anymore? Me and my brother ain't had nothing to eat all day. If it's all the same to you, we'll head to the kitchen and rustle up something. It's a fair piece back to our place, and Dewey might not make it on an empty stomach."

"What's the matter, boys? Got no gumption for what comes next?"

Hickory slid the blade down the meaty part of his palm, and a thin red line appeared. Holding his hand out, he let a few drops of blood fall to the floor. The Butts made a beeline for the door, Dewey leading the way.

"Queasy at the sight of a little blood, are you?" said Hickory. "Well, go ahead, pansies! Feed your faces! But I'll be needing your help later moving the body when I'm finished here."

Alone now, Doc moved the oil lamp closer to the bench. First he loosened the twine around the bundle. Then, ever so slowly, laid back the soiled blanket.

"Have you ever seen a more magnificent specimen?" he whispered to himself. "Time for the good doctor to operate."

The shiny knife still in his right hand, he put his left palm on Micah's belly. And in one quick motion, he began to open my brother up.

At that, Hattie stopped talking. She lowered her head. Gave out a long sigh.

"And there wasn't a damn thing I could do about it. I was still back at the graveyard."

EIGHTY-THREE

"With my heart hanging heavy in my boot heels," said Hattie, "and my mind tangled up in a rush of yesterdays, I don't know how I made it home that day. All I remember was a sea of blurry faces chin-wagging at me, probably offering more of their so-sorries and if-there's-anything-I-can-dos."

❦

I'm sure they was all well-meaning folks, but to this very day I can't recall who most of them were or a single word they said. I don't even remember getting in my buggy, much less the ride home. Going through our front door, either.

Hours later, still stone-cold dead from the neck up, I chanced a look out the kitchen window to see the full moon hovering high above the trees. I must have sat there all day in the dark, staring at the walls like a lump of clay. It wasn't like me to be so tumble-minded. In such a pity-bound state, I was no good to anyone. Not me, and especially not to Micah's memory.

Even in death I'd failed him. I'd let Abel Hickory, that snake with legs, spirit his body away right from under my nose. I didn't know when or how he did it, but I knew it was him. Who else? The doc had outsmarted not only me but the whole damn town. Probably planned it months in advance. The Butt brothers provided the muscle, no doubt, but sure as eggs is eggs, Hickory had been the brains behind it all. My worst fears had been realized. The milk had been spilled, and there was no putting it back.

But I'd be damned if I was going to let that son of a bitch keep my brother's bones. I know the Good Book says revenge is supposed to be up to God. That it's His will alone, and His alone. Ye who are without sin, or something like that. Turn the other cheek and some such nonsense.

But deep down, in my heart of hearts, I knew that just this one time, He might be willing to leave the doc and his goons to me. So I made a solemn, hope-to-die promise that if He granted me this favor, I'd never ask Him for anything again.

I prayed for a sign from above. A bolt of lightning, a sudden gust of wind, an eagle flying through the moon, a rustle of leaves—anything to let me know that the Lord was on my side. But all remained hush quiet in the forest. Not even a mouse stirred. And that was good enough for me. To my way of thinking, sometimes the Lord says a lot by not saying anything at all.

First, I'd prepare a surprise for the Butt brothers. A special concoction, strong enough to stagger a mule, one I'd only had occasion to use once before. And that had been on a sick critter to cure rabies. I wasn't persactly sure how it would affect a walking, talking human being, but I was willing to give it a try. If it didn't work to my satisfaction, I'd try something else. "If at first you don't succeed" has always been a favorite motto of mine. I'm not sure, but I think that too may come from the Bible.

I had bigger plans for Abel Hickory. A tailor-made bushwhack, one I knew he would appreciate in the end. As ye sow, so shall ye reap. That one I know for sure comes from the Bible.

From a top shelf I took down three dust-covered jars I hadn't touched in years. I pried the first open and gave it a sniff. Stunk to the high heavens it did. That meant it still had teeth. The second jar didn't smell any better. Neither did the third.

I stirred three spoonfuls of each together, then added a pinch of diced snake root, four drops of toad piss, a ground-up ratsvein leaf, and a quarter cup of calf's blood. When it turned milky, I poured the mixture into a small ironstone pot and hung it high over a low fire. Too much heat would scorch the kick out of it, and I'd end up with nothing but a blackened pot. Not enough heat, and it would simmer away, leaving behind a useless black ring.

As you can probably guess, I wasn't baking no cake.

EIGHTY-FOUR

After patting down her skirts, Hattie picked up where she left off.

❧━━❧

Conjuring up the right proper medicine is tricky business. It requires a skilled hand and a sensitive nose. And you have to take your time. And be patient. Hover over it with a loving eye, waiting for that perfect, simmering moment. One of my eyes may not see so well, but I've got all the patience in the world.

As I was finishing up, I glanced outside to see a gathering of shadows on my front porch. Micah's animal friends had come to pay their respects. And wait for my word.

"I'll be needing your help," I says to them. "You all are an important part of what I've got planned for the doc and his two stooges."

I may have been a whiz with potions and spells, but crippled up like I am, there are things I can't manage. I needed some strong backs, and I was counting on the larger critters to provide me some.

The bull elk with a full rack of antlers snorted twice. His wifemate stamped her feet. At the other end of the porch, Mr. Black Bear plopped down on his haunches, waved his right hand. Two raccoons, a pair of vixens, a bobcat and a badger, as well as several rabbits and squirrels likewise made themselves comfortable, listening real hard to what I had to say. It was a time of truce in the forest for predator and prey alike. There would be no eating on each other that night.

Two curious baby mice came close to one of the open jars, and I shooed them away. Curiosity not only kills cats; it's worrisome for mice. And all kinds of furry creatures, for that matter.

"Stay clear of that stuff, little ones," says I. "One sniff, and your bellies will turn inside out."

I filled a pan with water. Ocho's great-great-great-great-grandpappy, an eight-legged bag of curiosity himself, lowered himself for a closer look at my simmering pot. One whiff, and he skedaddled back up his thread. He was one smart spider. After a few more stirs, I gave the pot a sniff myself.

"Smells about right," says I. "Looks about right, too."

I put that pot into the pan of water, and it hissed out a cloud of steam. In a few seconds, it was cool enough to touch. I scraped the powdery white ring around the top of the pot onto a plate. Not much more than a couple of pinches. Enough for my needs. When I trailed a silver spoon through the powder, it turned black in an instant. Then I held it up to my nose.

"Smell's gone, so she's ready," I says to the mice. The closest one nodded his approval. He couldn't smell it either.

The only question was where to put it. It had to be someplace on the body, warm and moist. Somewhere the Butt brothers would never expect. Mouth? Eyes? The nose? Nope. They were all too obvious. Places too difficult to apply.

In a flash, it came to me. I grinned.

"The Butt brothers! That's it!"

I funneled the powder into a small vial and capped it real tight. Stuck it into a deep pocket, gathered my shawl, and grabbed my cane. Before heading out, I turned to my wall critters.

"You fellers watch the place while I'm gone. I have to pay Nosmo and Dewey a quick visit."

Grandpa Ocho bobbed up and down. Two of the mice cocked their heads to the right and squeaked.

"Don't worry, little ones," says I. "I'm saving the good doctor for last. Him I want to savor."

I closed the door behind me and stepped out into the cold night air. The deep breath I took invigorated me from the tip of my nose all the way down to my little toes. Never had I felt so alive.

"It's time to revenge Micah," I said to my friends on the porch. "But I won't be needing you for this first part."

EIGHTY-FIVE

The Butts lived in a cabin of rotting wood surrounded by junk, garbage, and hardening dog turds. I made sure I was upwind as I approached their outhouse. Soon as I finished laying out my little surprise, I melted back into the forest to wait them out.

It was pitch black that night. No hint of a moon. So, I wasn't worried about anyone spotting me. But I still hid behind a short bush. Little as I am, it don't take much to hide me.

I heard the brothers finishing up dinner inside the shack. They sounded like two hogs slurping from a trough. Live like pigs, eat like pigs.

I'd just settled behind that bush, real comfortable-like, when the back door opened. Nosmo stepped out, a kerosene lamp in his left hand.

"Save me some of that pie for me," he calls out to his brother. "I'll be back in a few. Got some pressing business to take care of."

Scratching his unmentionables, he stretched. Yawned. Then headed off toward their outhouse. Probably for his evening constitutional. With that uncoordinated gait of his, he looked like a stork with a bad case of the corns. As he went, he was whistling something off-key. "Dixie," I think it was. Having a tin ear myself, I could be wrong. As awkward as he looked, I almost felt sorry for the ninnyhammer. Almost, but not quite.

Disgusting slob that he was, Nosmo didn't even bother to close the crapper door. Maybe he felt no need, what with his place being so isolated. But even a dog doesn't like doing his business out in the open like that.

I tell you, it unsettled me more than a mite when he dropped his drawers. Never in my born days had I been witness to such a bony white behind. Looked like a bucket of fish guts stacked atop two thin sticks. Turned my stomach, it did.

With his pants down around his ankles, Nosmo shuffled over to the outhouse hole, bent down, and took a sniff. He jerked back. Wrinkled up his nose. Waved a hand in front of his face.

As if that's gonna do you any good, I thought.

With a shake of his head, he sat down. Scooched back and forth a couple of times to get comfy. He reached into a pocket and pulled out a postcard of some sort. Waved his hand again.

"Next week I'll have to dig us a new hole," says he. "'Cause this one's sure enough full up."

I had to squint real hard, but I could see that the postcard was one of those naughty French thingamabobs. The kind with a naked women on the back. Nosmo pawed the card with one hand, a cathouse grin on his face. I may not be no woman of the world, or wise to the ways of men, but I'm not stupid. I knew what he was doing with his other hand. It didn't surprise me none. What chance did Nosmo have of getting the real thing? No self-respecting female would ever come within ten feet of the man.

If that wasn't bad enough, he gave the postcard a long sniff.

"Mmmm," he says, all dreamy-like, his eyes rolling back. "I got something in my right hand that would make you beg for mercy, pretty lady," he adds. "And show you what a real man is like."

I had to turn away. Real man my ass. Mountain out of a molehill, I'd seen bigger willies on a baby rabbit. Holding the card up to the light, Nosmo sniffed it again. Gave the French lady a critical eye. As if he were judging a beauty contest.

"Not bad. Not bad at all," says he.

My gore on the rise, I wanted to bean the pervert with a rock. I may not have the strongest arm on the mountain, but my aim is deadly as snake spit. But patience being the virtue that it is, especially in matters of revenge, I restrained myself. Let the windbag butter his corn in front of God and creation. When his time came, I wouldn't be the one explaining his actions on earth to Saint Peter.

EIGHTY-SIX

Nosmo grunted, then let out a revolting toot, like he'd stepped on a duck. My appetite shredded for at least a week, I waited for what had to come next.

"Job ain't over until the paperwork is done," he says.

With a chuckle, he wadded up a fistful of paper. Gave his bottom a healthy wipe. Then another. Before he could go for thirds, his forehead furrowed up. He squirmed around on the seat. Clearly something didn't feel right to him back there. His eyes went real wide. He bounced up and down.

"What the hell?" he yells. "My damn ass is on fire!"

He looked down at his hands. Then over at the wiping paper. Both covered with my powder.

"What's all this white stuff?" he shouts.

A cramp doubled him over. His left hand jerked forward, knocking the lamp over. The soiled paper caught fire first. Then his French postcard. Gasping for breath, Nosmo clutched at his throat. A second gut cramp knocked him against the far wall. A third threw him to the floor. Trembling all over, he tried to scramble to his feet. He started to moan.

"Shit! Shit! Shit!!" he bellows. *Kinda appropriate*, I thought.

Another cramp sprawled him across the outhouse seat. His head jerked to the right. He gurgled out another grunt. As flames danced around his entangled legs, he turned stiff as a board and twisted over backwards with a clipped grunt. And he fell, dead-stone flat, wedging his scrawny white ass halfway down the crapper hole in the process. Not the prettiest sight I've ever seen.

All that took but thirty seconds. Much too quick by my way of thinking. Maybe I should have used three drops of toad piss instead of four.

That's when the cabin door slammed open. Alarmed by all the yelling, Dewey ran out onto the porch, his expression twenty pounds of stupid. For a several seconds he only stared at the fire engulfing the outhouse. Dewey was good at looking stupid. Did it better than anyone I knew. Then something must have jabbed him in the fanny, because he leaped off the porch without touching a single step.

"Jesus, N-Nosmo!" he bleats. "Did you knock over the lamp again? S-shouldn't flog your mule on the c-can."

Twenty feet from the outhouse, the heat stopped him dead in his tracks. Dewey began to bounce on his tippy toes.

"Nosmo!" he shouts again. "Get yourself outta there!"

Shielding his face from the flames with his jacket, he summoned up a lifetime's worth of courage and charged forward. Have to give that tub o' lard credit. I didn't think he had it in him.

Born with two left feet and all thumbs, Dewey slipped sideways on the wet floor, then tumbled face-first on top of his brother. I'm not much of a carpenter, and was never that good at math, but I'm fair to certain that if that crapper had been a two-holer, it might have been able to handle the extra poundage. Howsomever, Dewey's added weight was too much. Quicker'n you can finish a good sneeze, the floor collapsed. And in a shower of sparking splinters, both Butt brothers plunged into the muck below.

Even trapped like he was beneath Nosmo's body, Dewey might have survived had not that hole been filled to the brim. They say hindsight is twenty-twenty. If only Nosmo hadn't put off digging a new hole, he might have survived. Just goes to show you how dawdling sometimes comes at a fearful cost.

Drowning in half a year's worth of your own shit ain't the greatest way to kick a bucket. I hadn't planned on killing those two knuckleheads, but I can't say I shed a tear At any rate, it saved the town considerable bother. No way was anyone going to dig Nosmo and Dewey out from all that crap. Two birds with one stone. That sort of thing.

Watching that outhouse burn to the ground didn't give me as much satisfaction as I'd been hoping for. It also wouldn't bring Micah back. When it finally collapsed in on itself to send a hissing stream of sparks skyward, my first thought was that I'd saved somebody the price of a funeral. Eventually a mound of dirt was shoveled over the blackened pit. Later somebody placed a cheap stone over it. And that was about it for the Butt brothers. As Reverend Yass liked to say, ashes to ashes.

I was basking in the warm glow from the fire when a soft chitter made me look skyward. Br'er Crow had perched himself two branches up in the tree to my right.

"Ah, my friend," says I. "Checking up on me, are you?"

After fluffing out his feathers, he cocked his head to the left, gave what was left of the outhouse a quick once-over. Then he tilted his head to the other side, clacked his bill twice.

"I agree," I said to him. "That takes care of Nosmo and Dewey. Two down, one to go."

EIGHTY-SEVEN

"**A**fter watching the Butts' crapper go up in smoke," said Hattie, "it took me the better part of half an hour to hustle back home. Twenty minutes later, I headed off to even the score with Abel Hickory. By then it was the middle of the night, and perfect for what I had in mind for the scum-sucking doctor."

———

With my animal cohorts hiding in the forest shadows behind me, I knocked on his door. None too politely, I might add. In my mind, I gleefully pictured him all warm in his bed, snug as a bug in a rug. Then, hearing my knock, bolting out from under his quilt, a scowl on his face as he struggled to light a kerosene lamp. That image warmed the cockles of my heart, it did.

"What the devil!" I heard him shout. "It's two o'clock in the damn morning! I don't see patients in the middle of the goddamn night! Whoever you are, come back tomorrow!"

To piss him off, I knocked louder.

"Alright! Alright! Hold your horses!" said the doc. "I'm coming! I'm coming!"

I heard feet shuffling across the second floor. Then down the stairs. Heard him mumble out a string of curses. "Tomfool idiot! Crazy bastard! No-account son of a bitch!" Something like that.

When I peeked through the window, I saw a light heading for the front door. I steeled my resolve. Inhaled slow and deep. No way would I let that man get the upper hand on me again. Still grumbling beneath his breath, he fumbled with the dead bolt for a few seconds. The doc was not a happy camper.

"This better be one hell of an emergency!" growls he.

I gave the door a final rap for good measure. Full-fisted enough to rattle the hinges. I may be small, but I'm wiry.

Finished with the bolt, the doc flung the door open. Raised his lamp high to get a good look at the "tomfool idiot" making all that racket.

"Now, what's so all-fired important that it couldn't wait until tomorr—"

His words stuck in his throat when he recognized me. I was the last person he wanted to see on his porch, especially at that late hour. Even in the dim light, I saw his skin had taken on a milky sheen. Paler even than his usual sickly self.

Doc blinked twice, sucked two gasps in through his nose. Then pursed his lips into a tiny O. A look somewhere between confusion and fear stitched itself into those beady little eyes of his. His cane hand took to twitching.

Past him I saw shadows dancing down a long hallway. Hickory's place was darker than the ace of spades, just like his black heart. Dark floors, dark walls, dark ceilings seemed to stretch on forever. I chanced a quick breath and inhaled the stink of things old and dying. That's when Hickory glanced toward his workshop. A pitiful attempt at a smile revealed his four gold front teeth.

"Hattie?" says he, his voice thick and clogged with phlegm. "I never expected to see you on my doorstep this late at night. What brings you out at this ungodly hour?"

I brandished my cane high above my head like the proverbial terrible swift sword. Hickory staggered backward. Tripped on his nightshirt.

"Out of my way, defiler!" I shouted. "You know damn well why I'm here! I've come for my brother!"

Standing between me and his workshop, the doc tried to play the fool. The look on his ferret face said, "Grief's gotten to the woman. She's gone daft."

"Micah?" says he, his mouth full of canary feathers. "I don't know what you mean, Hattie. You buried him yesterday. Don't you remember?"

Having none of it, I jabbed my cane to within an eyelash of his crooked nose.

"Liar! You stole Micah from me before I could give him a proper burial. Thanks to you and your chuckleheaded hired hands, I buried a pile of rocks. Now stand aside! I know his body's here!"

"Y-you can't go into my workshop," he said, almost whined. "It's private property. Y-you're trespassing, plain and simple. I'll sick Nosmo and Dewey on you. Maybe call the sheriff."

But I was a woman possessed. Neither Doc nor his recently departed, dim-witted thugs were going to hold me at bay. And least of all, no damn paid-for sheriff.

"You can call anyone you want, but neither of your goons will be coming. Not now. Not ever."

"I'll sue!"

"It's too late for that, Doc," I said.

With that, I pushed him aside and barged through the workshop door. Two steps in, the stink knocked me sideways. Foul as week-old cat piss. My eyes watered up, and I had trouble breathing. I put a hanky to my nose and took another step forward. After my eye adjusted to the light, I made out a large human form lying on the bench in front of me. Covered by a tattered, bloodstained blanket. The skeleton was all that was left of my dear, sweet Micah. Once again, I was too late.

"My poor brother!" I wailed. "What has he done to you?"

I ran a trembling hand over Micah's powder-white skull. His jawbone had been laid to one side, leaving a hideous scream on his face. Where once swam the clearest, greenest, most loving eyes in the world, there were now two black pits. I couldn't believe that this beautiful creature had been reduced to a pile of bones.

The sight was more than my heart could bear. My head swam.

The room tilted to one side, and as my legs failed me, my cane slipped. I dropped to one knee, dizzy and sick to my stomach. When I shut my eyes, tiny flashes popped off under my eyelids. I reached for the table to steady myself, and in the process, I touched Micah's hand.

It wasn't just bone I felt. I sensed his presence, speaking to me from beyond. Giving me strength for what had to come.

EIGHTY-EIGHT

"It's alright, Hattie," said Micah's spirit. "I'm in a better place now. It wasn't your fault. You did your best. I was dying anyway."

But I knew better. It was my fault. And come hell or high water, I was going to make it up to my brother.

Just like that, my stomach calmed down. The flashing lights faded, and I could see clearly. Knew what I had to do. Strength returned to my knees, and I stood to face the doc eye-to-eye. I pointed my cane at his chest.

"Now it's your turn, Abel Hickory! Time to settle up for the evil you've done!"

His eyes darted about like a caged animal. Fear filled his face. He cried out, "Nosmo! Dewey! Get your asses in here! I need your help! *Now!*"

"Save your breath, Doc," says I. "They won't be coming. Not in your lifetime, anyway."

His second attempt at a smile was more pitiful than the first.

"Now, Hattie, I know I did wrong, stealing away Micah's body like that. But I can make it up to you. Honest to God I can."

He shot a glance toward the back door, but it had been padlocked. No escape there. He looked to the front door, the one me and my trusty cane were blocking. He couldn't get through me without losing an eye or two. Trapped he was.

"I swear on my mother's grave, Hattie," he stammered, "if I had an inkling it would cause you this much grief, I never would have done it. As God is my witness, I wouldn't have touched a hair on your brother's head."

Too late for palavering. But I didn't say a word. Encouraged by my silence, Hickory kept on flapping his gums.

"Be reasonable, Hattie. What's done is done. Powerful sorry that I am, I can't undo the past. I'll admit I wanted Micah's bones for a long time. That I was obsessed with him from the start. Possessed by the devil, even. But I'm willing to make amends."

Not a peep from me. I slitted my good eye. I've been told by some that it can shiver a man to his spine.

"I know this may sound strange," he continued, "but a part of me wanted to save Micah from death as we know it. To preserve him for future generations. Whether you know it or not, your brother was unique, a once-in-a-lifetime find. A miracle, if you will. It would have been a shame to bury him in some deep hole. I'm willing to pay you handsomely for his earthly remains. Name your price, and you'll never have to worry about anything for the rest of your life."

Hickory pondered his next words. Tried to put a concerned expression on one of his faces. Failed miserably.

"Um, in a way I was resurrecting him from the grave's everlasting darkness." He continued his foul course. "Resurrecting him so mankind could remember how special he was. When you get right down to it, what better monument could a person have?"

I couldn't believe my ears. What a load of pickled bull crap! Not only was the man evil incarnate, but he didn't have a lick of common sense. First, he hounds my brother into an untimely death. Then he steals his body out from under my nose. To top it all off, he has the gall to treat me like the town fool! I should have laughed in his face, then skewered him on the spot with my cane. Instead, I pointed a finger at him. Spat on the floor.

"Mankind?! Monument?!" I screamed. "A pox on you and your twisted words! The only thing my dear brother wanted in this life or the next was to be left in peace. To live with his beloved animal friends. Away from the prying eyes of snakes like you."

When I raised my cane to strike him, Hickory cringed. Covered his head and cowered like the spineless rat he was.

"But you wouldn't let him be," I continued. "You hounded his every step while he was alive. Never let him have a moment's peace. He never once bothered nobody, never hurt a living creature. It just wasn't in his nature. But YOU! You walking piece of cow flop! Always lurking around the corner. Spying on him. Planting the seed of fear in his innocent mind. A day didn't go by he wasn't looking over his shoulder, afraid you'd pop up around the next bend, from behind the next tree. You and your damn offers drove him to an early grave."

I lowered my cane. Pointed it at Micah's skull.

"And now, *this* abomination! Even in death you won't leave him alone. You can take your offer and choke on it. All the money in the world ain't gonna buy me off. It's revenge I've come for, and it's revenge I'll be having."

That staggered Hickory back a step. Panic in his eyes now, he glanced again at the front door.

"I-I swear I'll make this right, Hattie," he says. "And I'll see to it Micah has a proper burial. Please, just give me the chance."

"It's too late for that," says I. "It's time you paid the piper. And that would be me!"

EIGHTY-NINE

Hattie paused to look out the window. A few seconds later, she glanced up at the ceiling. Shuddered, then took two deep breaths. Shaking her head, she gathered her shawl tight around her shoulders. Then licked her lips before continuing her story.

⌁━⌁

Ever so slowly, I swung my lamp back and forth in front of Doc's eyes. Its handle made a soft clicking sound, like the ticking of a clock. I stepped forward. Softened my voice to an even drone.

"I'll be the only one making amends here, Doc. No need to worry about anything anymore. You're in my hands now."

Every fiber in his body must have been screaming, "Run, Abel! Get yourself out of there!" But he couldn't move a muscle. He was mine, and he knew it.

"W-what are you going to do?" he asks, his voice dryer than a winter leaf.

Crooking my cane over an elbow, I reached into a pocket to bring out the vial. When I held it up to the light, it glistened like iced-over snow.

"I've brought you a present," says I. "Cooked it up special, just for you, Doc. Look how it shines. Kinda pretty, don't you think?"

I set my lamp on the workbench. Popped the vial open, tapped a smidge of the white powder into my palm. When I raised my hand to within a foot of his face, his body stayed rigid with fear. With his eyes white and wide as saucers, he couldn't even blink. Tears began to stream down his face. He broke out in a sweat. Started to tremble.

"W-what are you going to do with that?" he asks.

"Don't worry," says I. "You won't feel a thing. I promise."

Ever so slowly, I brought the powder close to his eyes. He began to beg.

"Please, Hattie. Have mercy."

"I'll show you mercy, alright. The same mercy you showed my brother."

With that, I blew the powder into his eyes and stepped back.

"Sweet dreams, Doctor Hickory," I said.

Hickory blinked twice. Coughed, then sucked wind. His eyes rolled back, and the starch went out of him. A twitch or two later, he collapsed, twisting around as he fell, like a yard and a half of wet, frazzled rope. His foot jerked once, twice, then stopped. I reached down to check his pulse. Slow but steady. Just like I planned.

But the job was only half done. Now came the hard part. With his head tilted back, Hickory looked like a broken rag doll. Hard to believe something so small and pathetic could be worth anyone's hate. With his eyes pinched shut, a small glob of drool hung from one corner of his mouth. For a fleeting instant, a hint of pity flickered in my heart. One look at Micah's skeleton on the workbench and the flicker was snuffed out.

He would be getting no pity. Not from me, anyway. The Lord? That was a matter above my lot in life, and the least of my worries. I tend to worry only about the things I have control over, and the rest usually work themselves out. Just another Melungeon motto.

I retraced my steps through his house. On the front porch again, I raised my lamp to signal my critter friends.

"The deed is done," I said. "We can take my brother home now."

While the animals gathered around the porch, I went back inside to swaddle Micah's bones in Momma's best quilt, the one that won her first prize at the county fair. Double tufted, soft and warm, it still smelled like Momma. Micah always went to bed with that quilt. Couldn't fall asleep without it. I figured it was only proper to bury him in it.

"Your journey's almost over," I said to Micah. "Soon you will be properly avenged."

I couldn't believe how light he was when I picked him up. A man that big, a giant in life, and barely more than a few feathers in death. As Reverend Yass had said, "Ashes to ashes, dust to dust." Made me mindful of just how little is left when we shuffle off this mortal coil. To sleep, perchance to dream.

The writer in me was confused. Despite my promise not to, I had to interrupt.

"I'm impressed, Hattie," I said. "You know your Shakespeare."

"Hamlet's always been a favorite of mine," she said. "Can I continue now?"

"Sorry. Please do."

Hattie rocked back. Scratched an arm.

"Now, where was I?" she said. "Oh yes."

My brother reduced to a pile of bones? It was more than a loving sister should ever have to endure. My eyes filled with tears. My throat went dry. A rock-hard knot of hate in my gut, I looked to heaven for an answer. I opened my mouth to scream, but nothing came out. It wouldn't have been Micah's way.

Outside again, I put him in our buggy, then turned to my friends.

"You can bring the doc out now. But be careful. I've got big plans for Abel Hickory and don't want him dying on me just yet. Don't worry. He won't give you no trouble. Now or ever again."

On the way home, the clouds began to break. When the moon peeked around a cloud for the second time that night, the forest took on a warm glow, as if nodding its approval.

Our entourage must have been quite a sight. Me and Micah in the buggy, followed by all them critters. Leading that pack was Abel Hickory draped over the big buck elk like a sack of shucked corn. It probably looked like a procession from hell.

And for Doc Hickory, it probably was. He may not have known it just yet, but his nightmare had just begun.

NINETY

"**I** didn't sleep a wink that night," resumed Hattie. "Restless as I was, I watched the sun come up from the kitchen window. Morning's first light brought a low-lying mist that would linger past noon. Sunrise comes quicker on the mountaintop than it does down in the valley. Sorta sneaks up on you, like a bobcat on the prowl. It's the main reason shadows lollygag in the flatlands."

Anyhow, as soon as Mr. Sun blinked an eyeball over Clingman's Dome, a hiccough or two right of Newman's Ridge, I knew the day was gonna be a chilly one. Soon, shapes began to ooze out of the gloom. And since revenge is best served cold, that shadowy gloom was perfect for what I had in mind.

Despite the nip in the air, I cracked open a window. I didn't want the cabin to stuffy up. Still standing guard around the porch, my animal friends hadn't left their post all night long. They sensed the job was not yet done. Not by a long shot.

"Good morning to you all," I says to them. "I'm mighty grateful you stayed to see this through. Micah would have appreciated your patience."

The buck elk to my right snorted, then pawed the ground as if to say, "Wouldn't have missed this for the world."

A low groan from inside told me Hickory was finally coming around.

I'd strapped him to a pole in the center of my tin washtub. Secured his head tight so it wouldn't loll forward. Spit drooled from his chin. And when he tried to say something, he only babbled.

"The doc seems to be up, but not so much about," I said to my friends. "You'll have to excuse me for a moment while I tend to business. I promise I'll keep you posted on how things are going inside."

I lit up an oil lamp. Hung it from a rafter a foot above Doc's head. Flickering in a draft, it cast a ghastly hue across his face. Spending the early-morning hours hog-tied to that pole hadn't helped his pale color none.

"Good morning, Doc," I said. Turned up the lamp flame a notch. "There. That should make it easier for you to catch this morning's festivities. Hope you slept well, 'cause I've got big things planned for you. The sun's already up and it's a bit chilly outside, but it looks like it's going to be a great day. For some, that is."

Grandfather chimed six times, then ticked on.

"I don't want to spoil the surprise, but I can tell you it ain't gonna be anywhere near pretty."

Unable to move his head, Hickory could only look around with his eyes. Drawn to the loud *tick-tock* to his right, he gave Grandfather a long stare. He tried to speak but only managed a hoarse croak. He swallowed twice, his Adam's apple bobbing up and down like a duck on a pond. His mouth fell open. Fear twitched into his eyes, and he had trouble focusing. It had been a rough night for the good doctor.

"W-where am I?" he finally says, his words coming out slow and slurred. "I-is that you, H-Hattie?"

"That be my name, Abel Hickory. And you're in my cabin. My forest friends outside brought you here in the wee hours. I guess you were in no condition to remember much of anything."

Confusion melded with the fear in his eyes.

"W-why can't I m-move?"

I came closer. Waved my hand two inches in front of his nose. His eyes followed the motion, but that was about it. The sweat forming on his forehead told me that even moving his eyes took a lot out of him. No doubt about it; my special potion still had him by the short hairs.

"First and foremost," says I, "you can't move because you're wrapped tight to that post behind you. Hand and foot. I tied the knots by my lonesome, used a double sheep shank. Right passable knots they are, too. So, there's not much chance of working yourself free. Wouldn't do much good even if you could. I gave you something last night to slow you down a bit. Make you easier to handle, so to speak."

"Y-you . . . poisoned . . . m-me?" he asked.

"Not poison, persactly. More like a sleeping potion. I slipped you what some might call a mickey. A real humdinger. It knocks you off your pins for a while, but it won't kill you. If I'd have used poison, you'd be dead by now. And that would have been too easy. I got bigger plans for you, Doc."

NINETY-ONE

I pulled a hairpin from my bun. Held it in front of his nose. The doc went bug-eyed. Began to whimper.

"W-what are you going to do with that?" he asks.

"Just a little test," I say.

I jabbed him in the thigh. Looking him flush in the face, I pushed it in as deep as it would go.

"Feel that?" I asked.

"N-no, but—"

"Good, good." I nodded, pulling the pin out to examine it. Not a drop of blood. "Nice thing about this potion of mine," I said, "it deadens the body real quick. All over, too. I could cut your thumb off and you wouldn't feel a thing. Bad part, when your feeling does return, it will be too late. Now that you're all numbed up, I guess we can begin."

"B-begin? Begin what?"

"Something you should appreciate, Doc. It's one of your favorite pastimes. You'll have to excuse me for a second while I fetch two bags from the porch. They contain a special present I've gathered just for you. I'm sure you'll find it—er, them—interesting."

The doc began to wail something fierce.

"Them? J-Jesus, Hattie! What are you going to do to me?"

"Calm down, Doc," says I. "Don't go all applesauce on me. Take a deep breath. Concentrate on Grandfather over there. His ticking can be soothing to the troubled mind. Always has been for me, anyway."

With that, I left him to stew in his juices. The two bags I mentioned were on the large size, double-tied with twine so they wouldn't spill out. Even so, they were mulish and hard to grip. The way their contents were moving about, it took all my strength to manhandle them through the door.

By the time I huffed and puffed them up to Doc's tub, I'd worked up a respectable sweat. Watching my struggles, his eyes went saucers again. And when he heard the buzz coming from those bags, he began to tremble all over.

"These buggerlugs of yours are a load and a half, Doc," I says. "And a bit on the skittish side. Damn noisy, too."

Hickory opened his mouth, but all that came out was a high-pitched jibber.

I set the bags down. Wiped my brow.

"By now I'm sure these fellers are ravenous," I said. "I'm guessing they haven't been fed recently. Probably not since you fed them Micah."

I nudged one bag with my cane, and the buzzing turned louder. Angrier. Hungrier.

"Th-this is an abomination, Hattie," managed the doc. "What would the Lord say?"

"The Lord, Doc?" I said. "Every God-fearing Christian—of which I know you aren't one—knows full well there's no rage in heaven. That's why I'm revenging Micah here on earth."

NINETY-TWO

"**N**ormally I'm not stonehearted," Hattie said to me. "Most folks say I don't have an evil bone in my body. That I wouldn't hurt a fly. I have to admit, however, on that particular day, I was beginning to enjoy myself. But I digress."

"I'd sure hate to be in your shoes when I turn these critters loose, Doc. Be thankful you're still all numbed up. 'Cause you ain't gonna want to feel what comes next."

I touched a finger to his lower lip. Dry as snake molt it was.

"Land sakes, where are my manners?" I said. "I can't have you withering up on me before we get to the main course."

I wetted a towel. Dabbed it across his lower lip. Then flicked a few drops into his eyes. My potion has a tendency to dry out things somewhat. Especially the eyes, nose, and mouth. I let him have a few sips of water from a cup. Didn't let him drink his fill, which might have weakened my brew's potency.

"W-why are you d-doing this to me?" he asked.

I wiped his upper lip. Then his brow.

"The reason is in the Good Book, Doc," I told him. "Plain as day."

I picked up my trusty Bible from the shelf. Thumbed through a couple pages. Way in the back, I found what I was looking for.

"Here it is," I said. "Galatians 6:7, if I'm not mistaken. And I quote, 'for whatsoever a man soweth, that also shall he reap.'"

I set aside the cup of water and the Bible.

"Time's running short, so we best get on with it. We can't keep your darlings waiting. I'm sure by now they've worked up a powerful appetite."

It was a chore, but I finally maneuvered the first bag to the washtub's edge. I used my cane to prop it up, then untied the knot, which took some effort. Cold weather brings on my arthritis. Especially in the fingers.

"Sorry, Doc. I apologize for the delay," I said. "I might have tied this knot a bit too tight. But I had to make sure none of these fellers got loose. Better safe than sorry, I always say."

As I pulled away the last of the twine, Hickory let out another moan.

A terrible racket rose when I dumped the bag into the tub. As soon as those beetles hit metal, they skittered straight for the doc's legs. I, for one, was glad I wasn't the one hog-tied in that tub.

"That sound must be music to your ears, Doc," I said. "Kinda like Grandfather's ticking, don't you think?"

I dragged the second bag over. It turned out to be heavier than the first.

"P-please . . . don't," said the doc, his eyes now shut tight.

"Don't worry, Doc," I said. "If my potion is up to snuff, you won't feel your friends eating away at you. Even after they get to your eyes."

"H-Hattie" was all he could manage. Saying my name must have drained what was left of his mettle.

"No need to thank me for the numbing medicine," says I. "As a good Christian, it's the least I could do."

NINETY-THREE

It took me longer to empty the second bag. It was twice as heavy, and I was getting tired.

"You know, Doc, I could be wrong," says I. "But it seems as if this second batch looks hungrier than the first. You know them better than me. What's your think-so on the matter?"

Dead silence from Hickory. I bent down for a closer look. What met my eyes was not an appetizing sight, I can tell you that. Those beetles didn't take kindly to the tight space I'd put them in. Thank goodness they couldn't get a toehold on the tub's metal sides, or they'd have messed up my kitchen something fierce.

"Are they always this rambunctious, Doc?" I asked. "Something's sure got them riled up. At the rate they're going, it probably won't take them long to reach your belt buckle. Less than a day, I'm guessing." I looked over at Grandfather. "Well, I'd better make myself comfortable."

I dragged my rocker over. Then a small table for my knitting, to while away the hours. Next, I went to the kitchen to put on a pot of tea. I like tea in the morning more than coffee. It's not as bitter and still wakes me up. That done, I gathered a pillow and my shawl. Then I settled into my chair, front and center, facing Hickory.

"Don't mind me, Doc," I says. "From here on, you won't even know I'm here. But if you need anything, just give a holler."

But for the clack of my needles and the steady buzz of Hickory's beetles, a peaceful silence settled over the cabin. The doc had run out of things to say, but that was okay. So had I.

An hour passed. When I saw a beetle making its way up Doc's right leg, I leaned forward. Pulled at my chin.

"Looks like we've got ourselves an adventurous one, Doc. Little feller's probably looking for juicier stuff."

My fingers were getting tired, so I stretched them out. Cracked a few knuckles. At the rate I was going, I'd finish up my sweater about the same time the beetles got to the Doc's face. A second one started up Hickory's leg. Then a third.

"Your boys seem to be playing follow-the-leader, Doc," I says. "Sorry I had to use my washtub for this. That big vat you have in your workshop would have been quicker, but it was too heavy for me to move."

Knit one, purl two.

"They'll have to do a bit more climbing than they're used to. Insects are an adaptable lot, though. That's why they've been around so long."

Purl two, knit one.

"I see your friends like to work one layer at a time, Doc," I said. "Feeding their way from the outside in. Cleaning up after themselves as they go. I kinda admire that. Pretty soon there'll be nothing left of you but bones. Just the way you always like it."

Two fat tears made their way down Hickory's cheek.

"Land sakes, there I go again," said I, "chattering away like a schoolgirl. I can see you've got other things on your mind, Doc. From here on, I'll tend to my knitting. Keep my thoughts to myself."

NINETY-FOUR

"I spent the next eight hours knitting and rocking," explained Hattie. "Rubbernecking is never polite, so every so often I'd sneak a peek at the doc to see how he was doing. People tend to go all collywobbles when they know you're eyeballin' them, and he had enough to worry about that day."

After the first hour, he just hung there, eyes straight ahead, his face droopy as a shock of wilted lettuce. Two hours later, with the sun halfway across the afternoon sky, I noticed his tongue hanging out. I set my needles down and headed for the kitchen.

"I think I'd better fetch you some more water, Doc," says I. "Can't have you drying up on me. Not yet."

I pumped out a full glass of water. Returned to his side. Cupped his chin and trickled a swallow or two into his mouth. Parched as he was, he choked, and half of it dribbled down his chest.

"Easy does it, Doc. Take it slow and easy. Little bit at a time."

I wiped off his chin. Poured him another swallow. Wetted my fingertips, flicked a few drops into his eyes. He blinked twice. Finally, he focused on me. Sort of. The way his eyes were swimming around, I couldn't be sure. He moaned. Forced out four slow words.

"H-how . . . f-far . . . are . . . th-they?" he asks me.

I stood back to check. Those beetles had been going to town. Industrious little critters.

"Your friends are making good headway, Doc. Almost up to your waist, in fact. You probably can't feel them yet, but take my word for it, they're there. And from the looks of them, they're still hungry.

Something tells me they won't be slowing down anytime soon."

Grandfather chimed out four bells. It was turning out to be a long day for the doc. A very long day.

"Land sakes," says I. "Would you look at the time! There never seems to be enough hours in the day. I forgot I've got other things on my dance card today."

I gathered my shawl around my shoulders. Picked up a bag from the kitchen table. It wasn't heavy, so I had no trouble with it.

"Sorry, Doc. I have to leave you on your own for a bit. But I promise I won't be gone long. I wouldn't miss this next part come hell or high water."

At the door, I snuggled into my shawl. It was freezing outside. I'd come too far and didn't want to miss anything by catching my death of cold. I shifted my cane to my other hand. Waited until Hickory's eyes rolled over toward me.

"It's time to give Micah a proper burial," I said.

Maybe it was my imagination playing tricks on me, but it seemed as if Grandfather's ticking was growing louder. Or maybe the beetles had just kicked it up a notch.

My apologies made, I closed the door behind me, locked it tight. When I looked in through the window, I could see Hickory hanging there, his eyes wide, staring at the ceiling. He might have been praying, but I roundly doubt it. I can't remember ever seeing him in church. Not one single Sunday. Pity for him. If ever there was a time for a man to seek divine help through prayer, today was it.

Little good praying will do him now, though, I thought as I headed off into the forest.

NINETY-FIVE

When I got to Micah's special place, that small patch of meadow grass that he favored so, I saw a rough trench about four feet deep and eight feet long that had been gouged out by claw, hoof, and fang. A gathering of prey and predator alike were waiting for me in respectful silence, ringing that makeshift grave. This was Micah's day, and all in the wilderness this side of Newman's Ridge knew it.

Chilled by a crisp breeze, my breath whispered out white and thin as I spread out Momma's blanket. Then, one by one, I laid out Micah's bones as best I could. Into his left hand I placed the two silver-green stones he always carried. Momma's eyes. That done, I bent forward to kiss the crown of his skull.

"To guide you on your journey," I said to him.

I made the sign of the cross. Looked to the heavens. Then I bundled Micah up for the last time. From my pocket I pulled out a flat river stone. On it I had scratched a simple epitaph, the only words I thought appropriate. I cleared my throat, then read them aloud to feather and fur alike: "Brother Micah, an angel bound too soon for heaven."

I placed the stone on his right hand. When I sat back on my haunches, a stillness settled over the forest. Not a leaf stirred. Even the wind had taken pause.

"May you always rest in peace, dear brother," I said. "You're back home where you belong."

Soft though they were spoken, my words echoed from tree to tree, as if the forest was passing them along. Before they faded, a single acorn dropped from a nearby oak tree. It bounced once, then rolled into Micah's grave, coming to rest at his side. I saw no reason to remove it.

I don't know persactly how long I sat there. It could have been a few minutes. It could have been an hour.

Powerful as she is, Mother Nature is never silent for long. The wind soon remembered its gumption. Feeling the cold in my bones again, I stood to face my woodland allies. A fine snow had begun to fall, and already the treetops were dusted white, turning the forest into a living cathedral. I'm sure somewhere Micah was smiling down on us. He dearly loved the first snow of the season. I gathered my cane, bunched my shawl tighter around my neck. Nodded to the critters.

"You may cover him up now," I said.

By the time I got back to my cabin, the snow was coming down harder. An inch covered my roof. Too tired to knit anymore, I went to bed early that night. Before I did, however, I gave Doc another drink and a few swallows of broth. I didn't want him dying on me before dawn. I wanted him to see one last sunrise.

I slept like a log. Best sleep I'd had in years, in fact. I was up with the sun to check on the Doc. When I looked out the window, a winter wonderland was staring back at me. Over a foot of snow had fallen overnight. Fresh snow, virgin and white. The trees were covered with a thin layer of ice, making them sparkle in the sunlight, all colorful like a shimmering rainbow. I wished Micah was alive to see it. It was so beautiful

I couldn't say the same for Hickory. The beetles had made their way up to his mouth, a few reaching for his upper lip. I had to look away. Sensing my presence, the doc opened his eyes. He mumbled something I couldn't understand.

"What's that you say, Doc?" I asked him. "You want to see?"

I cocked my head to one side. Pondered his request.

"I don't know if that's such a good idea," I said. "There's not much of you left."

Hickory tried to take a deep breath, but only inhaled a beetle. After coughing it out, he mumbled something else. "Please" was all I could make out.

"Alright," I said. "If you insist. But don't say I didn't warn you."

I retrieved my hand mirror from the nightstand, the one with the fancy mother-of-pearl handle. Given to me by my grandmother, it was yellowed with age and cracked on one edge but could still hold a pretty picture. Depending, of course, on who was handling it. I held the mirror up to the doc's face. Ugly is as ugly does; there's no getting around that. A hideous sight met his eyes.

Most of his lower lip had been eaten away, exposing a rictus grin. His upper chest was a mass of churning insects. Several ribs lay bare, stripped clean by his ravenous cohorts in crime. When I looked closer, I saw the outline of his still-beating heart.

Hickory gasped in another bug. And choked as he tried to spit it out. His eyes rolled back in his head, and I lowered the mirror. No sense in overstaying one's welcome.

"I warned you it wouldn't be pretty," says I. "One good thing, there's not much blood spilled. I hear blood's the first thing your beetles go for. Then again, I'm sure you knew that already."

I pulled up my rocking chair. Picked up my knitting needles. I knitted one, purled two.

"With any luck," I said, "I might finish this sweater before your friends finish with you."

Half an hour and a ball of yarn later, I laid down my needles. The beetles had worked their way up to his eyes. I listened intently and heard a faint groan coming from what remained of his throat. In the only eye he had left was a plea for mercy. And again I almost felt sorry for the bastard.

"Take heart, Doc," I said. "It won't be long now. The worst is probably over."

NINETY-SIX

The batteries in my Sony picked a hell of a time to die on me. Enthralled as I was by Hattie's story, a couple of seconds passed before I noticed the blinking red light. I quickly rummaged through my pockets for the two spare DieHards I'd brought along. A seasoned reporter never goes anywhere without backups. It took me three fumble-fingered tries to snap them in.

"Sorry about that, Hattie," I said as I clicked the machine back on. Turned it toward her. "I hope I didn't break your train of thought. Please, continue."

An amused grin on her face, Hattie stopped rocking. Crossed her arms. Then looked out the window, her eyes somewhere long ago. The only sound in the cabin was the ticking of that grandfather clock. After several seconds, she turned back to me. A gleam returned to her eye, and she set to rocking again.

"There's not much more to tell, Mr. March. That was the long and short of my story. I have to give the doc credit. He lasted another hour or so. I never dreamed Hickory had that much gumption in him. At the end, his eyes rolled back in his head. He gave a little sigh, took his last breath, and finally gave up the ghost. By then the beetles had pretty much had their fill of him. Good thing, 'cause there wasn't much left of Abel Hickory. Just a few bits of skin dangling from a lot of bare bones."

I was stunned. Didn't know what to say. When Grandfather chimed out the hour, I nearly jumped out of my skin.

"Doc died about this time of day," added Hattie.

My mouth dry as sandpaper, I tried to say something but coughed instead. I pointed at my throat.

"Uh, could I trouble you for some water, Hattie?"

"Help yourself," she said. "Pump's in the kitchen."

At the sink, I poured myself a glass. Drank it down in three gulps. Poured another. Drank that down too. Then splashed some water in my face. Returning to the table, I cleared my throat. Had to muster up enough spit to speak.

"If you don't mind me asking, Hattie, what did you do with Doc's body?"

Hattie stopped her rocking. Looked out the window again. Tugged at an ear.

"I waited for another hour until his friends cleaned his bones up, all bright and shiny-like. Then I cut him down and put him away for safekeeping."

"What about the beetles?"

"I dragged my washtub out onto the porch. With all of them still in it. My bird friends waiting outside were mighty grateful for the bountiful feast I provided. Ate up all them beetles in no time flat."

"And that was it?"

"Yep. That was it."

"Nobody eventually came around looking for Hickory?"

"Nope. Why would they?"

"What about the law?" I asked. "There had to have been an investigation of some sort. Someone doesn't disappear into thin air without a few eyebrows being raised. The man was a doctor, for chrissake. Somebody had to miss him."

"Miss Abel Hickory? Not likely," said Hattie. "Oh, Constable Jenks, from down in Sneedville, did come by a week or so later. Told me the doc had gone missing and asked me if I'd seen him lately. I told him that was news to me. That he probably got himself eaten up by some wayward critters. That seemed to satisfy the constable's curiosity. When you get right down to basics, what I told him wasn't that far from the truth."

"And that was all he asked you?" I added.

"People around these parts don't like to ask me too many

questions. It ain't healthy in the long run. Besides, Constable Jenks didn't care much for the doc either."

"What about the Butt brothers? Didn't he ask about them?"

"Never even mentioned them."

At a loss for words, I scratched my head.

"To my way of thinking," continued Hattie, "and a lot of other people's too, Hickory got his just deserves, pure and simple. Nary a tear was shed on this side of the mountain. The town didn't even hold a service. Nobody would have come anyway."

Trying to make some sense out of what I'd been told over the past hours, my brain went into loop mode. And without realizing why, I felt a satisfied grin slide onto my face. I'd been privy to a cold-blooded murder more gruesome than most people could stomach. A surprisingly small part of me felt it was wrong. The rest of me wanted to jump up and down, pump my fist, and shout, "Yes!"

Deep down, I was also disappointed. Disappointed that Hattie's story had come to an end. The little kid in me wanted to hear more. I clicked off my recorder. Sat back to digest it all. It took several seconds for my reporter instincts to kick in.

"Hattie Sexton, I must tell you that was one hell of a story. Not to doubt your word or anything, but how do I know it's true? That you aren't pulling both of this city slicker's legs?"

Hattie stopped rocking. Leaned back. Another slow grin inched onto her face.

"Mr. John March, you mean you don't trust me?"

NINETY-SEVEN

"Trust isn't a working part of my profession," I said. "And in the long run, its highly impractical. A good reporter, one who doesn't want to get sued every other day, always verifies his sources. His ass would be grass if he didn't."

Hattie laughed from the belly. Slapped a thigh.

"Glad to see you're a prudent man, John. If I were in your shoes, I wouldn't trust me neither." Leaning forward, she shot a thumb toward the window. "You probably took a long, hard gander at that big oak tree out back when you arrived. The one even taller than the one next to my cabin?"

"How could I miss it? Biggest damn oak tree I ever saw."

She nodded toward the woods.

"That'd be Micah's tree. The one that came from that acorn."

The way she delivered this bombshell, so matter-of-factly, stunned me—"knocked me off my pins," as Leaton Scump would say.

"Hold on," I said. "That's a heartwarming sentiment, poetic even, but I'm afraid you'll have to do better than that, Hattie. It's a bit on the large size, but nothing special."

Hattie smiled as she bent down to grab her cane.

"I can see you're going to be hard to convince," she said. "A doubting Thomas, as the Bible hints at." She pulled a key from her pocket. Headed for the grandfather clock. "Well, if it's more proof you want, then more proof you shall have."

Stretching as high as her twisted body would allow, she unlocked a compartment below the clock's face and ever so gingerly extracted a round object wrapped in a small quilt. She relocked the compartment and returned to the kitchen. After placing the bundle on the table in front of me, she sat. Began to rock again.

"Go ahead," she said. "Have a look. That should be enough proof for anyone."

The stupid expression I'd mastered over the past day returned. I didn't know what to do. At first I only stared at the bundle. Hattie let me stew for a minute, then nodded.

"Don't be shy, Mr. March. I'm sure you're curious. Forget about all the dead cats in this prying world. Open it."

I reached out, my hands shaking like leaves, and slowly unwrapped the quilt. When I pulled it aside, a jolt shot up my spine.

"H-holy shit!" I stammered. "It's a damn skull!"

"Yep," said Hattie. "That it be."

A sudden frost swept through the cabin. Despite the chill, a trickle of sweat oozed down my forehead. My heart began to thump in two-four time. I felt dizzy. Couldn't find the words. Any word. I babbled out a "B-but . . ." instead.

"But this skull could be anybody's," I finally managed.

"That it could," said Hattie. "But it isn't. Take a good look at the teeth."

When I turned the skull around, I saw the gleaming teeth.

"Are these gold?" I asked.

"All four of them," said Hattie. "Twenty-four-carat beauties."

NINETY-EIGHT

Those teeth were a lot to take in. Even for a veteran scribe like me. My head spinning, I put both hands behind my head. Leaned back. Puffed out my cheeks.

"Well. I'll. Be. Damned," I said, slow and with feeling. And more than a little reverence.

Hattie picked up the skull. Stroked its crown with a finger and looked into its empty eye sockets. When she spoke again, she breathed out her words softly, talking to that skull as if it were an old enemy who, somewhere long ago, had turned into something not quite but close to a friend.

"All these many years, I've taken comfort in your company, Doc. Now it's time for us to part ways."

Balancing Hickory in one hand, she dislodged his four gold teeth easily with the other. No surprise, considering the skull's age. They glittered like four kernels of golden corn in her palm. She looked down at them for a few seconds, then nodded.

"They aren't as heavy as I thought they'd be," she said. "Back when I was a young girl, I thought these teeth of his were possessed, that they contained some kind of evil magic. Now I can see they're just teeth. And always have been. If it weren't for the gold, they wouldn't be worth squat."

She closed her hand around Doc's teeth. Rattled them next to her ear like a pair of dentine dice. A grin on her face, she rolled them across the table. Swear to God, I half expected snake eyes to come up.

After they came to rest, Hattie let out a slow sigh.

"I might burn in hell for the things I've done, but it'll be a small price to pay." She shrugged. "Of course, considering all the pain I've lived through, how much worse could hell be?"

Still discombobulated, I pointed a finger at the skull, then at Grandfather.

"So, you kept *that* in *there*, all this time?"

"Course I did," said Hattie. "Where else would I put it? Nary a day went by I didn't check on the doc to see how he was doing. As I said, revenge is best served cold. Savored to its fullest only when long moved from passion's hot breath."

"But over a hundred years' worth?"

"One of my few pleasures late in life," continued Hattie, "has been my daily visits with the doctor. In time, he became quite the conversationalist. Much better than when he was alive. The dead are good talkers, you know. Oftentimes more interesting than the living. All you need is the time and the patience to listen.

"Besides, I can't tell you how gratifying it has been, being able to stare at Doc's earthly remains and remember back to that stupefied expression when those beetles finally got to his eyes. I'll carry that look to my grave. With a smile on my face, I might add."

"So, let me get this straight," I said. "You're telling me that your story, everything you've told me, it all basically boils down to an eye for an eye?"

"I'm impressed, Mr. John March. You know your scripture. Although, some people would argue that the notion of an eye for an eye would turn the whole world blind. I, of course, am not one of those people."

I looked down at the skull. "What now?"

Hattie put two fingers to her lips. Let out a shrill whistle. Virgil pushed through the front door. After giving me a suspicious glance, he padded over to sit at her feet. Hattie scratched behind his ears. Then looked me in the eye.

"Now that I've told Micah's story, it's time to set the doc free."

She put the skull down in front of Virgil. He sniffed at it twice, then trotted out the door with it clutched in his mouth. From the porch came a loud crunch. Loud enough to make me shudder.

"Man, that's brutal," I said.

"No sense in letting it go to waste," said Hattie. "I'm sure the doc don't mind none. He probably got tired of being cooped up in Grandfather's belly. He might even appreciate the peace and quiet. And maybe the change of scenery."

"But a dog's belly?"

"Rest assured he won't be there long. By this time tomorrow, the doc'll probably be fertilizing daisies somewhere in the back forty. Kinda fitting, don't you think?"

Hattie gathered her shawl around her shoulders. Leaned forward.

"That said, you owe me one last favor, Mr. John March. No backing out now. A deal's a deal. And remember, we shook on it."

NINETY-NINE

I'd all but forgotten about my handshake contract with Hattie. Since we'd sealed it with spit, that meant it was "iron clad." At least in the hills of eastern Tennessee. I sure as hell didn't want to end up getting stashed in some grandfather clock for the next century, so I wasn't about to go back on my word. Besides, after being totally mesmerized by Hattie's story, I felt it only fair that I settled up.

"Go ahead, Hattie," I said. "Lay it on me."

Hattie turned my right hand over. Dropped Hickory's four gold teeth into my palm.

"Give these to my neighbors," she said. "My human neighbors, that is. They'll know what to do with them."

I stared at the teeth. The four pieces of gold felt both hot and cold in my hand, almost alive. A shiver ran down my spine.

"That's it?" I asked. "That's all you want from me?"

Hattie smiled. Nodded.

"Yep. That be all. I've decided to let you off easy."

"Uh, how do I find these 'human friends' of yours?"

"They'll find you." Hattie glanced over at Grandfather. "And unless I miss my guess, they're already on their way."

She began to rock again, this time along with Grandfather's ticking. Lost in thought, she looked around the room. When her good eye settled back on me, she wore a satisfied expression. With another nod, she rested her right hand on her cane.

"Well, that about covers it," she said. "I guess I'm finished here."

She adjusted her shawl. Sat back and closed her eyes.

"Time to rest a spell," she said. "All this jabbering has plumb tuckered me out."

I watched as her rocking slowed, and a peace seemed to settle over her. It may have been my overactive imagination playing tricks on me again, perhaps just the surroundings, or maybe it was one of Hattie's spells, but I swear, the longer I stared at her, the younger she looked. The years seemed to melt away, along with her wrinkles. Entranced by the transformation taking place, I didn't notice the host of small critters gathering at her side. When Doc Holliday slithered across my feet, I didn't feel a thing. Didn't even flinch when Ocho dropped from the ceiling to dangle a few inches from my nose.

I don't know how much time passed before Hattie stopped rocking. It could have been a minute or an hour. Hattie's chest was still rising and falling, ever so slowly now. Her head had lolled to one side, her mouth slightly agape. The soft, baby-like purr coming from the back of her throat told me she had fallen asleep.

Poor dear, I thought. It had been a long day for her. But I too was exhausted. Lulled by Grandfather's ticking, I drifted off.

A few minutes later, I snapped out of it when her cane slipped out of her hand and clattered to the floor. I rushed to her side.

"Are you sure there's nothing else I can do for you, Hattie?" I said. "Passing on these four teeth doesn't seem to be much of a favor."

But she was no longer breathing. And except for Grandfather's ticking, a liquid silence had engulfed the cabin.

"Hattie?" I said again. "Are you alright?"

Grandfather skipped a slower beat.

"Hattie?"

Then that old clock stopped dead.

I touched her hand. It was stone cold. My own grandmother's hands are always cold, and she's only in her seventies. They were never that cold, however.

"Would you like another blanket?" I asked.

Getting no response, I checked for a pulse. Found none.

Two antiques giving up the ghost at the very same time? Coincidence?

I think not.

ONE HUNDRED

Dead between the ears, gumpstumped, pig ignorant, gobsmacked—none of these mountain colloquialisms came close to my state of mind at that moment.

After fumbling with the door latch, I stumbled out onto the porch. Before I could call for help, I saw three figures heading up the path toward me. The lawn mower man, sans his Toro. Ike Goins, hat in hand. And most befuddling of all, Granny Godiva without her nag. But still naked.

"It's Hattie!" I shouted. "I think she's dead!"

Ike looked up at the fading sun. Took off his hat. Wiped the brim.

"We're well aware of that," he said. "We've come to bury her."

"But . . . she just died," I stammered. "Only a minute or so ago. How in hell did you—"

"You got something for us?" he asked.

Beyond bewildered now, I looked down at my right hand. When I opened my palm, the four gold teeth glistened in the sun. I felt like Jack holding the magic beans.

"Just these teeth," I said.

Still in a daze, I gave him all that was left of Doctor Abel Hickory. Ike nudged one tooth over in his hand with a fingernail. Nodded, then stuck all of them in a pocket.

"Them's the doc's gold chompers, alright," he said. "Should be more than enough to give Hattie a proper send-off."

Without another word, the three "human neighbors" headed up the steps. My mouth hanging open, I stepped aside. I wasn't about to stop them, but I'd hoped for some sort of explanation. After what I'd seen, what I'd been through the past few hours, I thought they owed me that much.

"I don't understand," I said. "What about—"

"Better head back to where you came from, sonny," said Granny. "Your work here is done. And if I'm not mistaken, don't you have a plane to catch?"

"But aren't you going to at least tell me—"

"Time waits for no man, Mr. March. And that be God's truth."

Where had I heard that little gem before?

All three of them headed inside. At the door, Stratton Briggs turned to face me.

"I wouldn't waste any more time jawing with us, sir. I'm pretty sure you've got a story to write."

As he was closing the door, he looked up at the sky. Then down at me.

"One more thing, though. You write a single bad word about Hattie, me and my friends will come looking for you. And you wouldn't want to meet up with Ike and his ax when he's angry. If you catch my drift."

Then he slammed the door on me.

That closed door will forever be emblazoned in my mind. Every grain, every wormhole, every nail. My heart pounding out of my throat, I had trouble breathing. I couldn't move.

A clap of thunder snapped me out of it. Two minutes prior, it had been a bright and sunny day. Now it was dark as night, as if a thick shroud had settled over the entire forest. A churning mass of angry clouds was swallowing up the mountaintop in big chunks. Within seconds, the storm would be on me. Shocked, I looked down at my watch.

"My plane! I'm going to miss my damn plane!"

A sudden bolt of lightning splintered a pine tree twenty feet to my right. That got my feet moving real quick. Realizing I could do no more for Hattie, I flew down the porch steps in a single stride.

Halfway to the path, a fat drop of rain hit me square in the eye, the first of many to come. With the clouds getting darker by the second, a yellow vein of lightning crackled off to my left, setting another tree aflame and ionizing the air with the smell of electricity. All hell was about to break loose, and I still had to run a gauntlet mile through the forest.

Knowing I had one chance in a hundred of ever finding my way back, I plunged into the trees. That's when it began to rain in earnest. A low-hanging branch hit me in the face. A hundred yards in, I was already hopelessly lost. In the back of my mind I cursed Herkie Bollinger for dropping me off in a godforsaken wilderness.

Beneath a roll of thunder, I heard rustling from the undergrowth. Probably a frightened animal running from the storm. *Just like me*, I thought.

ONE HUNDRED ONE

To my dying day, I'll never know how I made it out of that forest alive. My feet must have sprouted wings. Call it instinct, divine intervention, maybe even my dumb Irish luck, but somehow I managed to survive the deluge. During my mad dash, I kept hearing an owl screeching in the distance. With no other option, I crossed my fingers, lowered my head, and followed the screech.

Miracle of miracles, I stumbled across Herkie Bollinger waiting in his Studebaker. On time, and right where he promised he'd be. I was never so glad to see red hair in my life. Even my wife's.

Herkie must have known I was running late, because the minute I plopped my drenched butt into the passenger seat, he slammed the car into first gear and floored it.

"Sorry about all the water, Herkie," I said between pants. "I forgot to bring an umbrella. Hope I haven't ruined your leather seats."

"They'll clean up," he said. "Jesus, John! You look like you been put through ten wringers. What the hell did Hattie do to you?"

"It wasn't her," I said. "It was that damn forest. You were right. No one should be caught out alone in those woods. After dark or not."

He tossed me a towel, and I wiped off my face. The rest of me was beyond help. When we slid into a turn, I fastened my seat belt just before my head slammed into the roof. Compared to what I'd been through that day, however, my ride back to Sneedville would be a piece of cake. I took a few minutes to catch my breath.

"Hattie's dead, you know," I said. "She passed away right before my eyes. Damnedest thing I ever saw. One minute she was breathing, full of life. The next, she was not."

Struggling through a tricky curve, Bollinger had to concentrate on his driving. Finally he let out a soft sigh. Nodded over at me.

"I kinda thought that might be the case."

The back tires slipped in the mud, and the car jerked to the right. When Ginger regained her balance, Bollinger glanced over at me. Smiled sympathetically.

"Well, did Hattie teach you anything, my friend?"

"Tons," I said. "First and foremost, life is too short not to be your own man. Or woman, for that matter. You have to set your own priorities to survive what the world throws at you. Decide what's really important in life, then go out and get it. No matter how much it may cost you."

"That's not bad advice," he said. "Although these days that's probably easier said than done."

"Who says life is supposed to be easy? Look at Hattie. And all the bad things that happened to her. All the hardships she had to endure over the years."

"Good point," said Herkie.

"One thing's for sure; things are going to be different if and when I make it back to Boston. There's going to be some big changes in this humble reporter. You can bet the farm on that."

"You're beginning to sound a bit like Hattie. I take it, then, this trip of yours was worthwhile."

Herkie noticed me scratching my palm. I'd been doing it ever since I got in the car.

"Got an itch, John?"

"I might have touched something in the forest I shouldn't have. Poison ivy, maybe."

But I knew better. I could still feel those four gold teeth burning my hand. As if I'd been branded for life.

"You know," said Herkie, "an itch in your left palm means you're about to come into money."

"Another Melungeon superstition?"

Herkie looked out his window, scratched his head. Then winked.

"Um, could be."

ONE HUNDRED TWO

B y the grace of God—and perhaps helped along by Herkie's expert driving—I made it out of the hills in one piece. But how my rental car and I navigated through that storm to Knoxville's airport without getting a ticket is beyond me. A double dose of luck must have been riding shotgun. Had a traffic cop clocked me, he would have locked me up and thrown away the key.

At the terminal they were closing the airplane's door when I came charging down the concourse. Disheveled, wide eyed, and still soaking wet, I probably looked like a deranged terrorist. The air marshal standing by fingered his holster with one hand. Raised his other to slow me down. Half expecting him to slap the cuffs on me, I blurted out that I was a friend of Hattie Sexton. Better than flashing a get-out-of-jail card, it brought a smile to his face, and he motioned for the flight attendant to hold the door open for me.

"Hattie Sexton?" he said. "Why didn't you say so? Have yourself a good flight, sir."

Sometimes it pays to be a name-dropper. And in Tennessee, Hattie's was apparently the most potent name I could have dropped. After a quick pat down and a perfunctory wand wave, they let me board. Luck still with me, I discovered the plane was only one-quarter booked. As I said in the beginning, red-eye flights are the only way to travel.

I plopped down in the first vacant row with relief. A puddle quickly formed at my feet.

"Sir?" said the pert, strawberry-blond attendant. "Would you care for a drink?"

"The strongest you got," I said. "And keep them coming. After the day I've had, I'll be needing more than one."

As I settled into my first-class seat—thank you again, Helen Collette—the passenger across the aisle shot me a megawatt glare. Couldn't blame him. I'd delayed the flight's departure a good twenty minutes.

By the time I got comfortable, we were rolling down the runway. I watched the lights of Knoxville fade away into a soft, incandescent blur as we climbed. Ahead and a few degrees to the right, the last purple blush of a glorious sunset was turning gray. The sudden storm that had drenched me to the skin was still peppering Hattie's mountain with lightning bolts in the distance. Even at thirty thousand feet, I could feel the vibrations. I couldn't believe that less than two hours ago, I was caught in that very same maelstrom.

When we angled north toward Boston, the lightning disappeared beneath a wing, and the thunder dwindled.

I sat back and thought of Hattie. How could anyone experience all that history? Do all she did? See all she did? And in only one lifetime? It was more than my warbled mind could fathom. My thoughts a kaleidoscope of jellied sights and sounds, I tried to digest the last twenty-four hours.

Maybe it had all been a dream. Maybe it still was. Could it be that this was still Friday morning? That I was still asleep, lying next to Abby, safe and sound in my own warm bed? Maybe the alarm would go off in a few seconds. I'd wake, wolf down breakfast, make my usual ass-over-tea-kettle mad dash to the office.

When another flight attendant asked me if I wanted something to eat, I politely declined. A first for me. I never, ever pass on the offer of free food. But I had a story to write.

How do I write it? I asked myself. *Or should I even write it at all?* If word got out about what happened in Tennessee—the strange incidents up on that mountain, the even stranger characters—their lives wouldn't be the same. Notoriety would bring an end to their way of life. At best it would be an invasion of their privacy, something no self-respecting Melungeon could tolerate. They'd be set upon by hordes of curious tourists and opportunistic types. Or even worse, more reporters. Was that something I wanted on my conscience? And what about Hattie herself? Would she have wanted her quest for revenge broadcast to the rest of the world?

"But she sent for you, John," I debated the window. "And you alone. So she must have wanted her story told."

At best I was rationalizing. But for the reporter in me, it would have to do. I closed my eyes, racking my brain for a killer opening line; in the business, they call it a grabber. After four not-good-enoughs and a tenuous maybe, I dozed off. To dream of lawn mowers, sombreros, peg legs, and naked ladies.

And finally, four gold teeth.

ONE HUNDRED THREE

Rummaging through my pockets for quarters to feed probably the last operational pay phone in Boston, I was still a disheveled mess. My cell phone had popped out of my pocket during my frantic escape from the forest. I readjusted a damp wedgie, ignoring the stares of my fellow passengers. They were just a steady stream of faceless creatures on their way to nameless places, all of them less interesting than my mountain.

"Hello, Abby?" Concerned about Helen forcing this last-minute trip, she'd insisted on meeting me at the airport this time. "I just landed at Logan. Don't bother picking me up. It'll be quicker if I take a cab."

"John? Is everything alright? I know how you hate cab rides."

"I'm fine. It's been a hell of a day, but I couldn't be better."

"Are you sure? You sound . . . different."

"Different?" I took a second to roll the word's nuances around in my brain. "Yeah, you might say that. But don't worry. I'm still in one piece. With all my appendages attached, thank God. My ears have been lowered a few inches, but nothing life threatening. In fact, you might like the new me."

"You didn't join some backwoods cult, did you?"

"No cults. I may have had an epiphany or two. But I didn't even kill a 'bar' with my bare hands."

"'Bar'? Bare hands? What the devil are you talking about? Did you tip a few too many on your flight?"

"I ordered quite a few but only drank one," I said. "A small one at that. And I only finished half of it. I'm still a bit wet, but I can assure you I'm stone-cold sober."

"Wet? Are you in trouble, John? Are the police after you?"

"Hey, I'm supposed to be the semi-successful writer here, the one with the hyperactive imagination. Don't get carried away, Abby. You'll give your brain a hissy fit."

"Hissy fit?"

"It's an expression I picked up in the hills."

"And what else did you pick up in those hills?" she asked.

"Nothing contagious, I promise." A car honked, and I glanced down at my watch. "Look, it's already well after midnight. I'll fill you in when I get home. How are the kids?"

"They're both fast asleep."

"Good. Don't wake them. I should be there in half an hour or less. One more thing. You know that black teddy I got you last Christmas? The one you wore once, then packed away somewhere?"

"Yeah?" said Abby.

"Meet me at the door with it on."

"What!? Now I know you're drunk."

"Humor me. Just put it on."

"It's late, John. You have to be exhausted. Shouldn't we wait until tomorrow?"

"Nope. We can't."

Out of quarters, I cut it short.

"Love you. Gotta go."

On the way home, my cab driver was polite enough not to mention my appearance. Good trait, politeness. More people should try it. Especially we Americans.

ONE HUNDRED FOUR

Abby met me at the door wearing her ratty terry cloth bathrobe, the one she's had since college. On her feet were those threadbare fuzzy bunny slippers that always made her look like Bozo the Clown. To say I was disappointed doesn't cover the half of it. I set down my briefcase. Screwed a question onto my face. Raised an eyebrow.

"There better be a black teddy underneath that old thing."

For years I'd been begging her to turn that robe it into a dust rag. Her counter had always been "As soon as you get rid of your raggedy-ass Red Sox hoodie."

She parted the robe slightly to reveal the teddy. Then slammed it shut again.

"Satisfied?"

I swept her into my arms. Kissed her, then headed up the stairs.

"No," I laughed. "But I soon will be."

She thumped me on the arm. Raised an eyebrow of her own.

"Aren't you at least going to tell me what's going on?"

"Later," I said over my leer. "Right now I've got more important things on my mind. As they say in the hills, time's a-wastin'."

ONE HUNDRED FIVE

If not for the distant peal of steeple bells echoing off the Charles River the following morning, I would have slept past noon. Even so, there was no way I could drag my exhausted butt out of bed that Sunday. Church would have to wait another week. It took me two bleary-eyed squints to decipher the digits on our clock radio. Considering the protracted revelry of the night before, ten o'clock seemed a totally inappropriate hour to face the world.

Spooned around Abby's supple body, I raised my head slightly to survey our bedroom. The trail of clothes leading from the door to the bed said it all. Abby's ratty bathrobe, my wrinkled pants and shirt (still damp from the Tennessee thunderstorm), a pair of Hanes tighty-whities, the fuzzy bunnies, and finally—the pièce de résistance—the sacred black teddy. One lewd picture is always worth a thousand words. It had been a long time since Abby and I had gone for seconds. Last night, we'd gone for thirds.

I kissed Abby gently on the shoulder, a satisfied smile on my face. She made a slight movement but did not wake. Wanting to share the moment, I blew in her ear.

"Rise and shine, love of my life. Time to join the world of the living."

She arched her back. Stretched out her arms. Yawned mightily. Shaking her hair out, she rolled to one side to prop her head on her right hand. Smiled over at me.

"Good morning, stud. Not that I'm complaining, but what the hell got into you last night? It's been years since we made love like that."

I leaned back against the headboard. Opened an arm to make room for her. She snuggled closer.

"That trip did wonders for me. I feel like a new man."

Abby traced a finger down my chest.

"What happened to you in Tennessee?"

"Must have been something in the water," I said.

"Well, whatever it was, they should bottle that stuff. I for one would order a lifetime supply."

I pulled her tight. Kissed the top of her head.

"Actually, I think Hattie Sexton was responsible for the change. What an amazing woman she is. Er, was. The life she lived, the things she saw. You wouldn't believe the stories she told me."

The phone rang. Startled us both. When I reached for it, Abby slapped my hand away.

"Don't you dare answer that. It can only be one person."

I kissed her on the fingertips but still picked up the phone.

"Don't worry. Things have changed." Abby donned a skeptical grin, so I kissed her again. "Trust me."

As expected, it was my boss calling.

"Hello, Helen, I thought it might be you."

Wearing her best I-told-you-so smile, Abby pinched my right nipple. I punched the phone to speaker.

"Sorry to bother you on a Sunday, John," said Helen. "Am I disturbing anything?"

I shot Abby a wink.

"Not yet you're not. What can I do for you, boss?"

"You didn't call when you got back last night."

I pulled up the sheets. Looked down at my crotch. I was already up to half mast. And climbing. Not bad, considering last night's ribaldry.

"Something came up," I said. And left it at that.

Abby clamped both hands to her mouth. Fought off a snicker.

"I'm dying to know how your trip went," said Helen. "Did you get the old woman's story?"

"Every last detail."

"And it's good?"

"Better than good," I replied. "It's great! Solid-gold, hold-the-presses, pass-the-Pulitzer, soon-to-be-made-into-a-movie great."

"Fabulous! I had a feeling this might be a blockbuster. So, can I expect to see a rough draft on my desk tomorrow morning?" she asked, more statement than question.

"I don't think so, Helen. I'll get it to you maybe on Tuesday. Wednesday at the latest. I'll be taking Monday off."

A pregnant pause from the speaker. Then: "I thought you'd want to run with this, John. Put it to bed right away."

"Let's just say I've had a change in priorities. Altered my way of looking at things. At life in general."

"What could be more important than a gonzo story?" asked Helen.

"Taking my kids to the zoo, for one. Enjoying a picnic in the park with my family, for another."

More silence from the speaker.

"Um, this isn't like you, John." Then Helen hit me with her big gun. "Remember, *TIME* waits for no man."

"Nice try, Helen. Two days ago that broadside might have worked on me. But no more. Like it or not, I'm a changed man." I bent down to kiss Abby full on the lips. "And if *TIME* doesn't like the new me, maybe I should seek employment elsewhere. I'm sure there are other periodicals in this wide, wonderful world of ours that would be eager to provide me with a pencil or two."

That brought a gasp from the other end of the line. Not too often Ms. Helen Wentworth Colette gets hit between the eyes with a solid "No." Finally, a soft sigh from her.

"Then I guess I'll see your draft on Tuesday."

"Come to think of it, Helen, better make it Thursday." Abby gave me two thumbs-up. "I'd like to cover all my options."

"Alright, alright," said Helen. "Thursday it is. But your piece better knock my socks off."

"Socks off and skirts up, boss. I guarantee it. Have yourself a great day."

"You too, John," she said. "Enjoy the zoo."

Abby punched off the phone for me. Rolled up to straddle me. Bent down to kiss me on the neck. Then began to slowly grind her hips into me.

"Mighty impressive, the way you handled Helen there," she said. "Now, where were we?"

FUTURE EPILOGUE

Many, many years later

Today I turned a hundred. Me, John March, a centenarian? Go figure. It's hard to believe I've ventured into Hattie Sexton territory—if only by a few feet.

A lot has transpired since I interviewed her a mere sixty-three years ago. The story I wrote about her wasn't half bad, if I do say so myself. A year after I won the Pulitzer for it, Paramount paid me an ungodly sum to work up a screenplay. The movie starred Linda Hunt. She did a bang-up job, even earned an Oscar nomination. Partially for my effort in Tennessee, when I turned forty, *TIME* made me a managing editor.

I never forgot Hattie. As if anyone could. Until the day I retired, her photo sat on my desk, right next to the one of my four grandchildren. After I got back from the Smokies, I had Herkie Bollinger make a copy of that old tintype and send it to me.

By the way, Rusty, my eldest great-grandchild, is now playing triple-A ball for the Yankees' farm team. I'm still a diehard Red Sox fan, so that took some getting used to. Thank goodness the Sox won the American League pennant last year. Too bad they lost to the San Diego Padres (of all teams) in the World Series. There's always next season.

Big political changes occurred as the twenty-first century plowed painfully on. After our debacles in Iraq and Afghanistan, the United States wised up and took a step back toward big-stick isolationism. More emphasis on self-sufficiency than the big stick. As a consequence, no Middle Eastern country has told us to stuff it in years. The world in general seems to be a much safer place now. Unfortunately, it came at a high price. After North Korea accidentally detonated a nuclear device in its capital, disintegrating a million of its own people in a flash (including a large portion of its standing army), the world took proper note and gave the "new and improved" United Nations firm control of the bomb. That included all of America's.

And hallelujah! Since the late '40s, we haven't been dependent on fossil fuels. We now utilize both animal and human waste to propel our vehicles. Shortsighted skeptics call them crapmobiles. Even though you can smell them a hundred yards downwind, they seem to be working out. Mine gets over a hundred miles to a healthy bowel movement. No shit!

On March 31, 2034, a probe returned from Mars with a fifty-pound sample of the red planet's soil. It contained a dormant strain of bacteria that proved once and for all there was life elsewhere in this crazy universe. And miracle of miracles, when scientists reactivated the strain, they were pleasantly surprised to find that it had a voracious appetite for every type of cancer known to man. Within a year, the dreaded disease was wiped out entirely.

In addition, after the coronavirus pandemic of 2020, they came up with a universal vaccine that eliminated such threats. Those discoveries are two of the many reasons my cake today had a hundred candles on it. Combined with the quantum leaps in stem cell research, mind-boggling advances in subatomic nanotechnology, and the long-awaited perfection of the artificial heart, it resulted in almost doubling human life expectancy by 2075. Average retirement age in this country is now a robust ninety-one. However, a cure for the common cold still eludes us.

About thirty years ago, microchips replaced books entirely, saving a hell of a lot of trees. With a single outpatient implant, people are able to download entire libraries into their brains over the airwaves. *War and Peace* can now be "read" in a few minutes. Thankfully, a few nostalgic publications like *TIME* still crank out glossies for old farts like me who prefer to linger over the pretty pictures in our hands.

Two years before I retired, and mostly on a whim, I sent one of my star reporters back to Tennessee to do a follow-up story on the good people of Mulberry Gap. Unfortunately, two elderly gentlemen peppered his backside with buckshot the moment he let loose his Boston accent. One had a peg leg and was missing an eye, an arm, and an ear. The other was in a wheelchair, both of his legs gone below the knee. He had a hook for one hand and a metal plate in his head. Apparently the Goins brothers were still at it.

I guess some things never change.

Thank God.

THE END

OVER AND ABOVE:
THE WORLD'S TALLEST MAN

Robert Pershing Wadlow was probably the tallest person in history. Born in Alton, Illinois, on February 22, 1918, Robert eventually grew to be eight feet, eleven inches tall and weigh 439 pounds. His great size was due to hypertrophy of the pituitary gland. In comparison, if basketball great Shaquille O'Neal (a mere seven feet, one inch) stood next to him, he would have come to Wadlow's armpit.

A gentle giant who once said people "should utilize their handicaps instead of fussing about them," Robert toured with the Ringling Brothers' Circus for a short period but quickly tired of the "freakish" nature of the business. For most of his tragically short adult life, he served as a PR representative for the International Shoe Company, which provided him with his size-37AA shoes.

On July 15, 1940, Robert died from an infection of his left ankle caused by the heavy metal braces he was forced to wear. He was only twenty-two. His coffin weighed over a thousand pounds, was nearly eleven feet long, and required twenty men to maneuver it into its grave. At the time of his death, he was still growing. Had he lived until his midforties, doctors predicted he would have been over ten feet tall.

ACKNOWLEDGMENTS

Many thanks to my best friend Jim Maurer for his thoughtful insights. And for offering a hand to pull me up out of the path of a ferocious bovine beast.

BIBLIOGRAPHY

Aswell, James R. *Liar's Bench Tales*. Chapel Hill: The University of North Carolina Press, 1940.

Berry, Brewton. *Almost White*. New York: Macmillan Co. 1963

Botkin, B. A. *A Treasury of American Folklore*. New York: Crown Publishers, 1944.

Haun, Mildred. *The Hawk's Done Gone*. New York: The Bobbs-Merrill Co. 1940.

Milling, Chapman J. *Red Carolinians*. Chapel Hill: The University of North Carolina Press, 1940.

Davis, Wade. *The Serpent and the Rainbow*. New York: Simon and Schuster, 1985.

Cubbage, Eric. "The Tragic Story of Charles Byrne" PDF: "The Tallest Man." Retrieved May 2011.

Muinzer, Thomas. "A Grave Situation: An Examination of the Legal Issues Raised by the Life and Death of Charles Byrne, the Irish Giant." *International Journal of Cultural Property*, 2013.

Morning Herald Newspaper. London, 17 July 1782.

The Guinness Book of World Records.

Drimmer, Frederick. *The Tallest Man in the World*. New York: Bantam, 1991.

9 798888 241509